PLAID *and* PLAGIARISM

PLAID *and* PLAGIARISM

Molly MacRae

WORLDWIDE®

TORONTO • NEW YORK • LONDON
AMSTERDAM • PARIS • SYDNEY • HAMBURG
STOCKHOLM • ATHENS • TOKYO • MILAN
MADRID • WARSAW • BUDAPEST • AUCKLAND

This story takes place in Scotland, but it's narrated through the eyes of a newly transplanted American and filtered through her American thoughts and vocabulary.

Plaid and Plagiarism

A Worldwide Mystery/January 2018

First published by Pegasus Books Ltd.

ISBN-13: 978-1-335-50641-2

Printed in U.S.A.

For Cammy, Jenny, Jeb, Andy and Jack
—all the wild MacRaes

From the Inversgail Tourist Board's
***Welcome to Inversgail* brochure**

Welcome to Inversgail—story capital of the Scottish Highlands! When you arrive, lift your hat to our statue of Scotland's most famous storyteller: Robert Louis Stevenson.

Why not start your visit with a story about our name—Inversgail? The story begins with the small river that flows from sheep- and heather-covered hills and spills into the sea at Inversgail. There's no question about the "inver" part of our name. "Inver" means both "river mouth" and "confluence of waters." The river's name, though, is the source of some debate. On modern maps it's the Sgail. But once upon a time, and since maps of the area have existed, the name has been spelled Sgail, Skail, and Sgeul. Which is correct?

Some folk say that Sgail is an Anglicization of *sgeul*, a Gaelic word for "story." Legend has it that a family of noted storytellers and bards lived in the area and the "Sgeul" folk believe the river was named to honor them. And because stories, storytelling, and mouths all go together, they find the name Inversgail particularly apt. Other folk say Sgail is a misspelling of *skail*, a Scots word meaning "to spill." Rivers naturally spill their waters at their mouths, and thus the name Inversgail. A third group believes that *inver*—meaning both "mouth" and "confluence"—holds the key. The name Inversgail, they say, results from a confluence of meanings. The storytellers lived and told their stories beside the river, and the stories spilled from their mouths, just as the river spills into the sea at Inversgail. Which origin story should you believe? We leave that to you, our visitors, to decide.

Inversgail is a west Highland gem. We're a resort town within easy distance of Oban, Fort William, and Dornie, located in the Argyll and Bute council area. Our natural harbor and white sand beaches are protected from the open sea by the western isles. Our summer waters are warmed by the Gulf Stream, inviting bathers and boaters. Hills rise behind our charming houses and shops, creating a picturesque backdrop and fulfilling the dreams of photographers and hillwalkers. Fishing and crofting are the traditional ways of life in and around Inversgail. Tourism and our tradition of good stories allow our lovely area to thrive.

A friendly word of caution—once you've visited Inversgail, you'll want to call it home. But don't worry. We'll be here to welcome you!

ONE

"AND THERE'S NO need to cluck your tongue at my back, either," Christine said, not waiting for Janet to catch up. "You know well enough it's time we went to see the house for ourselves and find out what the delay is."

It should have been the best kind of morning the Highlands had to offer, and Janet Marsh was irritated that it wasn't turning out that way. Proof of the day's bright possibilities met her as she followed Christine Robertson out the door and down the steps of Yon Bonnie Books—*their* bookshop. Traffic along the High Street promised eager tourists. The breeze from the harbor carried the tang of salt and only a hint of fish. Water lapping the sand below the seawall matched the clear May sky, with no threat of rain. A swath of bluebells disappeared into the oaks fringing the banks of the River Sgail, and the river, not much more than a wide stream, splashed under the arched stone bridge she and Christine crossed. The hills rising behind the shops and houses and wrapping around the farthest ends of Inversgail appeared to embrace the village this morning, looking benevolent rather than brooding.

Janet wondered briefly about joining the bluebells and disappearing into the trees instead of following Christine down the street. "I don't want to intrude—"

"We won't intrude," Christine said. The soft burr of her accent took on a sterner tone. "We will simply walk past the house. We might go so far as to knock on the door."

"No knocking," Janet said. Her Illinois twang had the advantage of sounding firm and final. "I agreed to give the renters another few days."

Christine pulled up short. "Again? When did you agree to that? It's the first I've heard of it."

Rather than look Christine in the eye, Janet admired the red-tiled roof of Paudel's Newsagent, Post Office, and Convenience and pretended her short gray hair needed better arranging behind her ears.

"You've gone soft since leaving the States," Christine said.

"Not soft. I'm treading carefully and trying to fit in. I don't want to be one of those people who insist on things being the way they are back home, or try to impress people by throwing money around, or talk louder as if that will help people understand them."

Christine put her arm around Janet. "You never behaved that way before and you aren't going to start now. You and Curtis and the children were well liked all the years you came here." Christine's reassurance came to an awkward stop. Janet and her family had quit spending part of each summer in their Inversgail house when her husband, Curtis, a professor of economics, started an affair with one of his married graduate students. "Anyway," Christine plowed on, "Mum and Dad remember you and that's saying a lot, because half the time Mum might as well be away with the fairies. But to tell the truth, you and I are both strangers. All you have to do is listen to me to know that. I gave Illinois forty of my best years and Illinois paid me back by removing any trace of my lovely Scottish accent."

The women looked at each other and sputtered. Christine's native accent might have faded according to her aged parents' ears, but few Americans would agree.

"It is true, though," Christine said. "You should hear the dreadful things Mum and Dad whisper behind by my back. Except they're both so deaf they only *think* they're whispering." She eyed Janet up and down. "You're fine the way you are. All four of us are, and you and I and the girls are going to make a go of this move or die trying."

"The girls" were Janet's thirty-eight-year-old daughter, Tallie, and Tallie's former college roommate, Summer Jacobs. The four women—mother, daughter, and longtime friends—were now business partners and the new owners of Yon Bonnie Books, to which they ambitiously planned to add a tearoom and B & B.

"Here's a fashion tip, though," Christine said. "If you want to pass undetected amongst the natives, consider wearing something other than your orange-and-blue University of Illinois hoodie."

"The hoodie wouldn't be a problem if you would listen to reason and put off this *intrusion*. At least until tomorrow. I'm going to the launderette tonight." Janet congratulated herself for sounding only slightly defensive.

"And a trip to the launderette wouldn't be *necessary*

if you were already *in* your house, with your clothes and belongings *out* of their packing cases."

"Keep your voice down. I'll be in the house soon enough."

"And so you should be," Christine snapped. "You own the bloody place. If you're not the least bit curious about what's causing the delay, then you're soft *and* daft. *I'll be in it soon enough,* she says. We'll have this *sorted* soon enough. Come on."

Janet was about to protest but decided against it. Christine was right. She *was* curious about the delay keeping her out of the house she'd owned for thirty years. She and Curtis—Curtis the rat—had bought it after a sabbatical year at the University of Edinburgh and a summer holiday visiting the western Highlands and islands with Christine and her late husband, Tony. When Curtis had asked for a divorce, Janet engaged the best lawyer she could find and took the rat for as much as she could, including alimony, a decent lump sum (so decent it was almost indecent, which made her wonder what else the rat must have been up to over the years), and the Inversgail house free and clear. Jess Baillie, the estate agent handling the rental of the house, had begged for a few more days before turning it back over to Janet. Janet liked and trusted her, and she'd agreed without asking for the explanation Jess hadn't offered. But how could it hurt to walk past the house with Christine and see if the renters were at least packing?

"I knew you'd see it my way," Christine said when Janet gave a single, sharp nod and set off down the High Street.

They walked side by side, two friends comfortable in their similarities and either happy with their differences or able to put up with them. Christine Robertson, spare and angular, had grown up in Inversgail, the daughter of a district nurse and the Inversgail Grammar head teacher. Janet Marsh, shorter and better upholstered, came from a family of central Illinois corn, soybean, and pig farmers. They'd each followed their husbands to the University of Illinois and met when Janet had been her son's show-and-tell during third grade. Christine, by then a school social worker, had been walking past the classroom when Janet thrilled her son's classmates by demonstrating her state fair prize-winning pig call. Over the years Christine would tell people they'd bonded over Janet's reverberating *sooey* and Janet always returned the compliment by saying their friendship was cemented with Christine's recipe for shortbread. Christine's shortbread, they decided, would take pride of place as the first item on their proposed tearoom's menu.

"Look, isn't that Rab MacGregor?" Janet asked. She'd caught sight of a sandy-haired man and a sandy-colored Cairn terrier sitting on the seawall, faces turned to the sun like basking cats. In fact, there were two cats splayed on the wall, soaking up their share of the sun, beside the man and dog. From that distance, the ages of man, dog, and cats were equally inscrutable. "We should offer him the job at Yon Bonnie now, while we have the chance."

"Are you sure you don't want to advertise?" Christine asked. "Cast a wider net? The cats look more alert than he does."

"He always did fine work for us at the house," Janet said. "I don't see why he wouldn't be as good at general cleaning and odds and ends at the shop, too. Besides, he's always been nosy. *He* might be able to tell us something about the house. Hullo there, Rab!" she called. "Rab MacGregor!"

Rab looked around, and Janet waved so he'd know who had called his name.

Christine waved, too, and then stopped. "Did he just—" But the rest of what Christine said was lost in the noise of a motorcycle speeding past.

A day coach followed the motorcycle, frustrating the women by idling in front of them. They heard the magnified voice of the onboard tour guide telling her group what time and where to meet the bus later in the day and pointing out the public toilets. When the bus moved on, only the cats still basked on the seawall across the street.

"Where's Rab?" Janet asked. "Do you see him? I'm sure he heard me and saw us wave."

"He did. And then his eyes nearly popped out of his head. I think he's done as good as his name and scampered."

"As good as his name?"

"Rab, short for Rabbit, and it's what they do—leap and run."

"I thought boys named Robert were often called Rab."

"That shows you're not as nosy as Rab." Christine

scanned the seawall and street. "He got the name as a boy because he was fast off the mark in footraces. Good at jumping, too. But his name is Rupert. Blasted bus and blasted Rupert. He probably slipped over the wall when the bus stopped in front of us. Leapt and ran. And I'd like to know why."

"We don't *know* that he saw us," Janet said. "Maybe he had someplace else he needed to be."

"Not from the looks of him before he saw us, which he did." Christine looked ready to cross the street and organize a search party for the absent handyman.

"If you still want to be nosy about the house, let's get it over with," Janet said, "so we can get back to the shop." She started walking. "Honestly, I never knew you were so suspicious."

"Of course I am." Christine checked the seawall one last time before catching up to her. "If one of us is going to be soft, then the other one needs to be suspicious."

"I don't see the connection," Janet said, "and I don't want to argue about it."

"Explaining isn't arguing."

"And I won't like your explanation if the gist of it is that I'm soft. A person who figures out how four women can buy a business in another country and relocate three thousand six hundred and forty-three miles to run it is *not* soft," Janet said.

"You're right."

"There were hurdles covered in ridiculous amounts of red tape every step of the way and I got us over them."

"You did," Christine agreed.

"Do you have reservations? Are you sorry we took the plunge?"

"No. That answers both questions. What about you?"

"No. But I think we should add an addendum to our agreement stating that we ask each other those questions once a month."

"Once a quarter," Christine said. "The longer stretch will account for short-term vacillations of spirit. We're all bound to have small doubts and low periods from time to time."

"Only natural," Janet said. "I worry especially about Tallie and Summer. But we've had this conversation before. Please don't turn into a bully."

"As soon as your confidence in the way Jess Baillie is handling your property begins to waver, I'll revert to the cozy, comfortable Christine Creampuff you know and tolerate. In the meantime, I've got your back." She took Janet's arm as they continued down the street. "I love that phrase, but I don't think I've ever actually said it before. Thank you for giving me a reason."

"Always happy to help."

Janet noted the familiar businesses she'd passed or stopped in each of the summers she'd spent in the village—West Highland Wool, Howitt & Dugdale Solicitors, W. Brockie Greengrocer, MacBrayne's Pub. They were family-run and they'd occupied the same buildings for so many generations they might have been mortared into place with the stonework when the buildings went up. There were new businesses, too. Skye View Sea Kayak had moved into a building formerly occupied by a video store. Two shoe shops, rivals for decades, were now an Internet café and an outdoors shop. Janet was happy to see the optimism of the newcomers, but when she and Christine came to the chiropodist, the chemist, and the cheese shop—the trio her children had dubbed "the chops"—she was just as glad for the vigor of the long established.

A young woman came out of the cheese shop as they passed. She held the door open while a boy and girl jostled their way out along with the smells of cheddars, blues, and farmhouse.

"Mull Cheddar," Christine said in a reverent whisper. She dropped Janet's arm and spread both of hers, breathing in deeply and luxuriously. "I have so missed Isle of Mull Cheddar."

"You should've been called Mouse," Janet said. "We'll stop and get some on the way back. Oh, my." She'd started walking again, but immediately took two steps back, bumping into Christine, who gave a squeak.

"Sorry," Janet said, "but look who's moved her office out of Buchan Place and onto the High Street."

Christine stepped around her and read the brass nameplate beside the door of the business next to the cheese shop. "'Jess Baillie, Estate Agent.' She's moving up in the world. You didn't know this?"

"You'd think I would, but no. Good for her, though, right?"

"And handy for us. We can still go by your place, if we want to, but as long as we're here, let's intrude on Jess first."

Janet caught her arm. "Not me. You." Christine's mouth opened and Janet rushed to get her reasoning in first. “If I go in and give my name to her assistant, and if there really is something going on, we might not get anywhere. Jess might have told her she doesn’t want to see me. And if she catches sight of me before I see her—”

“Aha. Got you. Wait here out of sight. I’ll go and act the perfect mouse. And may I just say, Janet Marsh, Inversgailian incomer and soon-to-be successful bookseller, welcome back to the Sisterhood of the Suspicious.”

TWO

CHRISTINE CAME BACK out of the estate agency in less time than it took Janet to remember how to check her phone for missed messages.

"That was suspiciously fast," Janet said, giving up on the phone and slipping it into the back pocket of her khakis. "What could you possibly learn in three minutes? Or even twice that?"

"The assistant's name is Rosie. She's hardly more than a schoolgirl. She's open, friendly, and chatty." Christine ticked those points off on her fingers. Then she drummed the fingers against her lips for several seconds before going on. "She might be more chatty than usual because she's lonely. Or maybe I'm slipping back into my school social worker mode and overanalyzing. Anyway, Jess hasn't been in the office for the past two days. With no notice and without giving a reason."

"Does she have to give a reason?" Janet asked. "Maybe it's personal and she doesn't want to tell chatty Rosie."

"Rosie says it isn't like her."

"How well does she know her? I've dealt with Jess for the last seven or eight years and she's always been reliable."

"She didn't tell you why the renters need more time to clear out of your house," Christine said.

"That doesn't make her unreliable. Besides, I didn't ask."

"Maybe you should have. Or when you hung up your reference librarian hat, did you forget the art of asking essential questions?"

Janet looked at the toes of Christine's tennis shoes, now six inches from the toes of her own favorite old leather shoes. Hers could use a lick of polish, she noticed. Her sense of personal space could use another twelve inches, too, but she moved forward an inch, tipped her chin up, and met Christine's blue gaze. "I would make you blink first," she said, "but I have this terrible crick in my neck." She closed her eyes and massaged the back of her neck—which didn't hurt in the least. "I'm sure it's from not sleeping in my own bed with my own pillow." She dropped her hand and smiled. "You're a good advocate, Christine, and I appreciate your help with the house."

"Then why are we arguing?"

"We aren't. We're tripping over a bump in the road. Rosie *has* heard from Jess, right?"

"By text. She told Rosie to cancel her appointments, with her apologies. Nothing else, though. She didn't give Rosie a reason for the cancellations to pass along to the clients."

Janet shrugged. "Again, did she need to give a reason?"

"Rosie asked me if she should be worried about Jess,

which shows she's already worried. And then she asked me what she should do. Me—a stranger off the street."

"A stranger who listens," Janet said. "And who might be dressed like her safe and sensible grandmother. Plus, when you listen, you get that look in your eyes—"

Christine's eyebrows drew together.

"That's the one. Anyone within range of those eyebrows and that long nose will believe you're capable of getting to the bottom of things. Don't overdo the eyebrows, though, or you might scare someone. What did you tell Rosie?"

"That if Jess doesn't show up today, and if all she does is send another text, Rosie should ping her back immediately and ask when she *will* be in the office. Then I gave her my number and told her if Jess doesn't answer that question, she should phone me."

"Do you think she *should* be worried about Jess? Should *we*?"

Christine looked at the photographs of properties for rent and for sale taped to the estate agent's window for passersby to browse. "Cancelling appointments, staying away from the office, and not communicating with staff is an odd way to do business. I don't know Jess, though, and I don't know how excitable or prone to exaggeration Rosie is, so it's hard to say how worried she should be."

"Maybe no more worried than I've been about my house up until now. But that worry is ratcheting up since you talked to Rosie. What will you do if Rosie calls you?"

"Call the police. Or am I being *too* suspicious?"

"What would you tell them? That Jess is sending messages but not answering them?"

"And that she hasn't been in the office for a few days. But none of that sounds dire or urgent, does it? When did she ask you to give the renters more time?"

"Two days ago," Janet said. "By email."

"Maybe we should find out where Jess lives and cruise by her house, too."

"We do have a business to learn. We told the girls we wouldn't be gone long."

"I didn't mean we'd go now," Christine said.

"Good."

"We can go this evening."

"Going by my house can wait for this evening, too, then." Janet looked down at her orange-and-blue sweatshirt. "Although maybe not. In fact, now that my suspicion pump has been primed, let's walk faster."

They turned the corner into Fingal Street, taking the gentle climb toward Argyll Terrace at a pace that soon made Janet's prairie-born calves protest. She didn't slow down, though, even when Christine began to puff. The shops gave way to houses with front gardens enclosed by low walls. Fingal Street narrowed and they dodged around cars parked half on the street and half on the pavement. They crossed Gordon Street and then Ross. Christine fell behind and Janet didn't wait. When she reached Argyll Terrace, she turned right, and her feet carried her past two houses she barely glanced at. She stopped at the third house—a traditional stone detached cottage with four rooms down and two up—the house she and Curtis had been so tickled to own. Their house.

Standing in front of it now, she finally admitted to herself why she hadn't pressured Jess about the delays keeping her from moving in. She'd been uneasy because she didn't know how she'd feel when she saw the house or when she stepped inside. And she'd been reluctant to find out. She and Curtis and the children had been happy here. She'd *thought* they were happy. And when their son, Allen, married a young woman from Inversgail and moved to Scotland, to Edinburgh, and then with their retirements approaching, she'd expected to spend *more* time in this house. Not *no* more time.

The two of them, together, blessed and happy.

She stared at the house, lips pressed tight. Stared at the windows Curtis was so proud of reglazing with the antique glass he'd spent a summer searching for. Stared at the door knocker, a brass wolf's head she'd found in a shop in Tobermory on the Isle of Mull. Curtis hadn't liked the knocker, but he'd secretly bought it and put it up for her birthday. It had been a wonderful surprise, and she was surprised now at how angry the wolf's head and the reglazed windows made her. Because she *was* soft. Soft and weepy over the loss of the life she'd been so sure she was meant to live.

"It looks empty," Christine said, coming up beside her. "No curtains at the windows. It's a charmer, though, and always has been. I can't believe you haven't at least walked past it yet. To see if there's any garden left, if nothing else." She stretched her back, sore from wrestling the weeds out of her parents' neglected garden. Then, before Janet realized what she was doing, Christine walked up the flagged front path.

"Christine!" Janet hissed.

"Don't worry. I won't knock."

"All right—"

"I'll ring."

Janet rushed after her. She was too late. Christine had pressed the bell. When no one answered, Janet let her breath out. But Christine didn't give up. She pressed the bell harder, as if that would make it ring louder and bring someone running. It didn't.

In the silence after Christine took her finger from the bell, Janet imagined she heard her children's giggles on the other side of the closed door…heard the rustle of intimate whispers as Curtis slipped into bed in their room under the rafters…heard the clink of morning coffee cups on the small covered deck they'd built outside the back door so they could see the harbor and islands and watch for approaching storms. She heard Curtis teasing that she'd never been good at reading weather signs. She looked the brass wolf in the eyes and felt her anger shift.

She lifted the heavy ring the wolf held in its mouth, and brought it down—*bang*. She was the one in control. She was the strong one—*bang*. She was the one who'd figured out how she could make this move and make the bookshop work—*bang*. *This* was her life now. This was *her* house—*bang*. And Curtis could go—*bang*. She let the ring go. It fell with a last hollow *thunk*, and she stroked the wolf between its ears.

"No one's coming because the place *is* empty," Christine said. "But if the renters have moved out, why can't you move in? You've got your keys, haven't you? Let's go in."

"Not until I know they're truly gone."

"Then let's look in the windows."

"At the back," Janet said, and she led the way around the house.

"Act casual, though," Christine said. "If neighbors see us, we want to look like we're supposed to be here."

"I *am* supposed to be here."

"That's the spirit."

The small backyard—back garden, Janet reminded herself—sloped down to meet that of the house below on Ross Street. The renters had terraced the slope with three raised beds bordered by rounded lumps of granite. Curtis's ugly garden shed, which she'd never liked—*her* ugly garden shed—stood in a corner at the bottom of the garden. When he'd told her he bought a shed, she'd pictured something charming, one that looked as though a writer could turn it into a tiny retreat, as though Alexander McCall Smith might emerge from it and ask for a cup of tea. What Curtis bought was an aluminum-clad box with a door. When she got the chance, that *thing* would be replaced.

Christine nudged Janet. "Lettuce is bolting," she said quietly.

Janet nodded. "Maybe the renters did, too?"

"Why do I have the urge to slink low to the ground like Rab MacGregor or one of his cats? We made enough hullabaloo at the front door to scare anyone away."

"You have good instincts," Janet whispered in her

ear. "We won't slink, in case neighbors *are* watching, but let's go carefully. Let's stay off the deck, for now, to avoid creaky boards. Head for the kitchen window on the corner."

They walked to the mullioned window, appearing about as cool and casual, Janet knew, as a pair of amateur peeping Toms.

They lost that little bit of cool when they looked through the window.

"There are no words," Janet said faintly.

THREE

FROM WHAT THEY could see, the kitchen was covered in garbage. The window looked in over the sink—the sink that was hidden under a mound of papers and food wrappers. Everywhere else there were cans, wads of used paper towels, juice bottles, beer bottles, crusts, rinds, coffee grounds, cores and peelings, and things they couldn't or wouldn't want to identify.

"Is that a boot on the stove?" Christine asked. "And shouldn't I be able to see the floor? Where did it all come from?"

"They couldn't have been living this way," Janet said. "I don't understand. I don't understand."

"It's a dump."

"It's a disaster."

"I'm so sorry, Janet."

They stood side by side, hands cupped to the window, silent and staring. Until Janet saw movement.

"Holy—" She grabbed Christine's arm. Someone was in the kitchen. She was sure of it. Below the counter. Tossing more garbage into the middle of the room. "Did you see that?" she whispered. "What should we do?"

"Get away from here and call the police," Christine said through gritted teeth while trying to pry Janet's fingers from her arm. Before she could get the fingers loose, Janet curled her other hand into a fist and rapped on the window.

Someone screamed.

Christine grabbed Janet's rapping hand and dragged her below the window. "Are you crazy?"

"*I'm* crazy? *You're* crazy! You scared the heliotrope out of me, screaming like that."

"*I* didn't scream," Christine said. "I *never* scream. Have you *ever* heard me scream?"

They stared at each other, then turned to look up toward the window, and then looked back at each other. Christine pulled her cell phone from her purse.

"Wait," Janet whispered, putting a hand over the phone. "Why now?"

"Because when there's a screaming lunatic trashing your house it's the perfect time to call the police."

"No—"

Christine yanked the phone away.

"I mean why scream now?" Janet asked "We didn't hear screams when we rang the bell and knocked."

"Still the perfect time. Dialing nine-nine-nine. *Now.*" Christine turned away so Janet couldn't stop her. That also meant she didn't see Janet rise to peek in the window again, so she wasn't expecting or prepared for *Janet's* scream. *"Wha—"* Christine's phone flew from her ear and smacked the rock wall of the house.

"Jess?" Janet peered at the woman frozen on the other side of the glass. "What on earth are you doing?"

Jess remained frozen.

Janet glanced at the hand she'd slapped to her chest—

a reaction as effective as closing a barn door, she realized. Her heart had already leaped out and flown over her shoulder like Christine's poor phone. And poor Jess—she looked like she was in shock. Janet took a calming breath, smiled, and called through the glass, "Why don't you open the back door, Jess? We'll come in and help."

"Help her do what?" Christine asked as they waited to see if Jess would unlock the door that opened onto the deck. "How do we know she isn't going to attack us with a rancid leg of lamb?"

"We don't. Hang on." Janet ran to the first raised garden bed and came back with a fist-sized knob of granite from the border.

"And if she has a gun?" Christine asked.

"I don't have a gun," said a dull voice from the door.

"Hello, Jess," Janet said. "I've brought Christine to see the house. That's all right, isn't it?"

"It's nice to meet you, Jess," Christine said to the worn-looking woman framed in the doorway. "May we come in? We rang the bell and knocked, but maybe you didn't hear us."

Jess pushed lank hair from her forehead with the back of her hand, then let the hand drop to her side. "Bring the rock if it makes you feel safer."

She turned away without waiting to see if Janet kept the rock. Christine raised her eyebrows at Janet. Janet looked at the granite in her hand and then tucked it into the kangaroo pocket of her hoodie.

"I do feel safer," she whispered to Christine. "Also like a bit of a fool."

"And the fool is welcome to go in first." Christine waved Janet ahead of her, but Janet had a hard time making her feet move toward the door.

"Did you get through to the police?"

"Not before my phone ejected. I could call now, on yours."

"Let's hear what Jess says first."

Several boards squeaked when they crossed the deck, as Janet had predicted they would. Although it was more of a creak than a squeak, she thought, and sounded more like a greeting than a comment or complaint. Christine was right about the house being a charmer. The ancient granite of its blocks and its newer hardwood boards were much too stiff-upper-lip to complain and too stoic to make comments. Appreciating that restraint, Janet returned the favor and didn't mutter to the old church pew they used for a bench that it needed refinishing, or to the back door that it could use a new coat of paint.

The faded and peeling door opened into an entryway with doors to the kitchen and the family room. As soon as she stepped inside, Janet was hit by the smell. She immediately closed her eyes, as though that would protect them and her nose from the assault. She wished she'd taken a gulp of fresh air first, and started to back out, but Christine was close behind, prodding her in the spine.

"Huh," Christine said in her ear. "Odder and odder. There's no rubbish on the floor here, and look at the lounge."

Janet's eyes opened and she crossed the small space to the family room door. There were the tired, comfortable chairs and sofa, the mismatched bookcases and cupboards, the fireplace—the room where she, Curtis, and the children had spent so many rainy afternoons reading, working puzzles, knitting, and drinking pots of tea—and all free of garbage. Except for the pervasive smell, the room appeared to be spotless.

"I wonder what the rest of the place looks like," Christine said.

"It's only in here," Jess's flat voice said from the kitchen. "Like a bomb went off in here, but it's nowhere else."

Janet wrapped her hand around the rock in her kangaroo pouch and went to the kitchen door. She stopped there, brought up short by the smell and by the sheer magnitude of the mess. As though someone had upended ten bags of garbage to cover every available surface. Large bags. Maybe closer to twenty bags. There was nowhere to walk without stepping in it or on it—whatever "it" turned out to be. Janet looked over her shoulder at the family room—familiar, cozy, normal. Then she turned back to stare at the kitchen—an alien landscape with Jess standing with one foot in a pizza box, garbage bag hanging from her hand, shoulders defeated, chin low, sniffling.

"So, Jess," Christine said.

Jess looked up.

"Is your bin bag half empty or half full?"

The anguished cry from Jess was too much for Janet. She waded through the sea of trash to the sobbing woman, took her arm, and pulled her out of the kitchen, through the entryway, and out the back door.

She sat Jess down on the pew. She sat on one side of Jess, and Christine sat on the other and passed her a packet of tissues.

"I don't know how long it's been like this," Jess finally said after blowing her nose.

"A couple of days, at least, judging by the smell," Janet said.

"It's ripe," Christine agreed. "Ripe and smells like tripe."

"And I can't believe you think I might have done it. Or that it's happened again."

"What?"

Janet was sure their combined shouts would put Jess back over the edge into uncontrollable tears. She cringed in anticipation but sat ready to administer pats to shoulders and hands as needed. She wasn't quite ready for wet, shuddering hugs—and she felt bad about that. And she definitely wasn't ready for when Jess stood up and addressed them.

"The situation is under control." Jess looked each of them in the eyes. "Fully. Janet, if you'd kept your word about giving me two more days, and hadn't come around to snoop, I guarantee you wouldn't have known anything was ever amiss."

"Amiss," Janet echoed faintly.

"And I don't want anyone else to know anything about this," Jess said, "so if you'll excuse me." She looked at each of them again, then went back into the cottage and closed the door, leaving Janet and Christine staring after her.

"Call the police now?" Christine asked.

"Not yet." Janet went to the door. It wasn't locked. She opened it.

Jess, arms crossed, appeared to be waiting for them.

"Jess—"

"Come in. Close the door. Really, I can't let this get out."

"You could at least open the windows," Christine said, "and let the smell out. It's horrible."

"No! No," Jess said. "When I get it cleaned up, the smell will go away. This will all go away."

"Hire someone to help," Janet said. "*I'll* hire someone."

"I did," Jess said. "Believe me, I did. I hired a service from Fort William. I waited here for them, for hours, and then they phoned to cancel. So I phoned Rab MacGregor. He's good and I thought I could trust him, especially if I paid him enough to keep quiet. He backed out this morning. Phoned to say he had a 'subsequent commitment.' His words exactly. I doubt he even knows what 'subsequent' means. So I came to do it myself and found more rubbish than ever."

"Is that why Rab bolted when he saw us?" Christine asked. "He's not a rabbit. He's a weasel."

"This is appalling," Janet said. "It's vandalism."

"I'll take care of it," Jess said.

"But what makes you think it'll stop after you've cleaned it up and after I've moved in? How are *they* getting in? I didn't see any signs of a break-in. Is this the renters? Revenge for not renewing the lease? I gave them three months' notice. Have you had the locks changed? *I'll* have them changed and now I *am* calling the police."

"No!" Jess caught at Janet's hand. Janet pulled away and took the rock from her kangaroo pouch.

"I can't believe this is happening," Janet said to Christine. "I feel like a cavewoman."

"And now she's crying again," Christine said.

"For the love of—Stop it this instant. Jess Baillie, honest to Pete, I can't take much more of this. Explain yourself or I *will* call the police."

"I want to know why *she* hasn't called the police," Christine said.

"Don't interrupt," Janet said, rounding on Christine. "Now, pull yourself together, Jess, and sum it up."

"Och, fine. I can't say it simpler than this. It's Ug."

Janet threw her hands in the air, her right still holding tight to the knob of granite. But Christine scratched her head and Janet saw enlightenment spark in her eyes.

"Una Graham," Christine said, "advice columnist for the *Inversgail Guardian*. Is that who you mean?"

Jess nodded.

"She's a good old-fashioned agony aunt," Christine mused, "and affectionately known as Ug. You must have seen her column in the paper, Janet. Dad never misses it. Except for the tide tables, she's the only reason some people do read the *Guardian*."

"She's a real person?" Janet asked. "I thought the staff got together and answered the questions over pints. And made up half the questions, too. I'm sure someone told me that."

"If it was a skinny little shrew who told you, that

was Ug herself," Jess said. "Thinks she's quite the wit. And she thinks she's an investigative reporter now, too."

"We know someone who could give her a run for her money in that game," Christine said. "Except our Summer has given up journalism to come sell books with us. I find this fascinating, Jess."

Janet gave Christine a look, tossed the rock in the air, and caught it with a snap.

"But only fascinating from a sociological point of view," Christine added. "You think Ug did this?"

"She has it in for me," Jess said. "She'd like nothing better than to put me out of business."

"If you have proof," Janet said, "then go to the police."

"And I'll stick my question in again," said Christine. "Why *haven't* you gone to the police?"

Jess stared toward the kitchen. "There won't be any proof."

"How did she even get in?"

"Learnt how to pick locks from her brothers, because they were delinquents."

"She's a burglar?" Christine asked, sounding confused and unconvinced.

"No. She's not. Because she's smarter than that. But so am I, and I'm on to her."

"Why does she want to put you out of business?" Janet asked.

"You see," Jess said. "You don't believe me."

"We're trying to understand."

"And that's why there's no use calling the police. They won't believe me, and they won't try to understand, and they'll do nothing. Ug is trying to make me jump and scream, like she did when we were girls and she put spiders in my schoolbag. And the teachers did nothing. But I'm not screaming this time. I won't give Ug that satisfaction. I'm not saying anything about it. And that's why I haven't told Rosie anything at the office. Rosie's sweet, but what she doesn't know she can't blather about. Please, Janet, let me take care of the mess. Promise me you won't tell anyone about it. I'll knock the last six months off my fees for managing the rental for the trouble this has caused. I can't clear it all out today, but I'll have it finished by tomorrow. And it won't happen again. Una won't come back once you're living here. There'd be nothing in it for her."

"THERE ARE MORE holes in the Una 'Ug' Graham Theory of Rubbish Distribution than there are in the last scarf I tried to knit," Christine said on the way back to the bookshop. "Do you believe any of it?"

"Jess obviously believes it," Janet said, "but I think I'd like to explore other possibilities. And call a locksmith."

"Agreed."

LIKE SO MANY shops along the High Street, Yon Bonnie Books looked as though it could have sprung straight out of an illustrated classic. Something by Scott or Maclaren, Janet thought, or one of their sentimental colleagues from the turn of the last century. The shop's granite blocks and windows trimmed in dark green gave the exterior exactly the right look for a bookshop. The updated interior, with walls in primary colors and a mix of antique and modern fixtures, gave the shop humor and vitality. The background music, a mix of lilts, airs, and classical pieces, and the fireplace with its grouping of comfy chairs made everything cozy.

Janet was pleased to see browsing customers when they returned. She apologized to "the girls" as well as Pamela and Kenneth Lawrie, the former owners of the shop, for being gone longer than they'd meant to be. The Lawries, who'd owned the shop for fifteen years, were preparing for their own move to Portugal—or anywhere warm, as Pamela had told them. But as part of the sales agreement they were staying on for a week to train the four new owners and to ease the transition.

"You had a nice walk?" Pamela asked as she watched Janet's daughter, Tallie, ring up a sale. Pamela reminded Janet of a library patron she'd known over the years, but never more than in passing—pleasant enough, she assumed, if one were able to breach the barrier. Friendly greetings hadn't ever been enough to do that, though.

"It was a nice walk and it's a beautiful day," Christine said.

"The only thing making it more beautiful is being back here surrounded by new books and happy customers," said Janet. Her flowery remark earned a raised eyebrow from Tallie, and Janet could see questions forming above her daughter's head like smoke signals. Tallie had been practicing and teaching corporate law for most of her career—enjoying it, then enduring it, and finally telling Janet that if she stayed in it one more year, her soul might shrivel up and turn to dust. It was

Tallie who'd found the "for sale" notice for Yon Bonnie Books.

"That's all right, then," Pamela said. "We did expect you back sooner so we could go over the ordering process before lunch. It's somewhat important, with the Inversgail Literary Festival being the biggest book-buying week of the year, and only a fortnight away. But I expect the ordering process can wait."

"And we kept *you* waiting," Janet said. "I'm sorry we took so long."

"Well, it's no bother to me," Pamela said. "It's not as if this is my new livelihood, is it?"

"Listen to her." Kenneth, gap-toothed and soft in the middle, put his arm around Pamela. "There's plenty of time yet to go over ordering, and it could be they'll want to set up their own system, anyway. You're all naturals at the book business, ladies. Speaking of which, has Una Graham been in touch?"

Janet wondered if she looked as startled as Christine did at the mention of Una.

"No? Well, she wants to do an article for the *Guardian* about the changing of the guard," Kenneth said. "It'll be a companion piece to their annual splash about the literary festival. She said she might come round this afternoon."

"I hope she doesn't use 'Changing of the Guard' for the headline," Pamela said. "It was trite before she became trite."

"Wheesht," Kenneth said. "We feel very good about putting the shop in your hands, don't we, Pammy?" Kenneth tickled her earlobe.

Pamela flicked his hand away. “We’ve an appointment with the solicitor, Kenneth.”

AS SOON AS the Lawries left the shop for their appointment, and in between customers, Janet and Christine broke their promise to Jess. They told the story in turns, and Janet gave Tallie and Summer high marks for listening without interrupting and without steadily lowering jaws.

“This is… I can’t think of a good word for what this is,” Summer said when they’d finished. “And words rarely fail me.” Summer was a newspaperwoman who’d managed to hang on to her job during the downward spiral of daily newspaper readership. But she’d finally seen the writing on the masthead, and when the others had told her about the bookshop, she’d jumped ship, ready to reinvent herself.

“*I* can think of the word,” Tallie said. “That story is full of—”

“Holes,” Christine said. “That’s exactly what I told your mother.”

“I called the locksmith,” Janet said. “He was at a job in Dornie today, but he’ll be around tomorrow. And we have a plan for filling those holes.”

“And four of us will be more efficient than two,” Christine said. “Neither of you has plans for this evening, do you?”

DURING A LATE-AFTERNOON LULL, Janet showed off her favorite methods for identifying and finding books when given few and sometimes inaccurate details. The demonstration was part of what Christine, Tallie, and Summer called their "Book Goddess" training. Pamela and Kenneth had returned, and Pamela's hovering attention made Janet uneasy. But when she described some of the trickier requests she'd deciphered in her years as a librarian, Pamela applauded with the others.

"Brilliant," Pamela said. "You see, it's only a question of using your brain and your computer."

"And our patrons, our *customers*, will think we're magic," Janet said.

"Don't expect the ungrateful ones to thank you, though," Pamela said. "They'll say to whomever they're with, or to anyone at all, 'Look, I found it.'"

"Isn't that the truth?" Janet laughed, glad for this moment of comradery with Pamela. "Whatever makes them happy, though. Even when they were annoying, the patrons were always right."

"What makes our customers happy most often is browsing on their own," Pamela said, putting the comradery back in its place. She rearranged a stack of bookmarks previously straightened by Christine. "I don't know how it's done in America, and you'll certainly have plenty of them marching through here on the trail of their ancestors, but in general you don't want to be overly loud or jump out at people when they first come through the door."

Christine appeared to inflate. Janet would have loved to hear Christine's feelings about Pamela's latest advice, but the jingle of the bell on the shop door intervened. A woman came in, and Janet glanced sideways at the others, suddenly afraid to make a move too obviously "American." Pamela stepped back with a gesture as though to say, *It's all yours.* Christine accepted the challenge but, in taking a moment to pat her hair and her composure back into place, missed her chance.

"What, has the cat got all your tongues?" Kenneth asked, coming out of the stockroom and wiping his hands on a dustcloth. "I didn't hear anyone greet—Oh, I say, good to see you, Una. Here she is, ladies—Una Graham of the *Inversgail Guardian*. Una, I'd like you to meet the new proprietors of Yon Bonnie Books."

FOUR

Una Graham held up a hand, postponing further introductions while she gave in to a raspy cough. Her moussed hair was a mixture of gray and an unhealthy yellow, as though the decades of cigarette smoke that had produced her cough had also precipitated out through her scalp. Jess Baillie's description of her wasn't far off, Janet realized. Minus the hair, Una was about her own height, with a sharp nose and chin. And if shrews had dark and darting eyes, even while coughing into their sharp elbows, then that part of Jess's description matched as well.

"Sorry," Una said, putting a hand to her chest. "I gave up the pipes because of that cough."

"You never played the pipes," Pamela said.

"No, but it's a good joke on myself, don't you think?"

Shrewish she might be, but Janet found herself liking Una Graham. The quick eyes held a humor Jess's and Pamela's lacked. "I'm Janet Marsh," she said, stepping forward. "I wish you did play the pipes."

"People either run to them or away from them," Una said. "Myself, I'm from the 'stand back and wait for a kilt-raising breeze' school of thought." She pointed at Kenneth. "Mind you, I only said that to make Kenneth blush. I can take the pipes or leave them, but I'd happily die for a cup of tea right now. Have I heard right that you're putting a tearoom in the empty space next door? If it were open, we could sit down over a pot and plate of cakes for an interview."

"Does she stop talking long enough to *do* an interview?" Christine whispered to Janet.

"You'll find I do," Una said, "and you'll also find I have exceptional hearing." She turned in a circle, taking in the shelves and displays. Was she memorizing details, Janet wondered, or looking for a crack or flaw to stick her fingers in and probe? "Who's your spokeswoman?" she asked.

With little debate, they decided Janet and Summer would answer questions and give Una a tour of the planned tearoom. They told her touring the rooms for the B & B upstairs would have to wait until Janet and Tallie moved out of them.

"Left your beds unmade, did you?" Una asked. "Afraid I'll air your dirty laundry?" She paused long enough to cackle and cough, and then suggested they find a place to sit. "My feet will thank you," she said, hiking a trouser leg to show them three-inch heels.

Summer suggested sitting in the tearoom-to-be. "It isn't cozy, yet, but it'll be quiet and I can run upstairs and get the electric kettle."

"Then, do it, hen," Una said. "Run like the wind. Fly, fly!"

"Shall we go through to the tearoom?" Janet asked.

"We'll wait," Una said, turning away. "I won't be on my game until tea's up."

THE SPACE FOR the tearoom had been a baked potato shop in a previous life. Over the years that the Lawries had owned the building, they'd rented the space to a series of seasonal enterprises, most recently a shop selling t-shirts and other clothing of a more adult nature called Tartan Tees and Tease. The windows had been covered with tartan panels to avoid scandalizing passersby, and the door through from the bookshop had been kept locked.

"We'll take the panels off the windows when the work is far enough along to generate excitement," Janet said when they were sitting with their tea at one of the tables left over from the baked potato era.

"Excitement is exactly why the panels were installed." Una wiggled her eyebrows. "Very popular place this was for a certain segment of Inversgail society, in addition to the tourists." She pulled a small laptop from her shoulder bag and opened it. "Now, will your tearoom and B and B have names all their own, or are they part of the Yon Bonnie franchise?"

"We're calling the tearoom Cakes and Tales," Summer said. "And we're calling the bed-and-breakfast Bedtime Stories."

"You like words. That's lovely. You're the ex-newspaperwoman, aren't you? It's a glorious profession. Whatever made you give it up? But hold your answer." Una erased the question from the air with her hand. "We'll get back to you. First, my readers will want to know why, of all the book joints in all the towns in all the world, did you walk into this one and buy it? My Bogie is far from brilliant, but I'm sure you catch my drift."

Janet's teacup stopped halfway to her lips. She set the cup down, moved it a safe distance aside, and leaned forward to tell what she thought of as their fun and still somewhat unbelievable story—how they'd turned a decades-old game of *why not* into a daydream-come-true. "Why—"

"Why don't you start with your division of labor," Una said. "People love the DIY angle to small businesses, in case they fancy a go at one for themselves."

"Christine Robertson and Summer Jacobs will be in charge of the tearoom, and my daughter, Tallie, and I will be in charge of the bookshop. That's Tallie Marsh, short for Natalie. To be practical, though, we're all cross-training."

"Right." Una studied Janet, an index finger tapping pursed lips. "Nicknames are common enough, but does your daughter dislike her given name?"

"No. Not at all."

"Are you sure?" Una asked, but before Janet got over her surprise at the question, Una went on. "I only ask because if there's tension in the story—between partners, for instance—all the better. Books, tea, cakes, and pillows for strangers' heads are all well and good, but I'm looking for that jagged shard of tension for an article that really grips our readers' imaginations."

Janet turned to Summer. "Do we have tension?"

"I haven't noticed any."

"A shame," Una said. "Moving on, you mentioned practicality. Is there any actual, practical bookshop or tearoom experience among you?"

"Thirty-five years in public libraries, purchasing

books for a popular collection, and proactively connecting those books with patrons," Janet said, proud of being able to string those words together without spitting them at the woman across from her. The one she wasn't liking quite so much after all. "And Tallie spent six weeks at a bookselling course in Wigtown—a program you might have heard of, in the town called 'Scotland's National Book Town.'"

Una typed without comment, and then, without looking up, she pointed at Summer and said, "Cueing the tearoom experience."

"Two years in a steamy relationship with a master baker who taught me everything he knew, if you know what I mean, and then one day, between the yeast and the icing, we lost the magic, and I ran away to the Scottish Highlands to lose myself in tea and scones and ultimately find myself."

Una had stopped typing at the word "steamy." When Summer finished, Una pointed at her again. "Cheeky. I like that. And if your Christine is anything like her mother in a kitchen, between the two of you Cakes and Tales should do very nicely. Now, let's put the unsavory bits to bed, so to speak, and get back to my original Bogie question—why this bookshop in this town? I feel certain our readers will want to know if this is a trend, alarming or otherwise, toward foreign ownership of our homegrown businesses, a snapping up of our heritage, if you will. Although you, Steamy Summer Nights, raised another issue when you mentioned running away. Whether it's true or not, I've read that a great many of the American students who come to study at our universities are either looking for something or running away from something, not necessarily successfully. I wonder which you're doing—searching? Or running?" She studied Janet, lips pursed again and eyes narrowed.

The better to see into your motives, my dear, Janet thought with a shiver. *Or into your soul.*

"On the other hand, a more interesting angle for our female readers might be whether or not you've considered how dangerous an adjoining tearoom, run by Steamy Summer Nights and the culinary heir of Helen MacLean, will be to your waistline."

Janet put her hands in her lap, the better to avoid swatting gadflies. She felt a subtle pressure on her right foot and shot a glance at Summer.

"Why don't you write the article from another perspective," Summer said as she laid a business card on the table, "one with a more international audience in mind." Her fingers dallied over the card in such a way that Janet couldn't read it. Una couldn't, either, but her eyes didn't leave it as Summer slid the card several inches closer to her. "Think of the millions of Americans who identify as 'Scottish.'"

"Obsessive Outlanders," Una said. "Born-again Bravehearts. They're a beautiful people."

"Exactly. Think about attracting the attention of a mere fraction of them. A fraction willing, able, and, if you play them right, eager to support local initiatives. Think about economic impact. Think about a leap upward in your career. I'll give you my AP contact." She slid the card three inches closer to Una, then stopped.

"Better yet—" She put her hand over that card, produced another, and handed both to Una. "NPR will eat this kind of story, completely and totally, up."

The cards disappeared. Una looked at her phone and sang, "The texts, the texts are calling me," then scraped her chair back. "I don't do 'Danny Boy' any better than I do Bogie, I'm well aware, but I entertain myself and that's not a bad thing. Ta very much for everything. Sorry to sip and slide so soon. Is that your kitchen there? Take me on a whirlwind tour of it, and if I like what I see I'll be back tomorrow to record more of the color you're adding to our local vicinity."

Summer took her into the kitchen. Janet didn't follow, having had enough of Una for one "interview." She knew she'd made the right decision when she heard what sounded like every cupboard and drawer being opened and banged shut in quick succession. Then Una's voice came in rapturous tones.

"Ooh, is that one of those fancy instant-hot, instant-cold, instant-ooh-la-la taps?"

That was followed by the sound of gushing water. Una exited the kitchen before the water stopped gushing, and Janet pictured Summer flying across the kitchen to turn it off.

"Cheerie-bye, then," Una said on her way past. And she was gone.

Janet found Summer standing in the middle of the kitchen looking slightly shell-shocked. "Thank you, Summer. I would have completely bungled that without you. Or thrown my teacup at her."

"A small dog would need three extra shots of espresso to reach her level of hyper."

"How on earth did you come up with that international audience and local initiative concoction?"

Summer shrugged a shoulder. "Just something I've been thinking about. It might even turn into something for her."

"And your card trick—you're very slick. It's lucky you had them with you. Or do you carry them out of habit?"

"I grabbed them when I went up to get the kettle." Summer smiled. "I play a mean game of poker, too."

UNDER KENNETH'S WATCHFUL EYE, Janet and Tallie went through the steps for closing out the cash register for the day. Janet didn't mind telling anyone—and wished she'd had the chance to tell Una Graham—that she was endlessly impressed by her daughter. Tallie was the one who'd found the real estate listing for Yon Bonnie Books online two years ago. She knew the shop from their summer visits to Inversgail, and it fit perfectly into the *why not* game. Janet had started the game during a stretch of high mortgage bills, tuition payments, and budgetary stress at the library. *Why not buy a restaurant on the Outer Banks of North Carolina,* she'd asked, *so we can live at the beach? Forever?* Getting away from it all and making life changes were key elements of the game. Christine, an excellent cook, latched onto the game during the years of her husband's illness. She planned menus for the restaurant and convinced the others to add a gift shop where she could sell the miles of scarves she stress-knitted. Tallie had taken the game into the realm of possibilities when she asked, *Why not buy a bookstore?*

"FIRST THINGS FIRST," Janet said when the four of them stood on the deck behind the cottage that evening. "I'd like us to spread out and check the rest of the house. We took Jess's word for it that only the kitchen is trashed, but we need to see for ourselves. Take pictures if you find anything. And open the windows as you go. If that smell has seeped into the furniture and curtains, I don't know what I'll do."

"And then we need to be brave and muck through whatever rubbish Jess hasn't cleared out of the kitchen," Christine said. "We're looking for anything with identifying information. Envelopes, pill bottles, that kind of thing."

"Names won't prove anything," Tallie said. A slim version of her mother, she'd pulled her dark hair into a stubby braid at the back of her head.

"But they might tell us where the garbage came from," Summer countered. "And that could lead somewhere. What about checking the shed? We might as well be thorough. Will it be locked?"

"Much good that did the house," Janet said. She sorted through the keys on her ring, pulled off two, and handed them to Summer. "Do you mind? I think it's one of those."

"I'll meet you inside in a few," Summer said and hopped off the deck with a grace Janet envied.

"Tallie, do you mind checking the bedrooms? And,

Christine, you take the dining room. I'll open the window in the lounge and start on the kitchen," Janet said. "Call out if you find anything. Now take your last breath of fresh air," she said, and unlocked the door.

The smell was just as bad as Janet remembered. She went to the window in the family room, picturing herself staggering through a toxic swamp. As she wrestled with the catch on the casement, she heard Tallie taking the stairs two at a time the way she had as a child and a teenager, calling "Tally-ho" as she went. The catch finally gave and the window went up with a groan. She leaned out the window for another blessed breath of fresh air and heard another groan. An echo? Her scalp prickled.

The sound came again, higher pitched and rising at the end. Behind her she heard Christine opening and closing drawers, and above her were Tallie's feet. But at the bottom of the garden, Summer held on to the shed door, then doubled over, retching.

Afterward, Janet tried to imagine how she'd got to Summer so quickly. Her only memory was of flying, arms stretched out to gather her in. But she must have called Christine and Tallie as she flew, because they followed, and they were there when Summer told them not to look in the shed. But of course they did, and they all saw the crumpled woman, and the pool of blood, and in her poor, thin neck, the sickle.

FIVE

THE FOUR WOMEN waited for the police, sitting on the pew on the deck at the back of the house. Janet and Christine made comforting bookends for the younger women tucked between them. Four sets of hands were clasped in four laps. Three sets of eyes did not waver from the garden shed. Janet knew the door she'd closed didn't keep them from seeing what lay inside, but as she watched their faces, she gave silent thanks for their levelheaded natures. Christine had known the right words to calm Summer. Tallie made a clear, concise call to the nonemergency Police Scotland number. With no hope the poor soul in the shed was hanging on to life, there was no emergency. It was Janet who'd herded them back up the hill to brush last year's leaves from the pew and sit down.

"I think this bodes well for the bookshop," she said.

Three shocked faces turned to stare at her.

"Not *this*," she rushed to explain. "Not this unspeakable—" She fluttered a hand toward the shed, and for a moment she thought she might lose her own level head. Tallie took her hand and held it. "I mean us," Janet said. She squeezed Tallie's hand. "I mean the four of us, and how we help each other and how well we work together. This is an unusual kind of acid test, but I think we passed."

"Did you expect us to fall out and start accusing each other of murder?" Christine asked. "No, forget I said that. That was a poor joke. I know you didn't expect that. And to prove your point further, I agree with you. We are a good team. I just hope this unspeakable"—she mimicked Janet's hand flutter—"doesn't put a damper on our business. And I don't mean to be disrespectful of the dead when I say that, God rest her soul."

Four heads bowed. Then Tallie asked quietly, "Is that Jess? Do we need a lawyer? A solicitor? Are they going to think you, or any of us, had something—"

"It's not Jess down there," Janet cut in.

"They've a similar build, but didn't you recognize her?" Christine asked. "That's Una Graham in the shed."

"I didn't look that closely," Tallie said.

"Of course you didn't, and I wish I hadn't," Christine said. "But this doesn't look good for Jess. She wasn't overly fond of Una."

"Do you think Jess snapped?" Janet asked. "I've always liked her. I don't want to think she did this."

"Did she strike you as being entirely stable this morning?" Christine asked.

"Let's not jump to conclusions," Tallie said. She stood up. "Let's make notes. Mom, you and Christine go over the gist of what you saw and heard this morning, in the order it happened, if you can, and sticking to facts. Summer, you're the reporter—start reporting."

"But impressions should count for something, too," Christine said.

"Especially those of a trained professional," said Janet. "I said I like Jess, but I trust Christine's judgment. It comes from years of observation and working with people in all kinds of situations."

Christine nodded agreement.

"So why don't you mark impressions with a capital I in your notes, Summer," Janet continued, "and mark facts with an F."

"Reporter," Tallie said, pointing at Summer.

"I know, dear. I'm just suggesting a method." She was pleased when the younger women returned her smile, although she suspected Tallie's was somewhat forced.

"Notes will have to wait." Summer nodded toward the garden gate behind Janet. "Police are here."

"One, anyway," Christine said. "Local constable."

"Do you know him?" Janet asked.

"I don't know why you think I would."

The constable lifted his cap to them as he came through the gate, revealing a brush of salt-and-pepper hair. He took in his surroundings as he followed the flagged path toward the deck, appearing to take his time and looking as though he might be in the market for the property, eyeing the roof, squinting at the chimney. He stopped before he reached them and turned to look toward the bottom of the garden, his hands on his hips.

"Out for an evening stroll, are you, Norman?" Christine called.

"I thought you didn't know him," Janet whispered.

"I'm as surprised as you are. I used to change his nappies," Christine whispered back.

"Evening, Mrs. Robertson," the constable said. "Just giving Mr. Atkinson, next door, time to put his wellies on. Very keen on police work, is Mr. Atkinson. He writes crime novels. I don't imagine he'll intrude on us, but he might have a sudden urge to turn the compost." He looked at the open window behind the women and took a few tentative sniffs. His brow creased as he must have caught a compost-like whiff from the kitchen.

"I was sorry to hear about your mum, Norman," Christine said when he reached them.

"And she was very sorry to hear about your husband, as was I. Are you back for a visit?"

"To stay. Looking after my own mum and dad."

"They'd be about my gran's age, wouldn't they? Well, time does not stand still for the old dears. So, then." He straightened his back and saluted them. "Constable Norman Hobbs here, and I've had a report." He took a spiral notebook from his breast pocket and held it so they could see the princess on the pink cover. "A birthday present from my youngest niece," he said. "I promised her I'd let everyone I come in contact with admire it." He carefully turned the cover back and looked at Janet, Tallie, and Summer. "I don't believe I have the pleasure of knowing the rest of you. May I have your names and current addresses, please?"

"Atkinson," Christine said before Janet had a chance to speak. "Ian Atkinson, the author? *The* Ian Atkinson is living next door? He never did before."

"Incomer. Arrived two or three years ago," Constable Hobbs said with a barely suppressed sniff.

"The nerve," Christine said with unsuppressed satisfaction. "Not that I personally have anything against incomers."

"No."

"And I daresay his presence is a benefit to the community," Christine said.

"He takes an interest, and that's appreciated. In fact, I wonder why he hasn't shown an interest in our gathering here this evening, writers being naturally nosy types. Or so I gather." Constable Hobbs craned his neck to scan the house and garden next door. Janet cleared her throat, and he turned back to them.

"I'm Janet Marsh, Constable Hobbs. I'm sorry to say I'm also an incomer. This is my house."

"May I be the first to remove my foot from my mouth and welcome you to our community, ma'am," Hobbs said with another salute. "Please forgive my rude comment. Like Mrs. Robertson, I don't personally have anything against *new*comers."

Hobbs took down their names and contact information in a neat, if crabbed, hand in his pink notebook and didn't offer further opinions. But when he heard he was speaking to the new owners of the bookshop, he stopped and shook each of their hands. "I've been tied up with family troubles," he apologized, "or I would have stopped in to welcome you sooner. A lovely shop. It's a bit of a step, relocating such a distance."

"A retirement scheme of sorts," Janet said.

"A multigenerational concept," Christine added.

"When it gets to that point, I can bring Mum and Dad along and park them by the fire so they won't feel isolated."

"And Tallie and Summer are building viable second careers," Janet said. "We planned carefully before taking that bit of a step."

"Very interesting." Hobbs said. "Aye, well, that's grand. Now, which one of you reported finding a body in the garden shed?"

Tallie and Summer stepped forward, as caller and discoverer of the body, respectively. Hobbs listened intently, jotting notes, as Summer gave her account. Janet appreciated his matter-of-fact if somewhat cozy approach. It gave her a reassuring feeling, a sense that the stalwart strength of Police Scotland was there for them to lean on. She did wonder if Norman Hobbs had ever considered growing a mustache to help that impression along. He was at least forty, if Christine had indeed changed his nappies, and the salt-and-pepper hair seemed to prove that age. But his hair would be hidden under his cap most of the time, and she could picture certain elements of the community not taking his round baby face seriously. His demeanor was professional, though, and only a red flush creeping up his neck, and a tighter grip on his pencil and princess notebook, gave her the inkling this call might be something out of the ordinary.

"Right," Constable Hobbs said after hearing Summer's account. "Wait here, please."

Janet and Christine exchanged glances and followed

him. When Hobbs realized they were treading carefully behind him, he stopped and turned around.

"I meant all of you should wait." He hesitated, then closed the gap between them. "Twenty-three years on the force," he said quietly, "and not once have I had a murder. The BBC calls Scotland the murder capital of the U.K., and yet I have never had a single one, and never had the chance to show what I can do. Natural causes, accidental deaths, aye. And suicides, I've dealt with a sad number of all of them. But murder? No." He narrowed his eyes. "There is no chance this is any of the above, is there?"

"No."

"I'll be back shortly, then."

They watched him go.

"I suppose this means we shouldn't do any further rummaging or cleaning in the house," Christine said. "All that rubbish might be evidence. And you still won't be sleeping in your own bed."

"Is that a spring in his step?" Janet asked.

THE SUN WAS beginning to set as Janet and Christine rejoined Tallie and Summer on the deck. None of them sat now, preferring to stand. Gulls wheeled and cried in the harbor. In another month, toward the end of June, it would be light enough after nine to read a book outdoors. With uncharacteristic sourness, Janet hoped it wouldn't be another month before she was reading a book in her own bed.

"Imagine Ian Atkinson living next door," she said, changing this unhappy subject in her head. "I wonder if Jess knows that, and if she does, why she never said anything. I'm tempted to call her now and let her know what's going on."

"Probably shouldn't," Tallie said.

"No."

"I need to be getting home to Mum and Dad," Christine said, "before they forget I'm staying there. But here's Norman coming back."

Hobbs had switched on a flashlight. He swept it back and forth across the grass as he came back up the hill. He flicked it off when he stepped onto the deck.

"I've called the Specialist Crime Division," he said. His tone sounded as though he'd brushed his cap and tugged the shoulder seams of his uniform straighter. Janet glanced at his shoes. They were impressively large, but beyond that she had no point of reference to know if they measured up to Specialist Crime standards. "A Major Investigation Team will be on its way shortly," Hobbs said. "Although 'on its way shortly' does not mean the team will arrive anytime soon, as some of them may be coming quite a distance. Please don't take that remark as a comment on procedure. When they arrive, they'll want to speak to you. Mind you, we needn't wait out here." He cast a hopeful glance toward the house. "Perhaps a cup of tea would be in order, unless there's some reason—" He took several more guarded sniffs toward the open windows. "Forgive me, but there's a reek like a pot of three-week-old kale coming from the house. Can't you smell it?"

"Trust me, it's much worse inside," Janet said. "And that's something we should probably warn you about before your specialists get here." With a silent apology to Jess, she filled Hobbs in on finding the estate agent in the kitchen and what she'd told them about the vandalism. "Jess did ask us not to tell anyone. She's sure it was only directed at her and her business. She's certain it won't happen again after I move in. And this morning I could almost believe her, but now..." Janet's words trailed off under Constable Hobbs's gaze, which was really more like a glare, she realized. She revised her opinion: His round baby face didn't need help from a mustache. "So," she said, mustering her courage, "a locksmith is coming tomorrow, and the vandalism really won't happen again, but what all this means is that I can't offer you tea."

"You didn't think to mention Jess Baillie's presence here today, or the ongoing vandalism, when I first arrived?" Hobbs asked.

Tallie moved over to stand beside her mother. "The body seemed more important, and now you know the rest."

"Do I?"

"Sarcasm doesn't become you, Norman," Christine said. "At this point, you know as much as we do. And this is our first murder, too, so you shouldn't be surprised if we've made a few missteps. But you've gotten off to a brilliant start with our help. Think how difficult we could have made it for you if you'd found us weeping and wailing. Instead, we've been collected and coherent. In fact, we were in the process of making notes when you arrived and interrupted us. Now, here's what I suggest we do—you go on in the house and look around so you can further impress your specialists when they finally do get here. We'll finish our notes and make sure you get a copy. And you'll be able to trust their accuracy, because amongst the four of us, we have the best brains and background you could ask for—we are a reporter, a lawyer, a social worker, and, best of all, a librarian. Don't you worry, Norman; we've got your back."

It hadn't occurred to Janet, until then, how easily Christine might stand in for the queen, should Elizabeth II ever have something else going on when the guards at Buckingham Palace needed encouragement. And if Elizabeth didn't mind a stand-in wearing a comfortably worn twinset and jeans with elastic in the waist, or looking younger than her oldest child. It was too dark to gauge Norman Hobbs's reaction to Christine's speech, but he did leave them and go into the house. She found it endearing that, given what he smelled, he wiped his feet first.

"There," Christine said. "I've never used the phrase 'got your back' before, and now I've used it twice in one day."

"You probably shouldn't overuse it, though," said Janet.

"I feel invigorated."

"Nevertheless."

"I feel energized, and I think we should do something to help Norman make the best possible impression on these major criminal specialists of his."

"I have an idea that might work," Tallie said. She waited until her mother and Christine were looking at her. "We've done well. We've contributed what we know and we'll give Constable Hobbs our notes. Beyond that, we should let the police do their work."

"But—"

"No, really. We should stay out of it."

"Well, shoot."

"And don't say 'shoot.'"

FROM TALLIE'S FONDNESS for trousers with pockets to her decision to quit the law, Janet knew that what she said and did almost always made sense. She told Christine that before they repeated what little they knew to the Major Investigation Team when it finally arrived. She reminded Christine of it again, after they'd been dismissed—*"Dismissively,"* Christine said with a huff—and cautioned not to leave the area.

By then, the activity in and around the house had attracted the attention of neighbors and passersby. Janet saw the silhouette of someone watching from an upper window next door. Ian Atkinson? How fascinating for the crime writer to have this going on below his window. Unless he was annoyed by the commotion and looking out to see who was disturbing his peace. The local press came sniffing around, too, but the victim's name hadn't been released yet, so they weren't aware they'd lost one of their own.

"If you can leave your keys with me," Constable Hobbs said, "and postpone the locksmith, that will be helpful. The house will be safe enough with the experts in charge of it. Now, I'll see you safely past the gawkers." He walked with them, clearing his throat every few yards as though preparing them for something he had to say. After turning the corner into Fingal Street he said it. "You didn't hear it from me."

"Hear what?" Summer asked. She took her phone from her pocket. Hobbs looked at her and cleared his throat again. She put it away.

"That Jess Baillie isn't guilty," he said.

"You didn't hear any of us say that she *is*," said Janet.

"And what makes you so sure she isn't?" Christine asked on top of her.

For a brief moment, Norman Hobbs looked as though he might be sorry he'd broached the subject.

"He's speaking as an unauthorized source," Tallie said, studying his face as though looking for further nuances to interpret for the others. "What else shouldn't we hear, Constable Hobbs?"

Before he could add anything, or retract the little he'd said, voices rose behind them from the onlookers. Hobbs touched his cap and returned to the scene.

"I think they're bringing the body out," Christine said.

"I think he weaseled out of telling us something," Tallie said.

"Do you?" Christine asked.

Janet thought Christine might follow Hobbs and took her arm. "Come on. I can't bear to look at the house again tonight."

"Are you going to be okay?" Tallie asked Janet.

"Compared to poor Una Graham?"

"Compared to the mom who didn't expect to find her

house buried in putrid garbage. Or the one who didn't expect to find a murder victim in her garden shed."

"Well, if your dad hadn't bought the shed and had it installed in the first place, then we wouldn't have found a body in it." Janet immediately felt bad for being snarky. She gave Tallie a kiss to make up for it, and said she'd be along to their temporary accommodations above the bookshop before too long. "But first I'll walk Christine home."

"You know you can't blame Dad for Una ending up in the shed, don't you, Mom?"

"I do know that, dear. You and Summer go on, now. I'll be fine. Fix yourselves a tot of something when you get back. Summer's had a bigger shock than any of us."

Summer, bouncing on her toes, looked less shocked than she did ready to take a run in the heather-covered hills. "When I was at the newspaper," she said, "I learned that typing fast and pushing on through is the best way to get over shock. So I'll get on those notes we said we'd share with the constable. Sorry, Tallie. Notes first, tots later."

"No worries," Tallie said. "I'll use pre-tot time for a spot of online research. How's this for a topic—Scottish case law on meddlers and meddling?"

"Excellent," Janet said. "Information is power. If we know where we stand, those specialists won't be able to scare us with fancy titles or false threats."

"Not exactly what I meant," Tallie said.

"I know that, too, dear." Janet gave Tallie another kiss. "Remind me to call Allen when I get back. There's no telling how or when this will end up in the news, but we don't want Allen and Nicola hearing it that way first."

"I'll text him so he doesn't read it first in a tweet," Tallie said.

"Or hear it first from Nicola's mother," Christine put in. "She has that competitive streak."

"Oh, my word." Janet looked back toward the house. She hadn't seen her son's mother-in-law there, but she hadn't looked closely at any of the faces in the small crowd. "I've been terrible and haven't even called Maida since we got here. I'd better fix that in the next day or two. Tallie, dear, tell your brother I'll call him in the morning."

Janet gave each of the younger women a hug for good measure. She watched as they started down Fingal Street toward the High Street, Summer clearly on a mission, and Tallie with the backward glance of a sensible daughter who knows her mother well enough to have forebodings. Then, her arm linked with Christine's, Janet turned so they were heading up Fingal Street in the opposite direction.

"Come on, we should walk faster," she said.

"Cutting over on Victoria will get me home fastest."

"Not if we're stopping by Jess Baillie's on the way."

BEN NEVIS MEWS, where Jess Baillie lived, lacked the former stables that would make the street a true mews. It lacked a view of the mountain it boasted, too. A half-hearted streetlight showed Janet and Christine a short, narrow road with no outlet and three modern semidetached houses on either side. The light's brackish glow also showed them a half dozen people watching as Jess Baillie was helped into the backseat of a police car.

SIX

"Don't stare at her," Janet said. She turned her back as the police car bearing Jess Baillie came toward them. The windows of the car were closed, but she imagined she heard sobs as the car passed behind them.

"Well, that's a shame," Christine said.

"And *that's* an understatement. Who was that in the car with her? It wasn't Constable Hobbs. Didn't he tell them she wasn't guilty?"

"Would they believe him?" Christine asked. "*Should* they believe him?"

"They should take what he says into consideration. He's one of them. He knows the town. He knows the people. He's their man on the ground with local expertise."

"Maybe lack of familiarity with him, or prejudicial familiarity with the Highlands, has bred contempt."

Janet made a rude noise.

"Then maybe they found something Norman didn't know about," said Christine.

"When? They've hardly had time."

"A witness?"

"A witness who waited until the body was discovered to come forward?" Janet asked. "What a fine, upstanding citizen that would be. Okay, earlier today you wanted me to be suspicious. Now tell me *you're* not."

"They're creeping closer." Christine tipped her head toward Jess's neighbors. The neighbors had shifted their attention from the departed police car to the women standing at the entrance to their enclosed domain. "Let's take our suspicions for a walk."

"Fine." Janet didn't spit the word, but her walk was more of a stalk. "I had two small pieces of consolation to hold on to through this horrible evening. *First*," she said, jabbing a finger skyward, "that Una was killed in the shed and not in the house."

"Definitely a relief."

"Don't interrupt." Janet raised a second finger beside the first and stabbed both of them as though putting out the eyes of the moon as it shone its cheerless light on the street before them. "Two—that Jess isn't guilty. Because if she is, then all that garbage in the house will be considered evidence. The whole house will be considered evidence. And I'll be living out of a suitcase above the shop for who knows how long. And I'm a total, complete, miserable, and selfish so-and-so for thinking of my own comfort when—"

"Stop it." Christine grabbed Janet's hand and held on just as Janet turned the stabbing fingers toward herself. "I need to get home to Mum and Dad, and you need to go have your own tot and then have Tallie's and Summer's on top of it."

Janet pulled her hand away.

"We'll get through this," Christine said. "And don't

start grinding your teeth. I know you. You won't be happy with the National Health dentist."

JANET LEFT CHRISTINE trying to get through a creaky front door without waking her parents. She continued her stalk home, supposing she should feel uneasy being out alone with a murderer on the loose. "But I don't," she said aloud. She'd enjoyed jabbing her finger earlier, and jabbed it again, this time at a wheelie bin left on the pavement. "I refuse to be a cliché."

A startled cat hissed, making her jump. The cat slunk behind the bin, and Janet hurried to the next corner and into the better-lit High Street. The tide was out in the harbor, leaving moored boats tipped as though napping on their seabed. Her adrenaline had ebbed, too, and she wanted her bed. Her own bed. As she approached the bookshop, a figure sitting on the steps waved. Her sensible Tallie.

"I'd forgotten how everything sounds louder in the dark," Tallie said when Janet dropped down next to her on the stoop and sighed. "Things smell stronger, too. Or do you think that's an illusion?"

"If you're speaking in subtext, I'm not up for it."

"No subtext," Tallie said. "Just an observation. The harbor is full of good, basic smells."

"If you like stranded seaweed and muck. I'm not up for more smells tonight, either."

"Christine called."

"And I didn't think to call you. Don't fuss at me, Tallie. I'm especially not up for that. I was going to tell you about Jess when I got home."

"No fussing. I called Constable Hobbs. He might have been more surprised than you about Jess being taken in. He hadn't heard."

Janet stopped picking pills from the cuff of her sweatshirt. "What did he say when you told him?"

"He asked very politely for our notes."

"How is Summer coming with them? Wait, first, what did your research into laws about meddling tell you?"

"I made cocoa instead," Tallie said. "Let's go warm it with a tot."

THE LAWRIES BROUGHT fresh scones to Yon Bonnie Books the next morning. Janet hadn't expected Pamela and Kenneth for another hour. She hadn't expected the scones at all, and she felt bad for being tempted to leave all of them out on the stoop, no matter how persistently they tapped on the glass for her attention. She'd looked forward to getting the shop ready and to opening it solo for the first time.

Tallie was out for a morning run—her way of dealing with stress. Christine and Summer were driving the forty miles to Fort William for a meeting with a baking and catering supplier for the tearoom. Janet had phoned her son in Edinburgh, a necessarily short call because Allen and Nicola were getting the children ready for day care and themselves for work. She'd sung a quick "Itsy Bitsy Spider" for Freddy and Wally, the two-and three-year-old grandsons she adored, before disconnecting with a loud smooch for each of them. Then she'd planned to sweep, dust, polish, and straighten the bookshop with such muscle that she would force the worst of last night's worries out of her nightmares and into the rational light of day. But she was willing to see if scones from Paudel's Newsagent, Post Office, and Convenience could do that, as well.

"Pear ginger," Kenneth said, handing one to her. "Best take a serviette, too." The buttery, spicy scent of the fresh pastries soothed Janet's disappointment at having company. Kenneth passed a scone to Pamela and paper napkins to each of them. "Did Paudel have the shop the last time you stayed in Inversgail?"

"Yes. I remember Basant quite well," Janet said, "and his sisters, Arati and Puja." The siblings had emigrated from Nepal. Basant Paudel had been a teacher in their country. He'd given that up and bought the business as a way to support his younger sisters in their education.

"Arati makes these whenever she's home on holiday from her nursing course," Kenneth said. "Mind you, it takes second sight to know when they're available."

"Listen to him," Pamela said. "The man's havering. He saw the girl arrive home last night. She won't be making scones for the shop many times more, though. She's been offered a job in Glasgow when she finishes her course, so enjoy them while you can."

"They're delicious," Janet said around a mouthful. "Thank you. If she isn't going to be making them anymore, do you think she'd be willing to share the recipe, or maybe sell it?" She studied her scone after each bite. "These would be wonderful in the tearoom."

"She might," Kenneth said.

"Don't be daft," said Pamela. "You don't sell a recipe like this."

"Everything has a price, dear heart." Kenneth took the pastry bag from Pamela as she reached inside for another. "We'll save the rest for the others, shall we?" He folded the top of the bag and creased it. Then he went around behind the sales desk and made himself comfortable on the high stool. "Now that I think on it, Arati very likely bought the recipe from us in the first place. She came in for weeks on end, drooling over a cookery book we had on display, and if I recollect right, there were scones on the cover. This was two, three years ago. Then one day she up and bought it, and soon after that Paudel's started selling scones. There, you see? I'll give myself a pat on the back for having a good memory and for being the best kind of bookseller. There's a tip for you, Janet: Remember your customers' names, remember what they like, and remember what they buy for friends and family. We were quite good at it, weren't we, Pamela?"

"And the four of you will be," Pamela said with a smile for Janet. "Although it's a shame you've got off to such a rocky start in the community, what with the murder in your house, and all."

Janet choked on her last bite of scone. "She wasn't in the—"

"Now then," Kenneth said, "didn't we agree we weren't going to bring up Ug and that terrible business?"

"And I haven't, Ken. It's you who're being disrespectful to the dead by calling her Ug. I'm just saying how sorry I am to Janet."

Janet accepted pats on the back from Pamela, and if she could judge the depth of Pamela's sorrow by the zeal of those pats, then she had no doubt the sorrow was very real. She also had no doubt that Pamela and Kenneth had arrived early with every intention of bringing up the murder. And why not? It was shocking news. If Constable Hobbs was right, and this was the first murder in decades, then it was also extraordinary news. She thought of the times at the library when she'd listened to and fielded questions about unsettling events, feeling sometimes like a community ombudsperson and sometimes like a bartender. The Lawries would be bucking human nature if they didn't want to talk about the murder. And it was only natural they would come in to find out what she knew about it. Because of the dratted garden shed, she was part of the news.

"But there's an end to the subject," Pamela said with a final, unnecessary thump on Janet's back. "And an end to Una Graham, too. She was a nosy bisom, God rest her soul."

"Wheesht, woman." Kenneth's rebuke didn't seem to ruffle Pamela. It apparently didn't apply to himself, either. "She provided a service to the community through her weekly advice column. She listened to problems and provided answers."

Like I did in my position as librarian cum ombudsperson cum bartender, Janet thought.

"People like that," Pamela scoffed. "She caused as many problems as she solved. She was an agony aunt, nothing more. What do you suppose she was doing in your house?"

"Shed," Janet said. "She was in the shed, at the bottom of the garden, a bit of a walk from the house, and I don't know why she was there."

"Are you sure?" Pamela asked.

"Yes! I have absolutely no idea why she was killed there, or what she was doing there at all, or how anyone got into the shed. It should've been locked."

"I meant are you sure about it being the shed. I heard from someone, who is ordinarily a quite reliable source, that it was your house, not the shed."

The soft burr of Pamela's r's did make her source sound unimpeachable, but Janet corrected her calmly, clearly, and firmly. Then it occurred to her that, if people were saying Una was killed in the house, they must also be wondering—Good Lord. "Do people think *I* killed her?" That hadn't come out calmly at all and she must have looked as alarmed as she sounded. Kenneth hastily gave her another scone.

"You specifically?" Pamela shook her head in a pooh-poohing way.

"Who, then? *Tallie?* No. Absolutely *no*. None of us—not one of us—had anything to do with that woman's death. Period."

"Full stop, now you're living here," Kenneth said, "and we believe you. After all, they do have Jess Baillie in custody." He turned to Pamela with an accusing eye. "I told you it was unkind to come and spread gossip."

"No," Janet said. "I'm glad you told me. If that's what's being said, then I need to know."

"Forewarned and forearmed, eh?" Kenneth asked.

"As long as it doesn't lead to foredoomed," Janet said. Then, seeing what might be a look of contrition crossing Pamela's face, she decided to press her advantage. "So people don't believe Jess is guilty?"

"Hard to say."

"What do you know about Una?"

"Not much," Pamela said.

So much for the power of contrition, Janet thought.

Kenneth offered a bit more. "Her family wasn't local, you see. They first arrived about thirty years ago, but they never quite settled. They came and they went. Had a caravan for some of the years. Some sort of tent or another."

"Were they Gypsies?" Janet asked. "One of the traditional traveler families?"

"No. Hippies," said Kenneth.

"Unwashed, tatty, and tie-dyed." Pamela's lip lifted at the memory.

"At some point the parents moved on, or were asked to move on," Kenneth said, "and Una stayed."

"But she was never a regular customer," Pamela explained. "That would have been the best way for us to get to know her."

"She and I were on one of the literature festival committees for the past several years," Kenneth said. "Judges for the writing contest. We read the entries on our own, though, and only met to compare notes and choose winners. It wasn't the sort of committee where you share personal information. Husband or children or pets to mourn her?" He answered himself with a shrug.

"Not knowing makes it sadder and more awful," Janet said.

"No husband." Pamela held up her left hand and touched her wedding ring.

Janet looked at the gold band stuck on her own finger, stuck because of a stubborn arthritic knuckle and her own stubbornness in not wanting to pay for it to be cut off. *The ring cut off*, she liked to remind herself, *not the finger*. "Una was writing more than the advice column, though, wasn't she? She was here yesterday to interview us," she said. "And she was doing some investigative reporting. I'm sure I heard that somewhere." Where had she heard that? From Jess, who thought Una wanted to ruin her business…

But Pamela was laughing. "What did *you* think of Una's reportorial skills?"

"She needed some practice or polish," Janet said. She didn't see the humor in that, but she threw in a few *heh-hehs* to keep the conversation and information flowing. "What do you know about Jess?"

"The trouble with these business types," Kenneth said, "is that they're so often caught up in chasing success that they don't know how to relax with a good book."

"Speaking of books," Pamela said, "have you met your neighbor yet? Ian Atkinson? I had no idea it was your house he'd moved next door to. He's bit of a hermit, mind you. He's another who hardly comes in the shop nowadays."

"He's hardly a hermit," Kenneth said. "A recluse, more like."

Janet's comprehension stumbled when she thought they were calling Ian Atkinson a hairnet, but she recovered nimbly enough, realizing they'd said "hermit," which they pronounced "hair-met."

"Hermit, recluse—he spends most of his time alone, so it's the same thing," Pamela said. "Always claims to be writing, but he hasn't had but the one new book since he moved here."

"*The Bludgeon in the Bothy*?" Janet asked. "I haven't read that one."

Pamela looked scandalized and went to get a copy from the shelf. "You'll have to do better than that in keeping up with trends." She handed the book to Janet.

"You'll enjoy it," Kenneth said. "I've enjoyed him the few times I've run into him in the pub. He says he likes to 'muse and schmooze on or about the booze.'"

"His love affair with whisky, he calls it. He should watch who he keeps company with, in that case," Pamela said.

"Is he drinking too much?" Janet wondered what kind of neighbor he'd be if that were true.

Pamela intercepted a look from Kenneth and backtracked unconvincingly. "Oh, I really couldn't say." Then, with a sly look of her own, she added, "Mind you, Una might have known. She certainly aimed to find out."

"Did she?" Janet asked. "How do you know?"

"Wheesht," Kenneth said. "She knows nothing of the sort. The man likes a drink and there's nothing wrong with that. If Una was up to anything, it was her own ugly business and none of ours."

Said the man who obviously knows more than he lets on, Janet thought. *But again, why not? Why should they share all with a virtual stranger, and an incomer to boot?*

Janet checked the clock. Time to unlock the door and open for business. She was glad to step back from the Lawries' bickering. She was equally glad when they stepped aside and let her greet the customers. Remembering Pamela's admonition not to jump at people, and to let them browse, she found herself greeting them in a subdued manner. She couldn't help feeling that her style and movements were being scored by a panel of Olympic bookselling judges, but she refused to be totally cowed. She smiled and said hello to everyone who came in. And when a tourist couple came in looking for a guide to the geology and landscape of Scotland, she felt a solid ten was within reach.

They were dressed for the soft smirr of rain coming down now, said they were in the area from Lancashire to spend the week hillwalking. They'd seen the book in a shop in Glasgow and regretted not buying it. And although they couldn't quite recall the title, they knew there was a lot of blue on the cover, and the author's name was…on the tips of their tongues. At that, Janet knew she had the gold. Not only did she know the book—*The Landscape of Scotland: A Hidden History*, by C. R. Wickham-Jones—but she found a copy on the ornate antique shelf to the left of the fireplace, put it in their hands, and gave them directions to the standing stone alignment at Ardnacross on Mull mentioned in it.

"But did you remember to slip a bookmark between

the pages before you handed the book to them?" Pamela asked when the couple had gone. "Because you know your sale isn't really complete unless you do."

THE SMIRR UNDER the gray skies might last all day. Janet knew it wouldn't necessarily keep people indoors, though. At any time the smirr might progress to a drizzle, or move on to a shower, or develop into a downpour. Unless tourists were woefully ignorant of Scottish weather, they would have come raingear-prepared. Or should have. Wet weather back in Illinois had often meant more patrons in the library, rather than fewer, and Janet saw that the same might be true for the bookshop. The smirr did indeed turn into a drizzle, followed by a corresponding spate of visitors who didn't mind shop-hopping. Janet could see that the tearoom was going to be a hit on such a day. They expected the decorators the next morning, and if all went well, they'd be serving tea by the next weekend.

Tallie came in, her hair pulled back in a neat, if somewhat damp, braid, and her cheeks still pink from the run.

"Didn't mean to be gone so long," she said. "Sorry. The trail along the river was harder than I expected. I'll start earlier next time, or not go as far. My calves might give me an idea which that'll be."

"Pretty?" Janet asked.

"The bluebells? And the water splashing down the hill? And everything? Heaven. Oh, and I took a detour. It looks like Jess Baillie's home and no longer in custody."

Janet was relieved to hear it. “She’s in the clear?”

“I don’t know that. They might be digging deeper to prove a better case. Or they might be building a case against someone else.”

SEVEN

TALLIE HANDED JANET several folded sheets of paper. Janet said nothing and made no move to look at the papers. Tallie removed the papers from her hand, unfolded them, and wafted them back and forth in front of her mother's staring eyes. When Janet blinked, Tallie put the papers back in her hand. Janet glanced at them—the notes they'd worked on and Summer had typed. She refolded them when Kenneth came over.

"Good news about Jess, eh?" Kenneth opened the bag of scones and offered them to Tallie. When she hesitated, he wafted the bag under her nose the way she'd wafted the papers under Janet's. "Your mother declared them worthy of a place in the tearoom."

Tallie took one and was suitably impressed.

"Glorious, aren't they?" Kenneth asked. "Now it's time for your crash course on VAT and other taxes."

Tallie looked suitably chagrined. "I've been had. That was bait and switch."

"It's no use complaining to me," he said. "As it will be no use complaining to the queen herself when it comes to paying them."

Tallie gave in with good grace, but not before taking a second scone.

Janet wished her luck but had no doubt she was up

to the tax task. Tallie had taught tax law for ten years back home. She settled on the stool behind the desk as Tallie and Kenneth disappeared into the office area. In truth, she was glad Tallie was going to be otherwise occupied. She needed time to think through—and worry about—what it might mean that Jess wasn't being held. That she could at last move into the house? That she or Tallie or one of the others was under suspicion? No, she refused to believe that. Rumors were one thing. Facts were another. The four of them had been together between the time Una had left Yon Bonnie Books and the time they'd found her dead. *Except.* Except for the hour or so Christine ran home to have a meal with her parents. But that time would be accounted for, too. It could be proved. *If.* If Christine's parents remembered. Janet felt a tightness creeping into her shoulders. She rolled them, lowered them, took a couple of slow, deep breaths. And nearly jumped out of her skin when Pamela cleared her throat behind her.

"I didn't want to sneak up on you," Pamela said. "But I wanted you to know that we still have a few personal bits and bobs in the office to clear out."

Janet refolded the notes.

"We'll pack them up this afternoon," Pamela continued. "And there's the ordering process still to go over, but then I really don't think you need us for much of anything else. I said before, and I meant it, you're naturalborn booksellers. We should be getting out of your hair and leaving you to it."

"Do you think we're ready?" Janet looked at the rows and ranks of bookcases, and over at the window displays—her new domain. Shelves and shelves of books, and all of them bright and crisp and new. Buying the building, the business, and making this move had been a bigger leap of faith than the one she'd made when she married Curtis.

"Do *you* think you're ready?" Pamela asked.

"I do."

Pamela reached past Janet, fumbling for a tissue. "It's been a good life. But to be perfectly honest, I can't wait to be shot of it. Can't wait to be shut of this place and the everlasting cold and damp. I can't wait until I've had so much bloody sun that I weep buckets of tears for a breath of air-conditioning." She laughed, then blew her nose and wiped her eyes. "Not that I don't wish you the best. Inversgail's a bonny town, and there's nothing like the book business. It's just…"

"Cold and damp," Janet said. She handed Pamela the tissue box.

"I hope you didn't think we were gossiping earlier on, or that I was prying when I asked if you'd spoken to Ian Atkinson after the…last evening. It's just we don't get this kind of crime here. It's unsettling."

"To say the least."

"I suppose in America you get—"

"We don't," Janet said. "*I* didn't, anyway." She fanned herself with the folded pages of notes, then thought better of it. She folded them a second time and slipped them into a back pocket. "You said something about Una knowing if Ian Atkinson has been drinking too much, or aiming to find out. Do you really know if she was? Because that might explain why she was in my garden. If she was spying on him, if she was looking for a scandal…" She let that dangle and watched while Pamela thought it through. Pamela glanced at the office and checked for customers before answering.

"There's no knowing what she was up to. She couldn't be content to answer letters from the desperate and the daft in her column. She should have stopped there, but you're right, she started calling herself an investigative journalist. She *was* a nosy bisom, and interested in anything that crawled or stank or bled. But no one deserves to die like that, and I'm sorry that she died in your house."

"In my shed—my ex-husband's *shed*. Not my house."

"In the house is a rumor Una would have enjoyed starting herself." Pamela glanced toward the office again. "Americans like bottom lines, don't they? Bottom line, then. I said I didn't know her well, and I didn't. But it didn't take knowing well to know she was a vile woman. A vile creature. It's a terrible thing to say of anyone, but someone did the world a favor. Now, I'll tell myself wheesht and save Kenneth the bother in case he's heard."

"He doesn't agree with you about Una?"

"He doesn't like any sort of negative talk in the shop when it's open."

"It's a good policy to remember," Janet said. "It was the same at the library. Bad manners are bad for business."

"He carps on about it, but he's right. Now, you really don't need me hovering or havering, but if you don't mind a body in the reading nook—" Pamela stopped at an intake of breath from Janet. "Sorry, hen, sorry. It's a common phrase, but awful under the circumstances. Forget I said 'body.' I'll be over with the picture books. This business with Una is making me ill. I need the sweetness of kittens and fairies."

Janet could think of any number of fairy tales that had nothing to do with sweetness, but she saw no point in adding to Pamela's discomfort by saying so. She sat back on the stool, and between customers she read the notes Tallie had given her. The four of them had collaborated on the notes, but in the end, typed and printed, they took only a single page. The second sheet was just a copy for Norman Hobbs. Janet hoped that reading the notes—the facts they knew, and the few impressions they'd included—might calm her nerves. It didn't. The notes only prompted more questions than she'd already voiced to Pamela—questions she felt compelled to write in the margins.

What was Una wearing? The same clothes she had on when she came in the shop? The same ridiculous heels? If she was wearing the same heels, were the heels on those heels clean or muddy? Why does anyone walk around in heels like that? What was she doing in our garden? In Curtis's dreadful shed? Snooping? Snooping into what? Or into who? (Whom?) Jess? Ian Atkinson? Us? Was she meeting someone? Who? Why would she be meeting someone in our garden shed? What about the renters? Who are they and where are they? Who killed her? Who? Who? Who?

At the best of times her handwriting wasn't dainty. Now she was running out of legible margin space, and the last three one-word questions were engraved in the paper. The bell on the door jingled, saving her from the embarrassment of adding one last question mark and drilling a hole through the paper.

The woman who came in smiled pleasantly—perhaps more pleasantly than an ordinary customer. Janet returned the smile. Without hesitation, the woman came straight for her. *Aha*, Janet thought, *selling something.* She folded the notes and stuck them back in her pocket, and prepared to be buttered up to within an inch of her bank account.

"Welcome to Inversgail," the woman said in fluting voice. She held out her hand. Janet took it and was surprised when the woman added her left hand to the clasp. "May I say how wonderful it is to have you here. New blood is an immeasurable joy."

The woman completely engulfing her right hand sounded as though she might have been fresh blood in Inversgail at some point, too. Her accent was more Lowland than Highland, but Janet's ear for regional accents was rusty. "Thank you. I'm Janet Marsh."

"Sharon Davis. Fellow librarian."

Janet reclaimed her hand, wondering if she'd misjudged the woman. Maybe she wasn't selling anything; maybe she was just starved for the company of librarians. She looked safe enough—somewhere around fifty; hair going naturally from blond to gray in a stylishly short cut; comfortably padded rather than spare; about her own height; carrying a canvas bag from the Scottish Library and Information Council over her shoulder. Most reassuring, Janet didn't detect the jittery eyes or the sweaty palms she'd learned to recognize during interactions with some of her more "unsettling" library patrons.

"Between the Internet and the talk one hears in the shops, there aren't many secrets left in the world, are there?" Sharon turned when the bell at the door jingled. "Nice to see you out and about, James," she said. "A shame about—"

James, in crooked tie and trousers bagging at the knees, nodded once and limped over to the display of new arrivals.

"James is a fiddler," Sharon said. "Quite good, only he took a tumble off the stage at a ceilidh last week."

"Carried away by the music in my soul," James said, limping over to the desk. He gave Janet a nod that was neither unpleasant nor pleasant and paid for the latest Ann Cleeves crime novel. "Norman Hobbs says you don't know anything more about the murder than what's in the reports." James had the eyes of an overworked, or possibly hungover, sheepdog.

"Constable Hobbs is right," Janet said.

"He often is. Stick to that, then. My advice, for what it's worth." He nodded again, took his book, and limped out. Janet stared after him.

"He'll be hurting over Una Graham," Sharon said.

"Ah." Did that explain the odd conversation? Janet wasn't sure.

"Of course, you know she's the one who…in your house?"

"The shed, not the house," Janet said. "Were she and James close?"

Sharon shook her head. "Not in that way. She wrote for the *Guardian*. James Haviland is the editor."

"Oh. *Oh.*" Janet's second "oh" trailed off into a note several registers lower, and questions, like a cloud of biting midges, swarmed her head. Had he come in on purpose to look at her? To see what kind of person owned a garden shed where prized employees could be murdered? Of course he had. So was he going to write a scathing article for the *Guardian*, filled with flights of baloney because she couldn't give him facts? Even worse, what if the *Guardian*'s story was picked up? Was she going to be hounded by a full onslaught of the British press? Great day in the morning, as her father used to say. Was her idyllic Scottish retirement about to descend into a nightmarish hell?

"Oh," she said, again, when a different thought flew at her. *Have I just missed a great chance to pry information about Una from James Haviland?* She was about to bat that last thought away as opportunistic and unfeeling, when another "Oh" escaped her. She hadn't expected to see the brightness of unshed tears in Sharon Davis's eyes. "I'm so sorry," she rushed to say. "I didn't even think about how Una's death might have affected you."

Sharon touched two fingers to the bridge of her nose, head slightly bowed. The strains of "Loch Lomond" descended from the speakers near the ceiling, as though drifting down from the high road. Janet took that as an omen and ventured another consoling remark.

"I didn't know Una well myself, but I'm sure there are many people in the community saddened by her death." She hoped that sounded suitable and appropriate—it was certainly better than another "Oh." She also couldn't help thinking that sentiment might prompt Sharon to tell her *who* in Inversgail was saddened by Una's death. Not that she was after gossip. Information was the more accurate term. And who better to get information from than an information specialist—a fellow librarian? But her fellow wasn't following through. She tried one more nudge. "It was such a senseless act of violence."

Sharon's shoulders rose and fell with the breath she took, her head still bowed, and her fingers still on the bridge of her nose. "We were friendly more than we were friends, if you know what I mean. But all the same, it's hard."

"I know, I know." Janet located the box of tissues again and moved it closer. Sharon shook her head and looked up.

"Thank you. I really am all right. But I should tell you why I'm here, and then not keep you from your business any longer."

Asking for something rather than selling? Janet prepared herself to be firm if she needed to be. "What can I do to help?" she asked. *Not the kind of firm I meant,* she thought.

"Have you heard of the Inversgail Literary Festival? A silly question, really, because of course you will have. You're in the book business."

"I've been hearing and reading about it for years," Janet said. "I'm looking forward to finally being here for it. Pamela and Kenneth told us that books for the author signings were ordered weeks ago. They passed the paperwork along to us, and we expect them"—Janet quickly leafed through notes next to the cash register—"Friday, possibly Monday, and that should still give us time to make changes. *Are* there any?"

"Not as far as I know, but I'll get back to you on that. No, the reason I popped round to see you is that we need a judge for the writing contest. Short notice, I know, but I rather hoped I might prevail upon you, as someone who knows books and who takes a keen interest in good literature, to join our small committee."

"Oh." *Dratted word.* "That's…quite an honor." *And you must be scraping the barrel, if you're asking a virtual stranger,* Janet thought.

"We're the ones who'd be honored by your participation. I know you've got your hands full with the shop and settling in, but there isn't much involved. It's simply a matter of reading and scoring the entries, and then choosing and awarding the winners. I always look on it as a labor of love."

"You don't think someone with more longevity in the community, or familiarity with it, might be a better choice?"

"No."

Janet raised her eyebrows at the strength and alacrity of Sharon's answer.

Sharon darted a few surreptitious looks over each shoulder, then leaned closer and asked, "Are there customers browsing?"

"Not at the moment." Janet didn't think that Pamela

consoling herself with kittens and fairies in picture books counted as a browsing customer.

"Close to home hasn't always worked," Sharon said. "For various reasons." Her eyebrows drew together, hinting at the seriousness of those reasons.

Janet would have loved to hear what the reasons were, for reasons of her own, but the bell over the door jingled again. A trio of hikers tramped in and asked if they could shed their rucksacks somewhere. That wasn't a topic Pamela or Kenneth had touched on, though Janet imagined it might be a frequent request. It was certainly a reasonable one. She didn't like the idea of damp or wet gear dripping on or near the books. Then she had a brainstorm. She excused herself to Sharon Davis and went to unlock the door to the tearoom space. She let them know the tearoom would be open for business in another two weeks. They thanked her and said they'd make a point of stopping in when they came back to Inversgail for the festival.

On her return trip to the desk, Janet passed Pamela looking comfortable in one of the overstuffed chairs near the picture books. She appeared to be nodding over a copy of *The Tobermory Cat*. At the desk, Sharon was deep in conversation with another customer—Maida Fairlie, mother-in-law to Janet's son, Allen.

"Maida! It's been too long. It's so good to see you." Janet sounded overly effusive, but she didn't care. She hoped her gush would make up for not being in touch before now. Though they'd never been great friends—friendly more than friends, as Sharon had put it—Maida was one of the first people Janet had met in Inversgail all those years ago. Janet often came away from conversations with Maida feeling as though she'd been tested. Not by Maida, so much. Maida seemed to enjoy hearing about life in central Illinois, and Maida and her husband had given Allen their blessings to marry Nicola, their only child. But it was always clear to Janet that looking over Maida's shoulders was a long line of sober, solemn, and Sabbath-keeping ancestors, clucking their tongues, even though they'd been buried in the kirkyard for centuries.

"I'll have a look round the shop," Sharon said, "and leave you two to chat. I'll catch you again before I'm away, Janet." Sharon squeezed past one of the hikers engrossed in *The Illustrated Encyclopedia of Tartan* and disappeared into the aisle with the gardening books.

"The grandboys send their love," Janet said to Maida. "We flew into Edinburgh and stayed with them for a few days before coming here."

"Nicola told me."

"I can't believe how much they've grown in the few months since we came to sign our lives away into this book business. Freddy started calling me Nana Jana, and Wally immediately changed it to Banana Jana, and they laughed until they had the hiccups. I loved every minute of their silliness. But look at you, Maida; you haven't changed a bit in five years."

"Away with you," Maida said. "It's just that I'm wearing my same old coat." She looked down at the dark gray cloth, darker because of the rain, and flapped the hem. "And it's more like five and a half years."

"Where do the years go? And the time—I'm sorry I

didn't call you when we were here signing the papers. We were in and out like a boomerang. But oh, I've been so jealous of you."

"Jealous of me?" Maida took a step back. "Whatever for?"

"Living a whole ocean closer to those boys. Do you know what I did the morning after Freddy was born? I sat at my kitchen table there in Illinois, and I started thinking about how many more times in my life I might be lucky enough to see my grandchildren. How many more times I would *hold* my grandchildren. I did the math, Maida. If I was lucky enough that I could make the trip to Edinburgh once or twice a year, and if I could keep that up until I was in my eighties—"

"Or they might fly to see you."

"True. But it's more expensive for four to fly and more difficult with children. But suppose they made the trip every other year, even then I might see them only twenty more times. Thirty times, tops. That's if I was lucky. And that wasn't going to be enough and it wasn't acceptable."

"And if your daughter goes back to America? Surely she'll have a lovely big wedding someday. What if you have other grandchildren there? What will happen then? How does she feel about all this?"

"She's the one who found the 'for sale' notice," Janet said. "As for the big wedding—she's been there and done that, as the saying goes, but it didn't work out."

"Poor wee thing."

"Tallie?" Janet almost laughed; then she peered at Maida, sure the solemn, sober ancestors must be jockeying for position in the gloaming she seemed to be carrying with her this morning. "Sometimes these things work out for the best. Tallie's very happy. Frankly, so is her ex."

"Well, that's all right, then."

Janet was tempted to dig beneath Maida's response for a less agreeable meaning, but decided to take it at face value. Why project her penchant for sarcasm onto what might be an innocent comment? Because Maida was right; it *had* been five and a half years since they'd seen each other. Five and a half years since the occasion of Allen and Nicola's almost wedding. What a surprise *that* had been. In the midst of all the grand wedding plans and transatlantic excitement, the two had snuck off and eloped. *Utterly romantic*, Tallie had said, *and so much less stressful.* It had happened around the time Janet had been blindsided by Curtis. He'd snuck off, too. But his defection was absolutely *not* romantic. The rat.

Janet relaxed her grip on the pen she'd picked up and glanced quickly for nearby customers. "Of course you've heard about Una Graham?"

"Wickedness, pure and simple," Maida said. "But Inversgail's not the wee, quiet town you remember. There's all kind of people stopping through, these days. Some are staying, and more every year. And this festival brings that many more, and so many odd ones, you'd think it was part of the festival fringe from Edinburgh."

Janet immediately pictured a phalanx of unicycles ridden down the High Street by poets with multicolored mohawks and multi-pierced body parts, some spouting Burns and McGonagall, others blowing flames out of bagpipes. She hadn't heard about that aspect of the literary festival. "Really?" she asked Maida.

"Well, perhaps not quite that bad." A dimple in Maida's cheek betrayed the unsmiling ancestors. "Or not yet."

Janet laughed, but judging from Maida's flustered reaction, maybe the last word had come from the ancestors and hadn't been Maida's comic timing. To smooth the awkward moment, Janet spread her arms wide. "How do I look, Maida? Like a bookseller?"

"I'm sure you do. I shouldn't be taking up any more of your time. I just came by to see that you're settling in and to ask if you'd like a cat for the rats."

"Sorry?"

"The rats."

"What rats, Maida?"

"Did Jess not tell you?"

Janet looked at the pen she was still holding; she was wringing its neck. "No. She didn't. What rats, where?"

"Och, well. The renters had a terrible time with them, or so I heard. The rats in your house."

EIGHT

THERE WAS NO point in jumping up onto the sales desk. If the rats were in her house, they weren't going to bite her ankles here at the bookshop. Janet did wish that Maida's voice hadn't risen each time she'd said "rats," though. Now one of the hikers looked nervous.

Janet wanted, very badly, to call Jess Baillie—to ask her about the rats, to find out what else might be wrong in the house, and to find out what Jess was going to do about all of it. But there was no time. The three hikers were ready to make their purchases and reclaim their backpacks. Janet thanked Maida for the offer of a cat and said she'd think about it. Actually, the idea of asking a cat to face a horde of rats within the confines of her house gave her the willies. Maida waved and left, looking somewhat less ancestrally haunted. Janet allowed herself the sour thought that a plague of rats suited their sensibilities.

The nervous hiker cast uneasy glances as he paid for a collection of short stories by Janice Galloway and a Loch Ness coloring book. "Rats?" he asked with a squeak he tried to cover with a cough.

"A rumor of rats, *elsewhere*," Janet said. "*Not* here."

"Told you," one of the other hikers said. "And my nose told you. There's no stink of rats here."

"Thank you," Janet said.

"We'll stop back for tea in a fortnight," the hiker with the nose said. "Unless we're savaged by wild haggis in the hills."

The third hiker made a noise between a cow's moo and an elk's bugle in the nervous hiker's ear. The three left laughing, and Sharon Davis came back to the sales desk.

"I've always loved the fireplace in this old building. It's a cozy touch. I wish they'd made room for one or that we could add one at the library."

"I'm sorry I've kept you waiting so long," Janet said.

Sharon put the back of her hand to her forehead. "Spending time in a bookshop, oh, the trials I endure. Don't worry. I'll count it as work time. I found several new books we don't have in the collection." She tipped her head. "Will you be offering a discount to the library for the occasional purchase?"

"Has the shop offered one in the past?" Another point the Lawries hadn't covered and Janet hadn't thought to ask about.

Sharon started to nod, but stopped, and a slight flush crept up her cheeks. "No."

"I would have thought, as a courtesy—"

"Suffice to say I won't be the only one in Inversgail welcoming new owners and new policies to Yon Bonnie Books." Sharon spoke softly, but even so, she made Janet uneasy. Surely she'd seen Pamela sitting by the picture books? But Pamela had been nodding; maybe she'd fallen sound asleep with the book over her face? Surely not.

"Back to my reason for coming, though," Sharon said, "and then I'll leave you in peace. The bookshop has been a beloved part of Inversgail since Colonel Farquhar first put books on the shelves and opened the doors in 1918. Your professional background and your standing in the community as the new owner of Yon Bonnie Books make you the perfect person to join the committee of judges."

Janet didn't think she merited a place on the same pedestal as, or even one next to, Colonel Farquhar. She'd caught a glimpse of him, at a celebration of his hundredth birthday, during one of their first summers in Inversgail. Even tucked into an old-fashioned bath chair with a plaid blanket over his knees, he gave the impression of standing at attention. Not to mention she wouldn't like a pedestal; she didn't like standing at the edge of any high place. But she understood the wisdom of choosing an impartial outsider and moved on to her next question. "How many entries are we talking about?"

"It's only a local, well, a regional festival by now. In years past we've had no more than a dozen and a half."

"And what about meetings? We're still getting our feet under us in the shop, and we hope to open the tearoom the week after next. I hesitate to overcommit."

"There's only the one meeting after you've read and scored the entries. At that time, judges will meet, discuss their favorites, and choose the winners. We've perfected the process over the years so that it's well suited for busy people. I would consider your participation a personal favor."

"Personal" is laying it on a bit thick, Janet thought. "It sounds like a worthy—"

"Indeed worthy, and a wonderful way for you to feel as though you're becoming part of the wider community."

Without actually *becoming part of it?* Janet ignored that thought as unnecessarily snide and needlessly pessimistic. This pleasant woman was asking a favor and painting it as prettily as she could to make it more likely she would say yes. It was a fair strategy. She'd used it herself with volunteers and skeptical board members any number of times. "How soon do you need an answer?" she asked.

"I hate to put you on the spot, but sooner than soon, I'm afraid. Today—now—if possible. Oh, and did I tell you that Ian Atkinson is one of our judges this year, as well? Now, *that* caught your interest, I can see. Perhaps I should have mentioned him first."

Janet wondered why she hadn't.

"I think he's looking for ways to make a better connection with the community. From what I understand, that isn't always easy for a writer. In any case, his participation should increase our chances for press coverage at the festival."

"How long are the entries? Roughly."

"A good question, without a single answer, I'm afraid. We get a good many short poems of a local form called Skye-ku. Then there's the usual run of short stories. They make up the bulk of the entries. We get play scripts, the occasional television script, and on through to some quite good creative nonfiction."

"Novels?"

"Not so many. I will say this—the judges have generally enjoyed themselves thoroughly."

Janet restacked the bookmarks next to the cash register, giving Sharon time to add any further grace notes to her request, and herself time to think of any other pertinent questions before deciding. Sharon seemed to have finished, though, and stood across the desk from her, looking hopeful.

"What do you say?" Sharon prompted. "May I put you down as a yes?"

"I—"

"Wonderful! Absolutely brilliant! I'm so pleased you've said aye."

"What?"

"I can't thank you enough. I know you won't regret it. Here are the entries." Sharon took the Scottish Library and Information Council bag from her shoulder and set it down in front of Janet. It made a solid *thunk* on the desk.

"You've taken a tremendous burden off my mind," Sharon said.

Her shoulder, too. She lifted the bag. It easily held the equivalent of two or three reams of paper.

"Una's death is a shocking tragedy for the community," Sharon said. "She's been a stalwart member of the judging committee and a supporter of the Inversgail Literary Festival from the beginning. But the festival will go on. Una would have been the first to say it must. And the contest will go on, too. It would be a shame to disappoint the entrants. In fact, it's just occurred to me that we might rename one of the awards for her. In her honor. What do you think?"

Janet thought she might need to take several breaths on Sharon's behalf or offer a paper bag against the threat of hyperventilation. But Sharon's gratitude carried her forward.

"We'll have our preliminary get-together at the library tomorrow at noon, sort of a working lunch—"

"Whoa. Wait." Janet held up a hand. "I thought you said there was only one meeting, and that it comes after we've read the entries."

"That's right. Only the one meeting. Tomorrow is more or less a quick get-together to go over the ground rules."

"You can't email them?"

"We'll only be half an hour or so. An hour tops. It'll give the judges a wee bit of bonding time, as well. The instructions will be clearer this way, you see. No chance of misinterpretation. Make sure we're all on the same page." Sharon laughed at her joke. Janet didn't. Sharon didn't seem to mind.

"Despite the setback of Una's death, I feel the fates are smiling on the contest this year. I don't mind telling you, but I was that chuffed when I heard the bookshop had found a buyer at last. That gave us a graceful way to replace a certain member of the committee without causing ill will. And that's when Ian Atkinson agreed to serve on the committee—a coup for the festival, and thank goodness a bloodless one."

Janet didn't laugh at that joke, either. Neither did

Kenneth. He emerged from the office, visibly startling Sharon.

"Kenneth. Good heavens. You're here."

Kenneth crossed his arms and leaned against the door frame.

Janet rushed to fill an awkward silence. "Kenneth and Pamela are giving us a week of their time and expertise. Invaluable help. We can't thank you enough, Kenneth. Really."

"How nice," Sharon said. Her pleasant smile now looked somewhat plastic. "I've been so busy—you know me, with my nose always stuck in the library—I must have missed the details of the sale. I thought you were off and away. Going someplace warm, didn't I hear? Sounds lovely."

Kenneth hadn't moved. "That's been Pamela's dream. A move like that doesn't happen overnight, though."

"And how is Pamela?" Sharon asked.

"Dreaming of warmer…temperatures." Kenneth pushed away from the door frame and came to stand behind the desk. That put Janet, still sitting on the stool, between him and Sharon. *More awkward to stay, or slip away?* Janet wondered. She stayed but tried to make herself smaller on the stool.

"We'll be away in another month or so," Kenneth said. "I resigned from the committee because I didn't want to be irresponsible toward the writers. Because of selling the shop, and the details of transferral and planning a move and packing, I didn't think I'd be giving the entries my best attention or the attention they deserved.

But if I'd known you wanted me off the committee that badly, Sharon, I would have obliged you years ago."

"It isn't really like that, Kenneth."

"What's it like, then, hey?"

"It's not—"

"Go on. What's it like?"

"Are you threatening me, Kenneth Lawrie?"

Sharon took a step back, and in the same instant Janet stood up. But as Janet swiveled to face Kenneth, the bell at the door jingled, and Constable Hobbs stepped in. And in the fraction of a second that it took for Janet to blink, she felt the scene shift. Sharon turned to Hobbs with a smile, Kenneth called a cheery greeting, and Norman Hobbs removed his hat, tucked it under his arm, and stood dripping on the floor.

NINE

"AND?" CHRISTINE ASKED. "Don't stop there. What happened next?"

Janet, Christine, Tally, and Summer were sharing cheese and pickle sandwiches for supper in front of the fireplace after closing up shop for the day. Christine and Summer had returned from the Fort William catering supplier with samples of bread and rolls, and they'd stopped at the cheese monger along the High Street from Yon Bonnie Books to pick up the Mull Cheddar Christine had been craving. Janet and Tallie were eager to hear about the trip and, more to the point, the prices and delivery schedule Christine and Summer had negotiated. But when Christine asked where the Lawries were at the end of the day, Janet launched into the story of Sharon Davis's visit, starting with Sharon's request for Janet to become a judge for the writing contest and ending with Norman Hobbs dripping on the floor. She didn't mention the rats, because the thought of them still made her mind skitter, or the ginger pear scones, because she and Tallie had eaten the last two after Constable Hobbs left.

"Nothing really happened after that," Janet said. "One minute Sharon looked as though she thought Kenneth was about to leap over both me and the desk to get at her, and the next they were acting like best mates. It was all tooth and claw and thunderheads, and then it was handshakes, plastic smiles, and sunshine—artificial sunshine, because, in case you hadn't noticed, it's still raining."

"But it's a soft rain and hardly noticeable," Christine said.

All four looked out at the rain-glistened street and gray harbor.

"It's beautiful, isn't it?" Tallie asked.

"It's the kind of rain that makes me feel like I'm healthy and growing," Summer said.

"That's fortunate," said Janet.

"But get back to the argy-bargy," Christine said.

"The argument? That's all there was to it," Janet said. "Sharon said she'd see me tomorrow at noon. Then she wished Kenneth good luck with the move, and Kenneth all but sang, 'So long, farewell, *auf wiedersehen*, goodbye.' I gave Hobbs our notes, he left, and Tallie and I went about our business of selling books the rest of the afternoon." She stopped there and chewed the last bite of her sandwich, but held up a finger to indicate a further thought. "Here's something we might think about. Should we have a place for people to leave their wet things? Not just umbrellas, but bags and backpacks and whatnot. Customers might appreciate it, and it might save a few books from getting wet. I asked Pamela what they did about wet raincoats and such and she said, 'Let there be drips.' That sounded uncharacteristically cavalier. I think she's already severed the metaphorical apron strings of the book business. And I wish I'd just said 'cut' instead of 'severed.'"

"Here's something that might make you feel better," Summer said. "It's an idea I had. Wouldn't it be fun to offer slippers to customers? We could have a basket of them by the door with a sign that says, 'take off your wet shoes and slip into cozy, knitted comfort.'"

"I like that," Janet said. "I wonder if they'd go for it? I know *I* would. I would love it. But we'd end up with a lot of extra washing every day."

"Or we could see if the laundry service for the tearoom will take them, too," Summer said.

Christine stared at Summer, then at Janet, and turned to Tallie. "Exactly how threatening was Kenneth this morning? Is your mum exaggerating the situation, underreporting, or avoiding an unpleasant truth by digressing into woolly footwear?"

"The only unpleasant truth is that we can't get into the house for a few more days," Tallie said.

"Oh, Janet, I'm so sorry." Christine put a hand on her friend's shoulder.

"Hobbs was sorry, too," Janet said, "so I didn't throw a book at his head, like I wanted to."

"Because you're good." Christine said. She gave Janet's shoulder a squeeze. "Notice I didn't say soft. But I should congratulate you on being made a member of the literary festival committee. A contest judge. Very good. It's exciting, don't you think? Or awful, depending on the entries. How many are there?"

Janet brought the bag from where she'd left it behind the sales desk. "I don't know the breakdown by type or number of manuscripts," she said, hefting the tote up and down, "but at a guess, I'd say between ten and ten and a half pounds."

"Good Lord. Well, I'm sure it'll be jolly fun."

"I hope so. I was looking forward to reading Ian Atkinson's *The Bludgeon in the Bothy*, but these better come first."

"When do you have to have them read?"

"Now you can call me soft, because I forgot to ask. I guess I'll find out tomorrow."

"Just as well you are soft, too," Christine said, "so that you *didn't* throw a book at Norman's head. Mind you, I'm sure Norman's had worse things hurled at him than books, and no one would blame you if you had clocked him. Did he say how much longer before you're in the house? His crime specialists must have found something of interest. He didn't let slip what, did he?"

"Tallie asked him both questions. He couldn't say about the house and wouldn't say anything about the investigation."

"Even though we gave him our notes? Ingrate. I wonder if there's any way we can find out without him."

Tallie cleared her throat in a lawyerly, law-abiding way. "Back to Kenneth," she said, "and how threatening he was or wasn't. The situation was definitely tense. But only briefly, like Mom said. And I've never gotten that vibe off him before. I was watching from the office door, and except for moving closer to Sharon—which wouldn't strike anyone as unusual under ordinary circumstances—Kenneth didn't do anything that *looked* threatening. His words weren't really threatening, either. It was in his voice."

"Of course, you and I didn't see his face," Janet said, "and Sharon did."

"True."

"But I honestly didn't feel like I was in any kind of danger sitting there between them," Janet said. "Or much, until she backed away from the desk."

"And then it was over, *poof*," Tallie said, splaying her fingers when she said "poof," and making Christine jump. "It was practically surreal. Sharon left. The Lawries left. Constable Hobbs probably couldn't tell that anything had been going on. He looked around the shop, Mom gave him the notes, he disappointed her about the house, and then he left, too."

"Inspecting," Janet said. "I got the impression Hobbs was inspecting the place."

"You got that feeling, too?" Tallie asked. "Yeah, definitely checking it over. He asked about the tearoom—like how long would the redecorating take? Did we expect it to be noisy with hammers or a power saw?"

"He asked me if we expected the work to disrupt the nice yet quiet and tasteful music and the calm atmosphere," Janet said. "I asked him if he wanted a job writing our advertising copy."

"What do you think he concluded?" Christine asked dryly.

"Not interested in the job, but pleasantly surprised by the bookshop and tearoom," Tallie said. "Maybe I'm reading too much into the way he nodded. Happy enough, though."

"There is still one thing I don't understand," Janet said. "Pamela was sitting in one of the chairs near the picture books this morning, reading. Starting to nod off. Maybe *did* nod off, because I thought I heard a snore. Then Sharon Davis came in and we talked for a while. And then Maida Fairlie came in."

"How is mousy Maida?" Christine asked.

Mousy Maida—Janet still didn't want to say anything about the rats. Time for that later. In fact, maybe the delay over getting into the house was a blessing in disguise. Now she'd have time to deal with *that* setback.

"Maida's fine," she said, "but calling her mousy is unkind, and we all need to be careful what we say in front of customers. That's something Pamela said Kenneth is big on, and it's something I firmly believe in." She was thoughtful for a moment. "That's interesting, though, now that we've witnessed Kenneth's nonthreatening threats. A little disconnect there."

"He wields careful words that hide a cudgel," Tallie said.

"Passive-aggressive behavior at its nastiest," said Christine, "if it's a pattern. But go on about Maida."

"It's really about Pamela," Janet said. "Maida came in, and Sharon went to browse. And when Sharon came back to the desk, she came down the aisle, past the picture books. And yet, when Kenneth popped out of the office, she was surprised and said she thought they'd already left Inversgail."

"Your point being?" Christine asked.

"That she couldn't have missed seeing Pamela. So why was she surprised to see Kenneth?

"Or," said Tallie, "where was Pamela?"

"That's really what I'm wondering," Janet said. "Sharon made a complete tour of the shop and didn't see her. And I didn't see her go out the front. So where was she?"

"In the stockroom," Christine said with a shrug. "Or she was taking a last look around the tearoom to make sure they aren't leaving anything behind. Does it matter where she was?"

"I'm not sure," Janet said. "I guess it made me think about opportunity. About who had the opportunity to kill Una. How easy it is for people to slip away and back again. How normal it is. Pamela was gone long enough that Sharon didn't see her and long enough that she missed the words between Kenneth and Sharon."

"'Tension' and 'words' are nice euphemisms," said Christine. "Thank goodness it didn't turn into a full-fledged rammie between them. Can you see the headline? 'Bookseller Linked to Brawls and Bloodshed.'"

"Classic," Summer said. "And then there'd be a picture of the garden shed with the caption 'Blood Shed.'"

"Those are horrible things to say or think." Janet crumpled her paper napkin, squeezing it into a tight ball. "But that sort of thing occurred to me, too. *Not* the picture and caption." She shot an aggrieved look at Summer. "But unfavorable press, yes. We might at least be safe from the *Guardian*, though." She told them about meeting James Haviland.

"I wouldn't mind repaying his visit," Summer said. "If nothing else, I'll express my interest in a sister news organization and see if he'll give me a tour. But maybe I can appeal to his better nature and try to ensure friendlier headlines. It's worth a shot, anyway. I'll do that tomorrow, after the decorators get started."

"Sounds like a plan," Christine said. "What are you doing with yourself this evening, Janet?"

"Reading entries. And laundry."

"You could drop the laundry off and have it delivered," Christine said.

"It won't hurt me to get out."

"Oh, aye. The launderette is a happening place, I'm sure."

AT STREET LEVEL, between the bookshop and the tearoom, was a chalky gray door. A coat of shiny dark green paint for the door was on Janet's list of things to do. The door opened onto a landing, and once inside and out of the rain, or possibly out of a squall of sunshine, there could be seen two more doors, one to the left and one to the right. The left-hand door opened into the bookshop. The right-hand door opened into the tearoom. Straight ahead, as one entered from the street, a stairway rose to the first floor, where Janet, Tallie, and Summer were staying in rooms not quite ready for paying guests.

The four partners had jumped feetfirst into the routine of running the bookshop—phase one of the business plan they'd drawn up. Opening the tearoom was phase two. They were giving themselves a month or two beyond its opening date to discover and smooth out any kinks in its operation—so that it ran like a well-oiled stand mixer, as Christine said. In phase three, after the addition of mod cons and more comfortable beds, Bedtime Stories, their bed-and-breakfast, would open. Summer would stay on in a small, private flat, after the Marsh women were finally able to move into Janet's house, looking after the guests. Janet assured Summer that their timeline gave her plenty of time to come up with a title for her position. Summer had cast aside "manager" as too prosaic but had also rejected Tallie's suggestions of headmistress, room mother, and wrangler.

That evening, Janet reluctantly left Ian Atkinson's *The Bludgeon in the Bothy* on the three-legged chair she was using as a bedside table. After hefting the tote bag of contest entries again, she decided against carrying the entire weight with her to the launderette. Instead, she took an inch of manuscript pages off the top, put them in a file folder, and then tucked the folder in the bin liner she was using as a laundry bag. Looking down onto the street, she saw that it had stopped raining, but she didn't want to count on the period of no rain to last. Stringing wet laundry around the bookshop wasn't an option.

She locked the street door behind her and wondered how soon she would think nothing of the simple act of walking down the High Street. How soon would she glance at the harbor and find a text on her phone more engaging than the possibility of a seal swimming by? *Although,* she thought, *anyone seeing me now, slopping along in my oldest sweatpants with my elegant bin liner, might think I've been on the dole here for years.*

She stopped first at Paudel's Newsagent, Post Office, and Convenience for soap powder and coins. The launderette likely had both, but it wouldn't have the scones Basant Paudel's sister baked. There might not be any scones left at this hour, but Janet hadn't made time to stop in the shop yet. The slim, dark-haired, dark-eyed young man behind the counter, Basant Paudel himself, stood up when she walked through the door.

"Mrs. Janet." He marked his place in the book he was reading and laid it on the counter—*The Bludgeon in the Bothy,* Janet noted with an inward sigh. "How are you today?" he asked.

"You have the most amazing memory, Basant. It's been more than five years since I've been in your shop, and you not only recognize me, but you say hello as though I picked up a pint of milk yesterday."

"Which Tallie did do. An Irn Bru, too." He made a mock toast with his own bottle of the fluorescent orange drink and took a sip. "I couldn't tell if she actually likes it or is simply approaching the liking of it with her usual concentration of effort."

"She does have that way about her." *And is it interesting that he knows that,* Janet wondered, *or just more evidence that he's a keen-eyed people-watcher with a good memory?*

She asked after his sisters. He told her how well they'd each done on their school-leaving examinations and were now doing in their further studies—Arati in nursing and Puja reading history at St. Andrew's.

"Puja is even studying the Gaelic. She says it is not

as difficult as English, which she learned to perfection," he said proudly.

"And Arati's scones?" she asked, knowing she didn't need a third—a *fourth* today. Still, she was disappointed when he confirmed her fears that they were long gone. And then annoyed for being shallow and needy. Or was it greedy? No matter, it was time to show concentration of effort.

"Where do you keep your laundry soap these days, Basant?" She went where he pointed, ignoring the display of crisps whispering her name on her way back to pay for a box of Fairy washing tablets. "And coins for the machines, please," she said, handing him a twenty-pound note along with a ten.

"I hesitate to bring up the shocking news of last evening," he said as he handed her a shocking weight in coins.

"Una Graham?"

He pressed his lips together and nodded.

"It's a terrible thing, and I know Una will be missed," Janet said.

"For her advice as well as her lively personality. But I'm also sorry that it happened on your property. In your shed."

She looked up from distributing the coins between her pockets. "Thank you, Basant. I've been hearing all day from people who believe it happened in my house. I've been trying to convince myself that it's a small thing, whether it's the house or the shed, and it is compared to the enormity of the crime. I should let it go."

"But it isn't really a small difference. And too often people hear but don't listen. If there is anything I can do, please let me know." He looked steadily into her eyes for a moment, then put his hands together in a muted clap. "Now, we will end our visit with happy news. You are living in Inversgail, a place second in beauty only to my dear Nepal. Arati will make more scones in the morning before she returns to Glasgow. And you are no longer lending books, but you are selling them, and that is also good. '*Books!*'" he said with sudden animation. "'*The best weapons in the world.*' Una was fond of quoting Humphrey Bogart. I'm fond of quoting the good Doctor." He patted his chest, and she realized he was wearing a *Doctor Who* TARDIS t-shirt.

"It's good to see you, Basant. I'll see you later and, I hope, often."

"Wait one moment, please." He turned to scan the glass jars of old-fashioned sweets on the shelves behind him. He touched the lid of one jar, moved to another, then jumped to a third and took it down. He unscrewed the lid, scooped a small portion of the sweets into a bag, and handed it to her. "Licorice allsorts are your favorite, aren't they?"

"You are amazing," Janet said, tucking the bag into one of her coin-laden pockets. "A wonderful treat. Thank you."

When she got outside, and far enough down the street, she laughed. She liked licorice allsorts well enough. They were never her favorite, though. Curtis the rat was the one who'd loved them, and she'd always bought them for him. But that, she decided, was a difference as small and inconsequential as Curtis the rat's understanding of devotion and faithful love.

THE LAUNDERETTE, ON a street several blocks back from the harbor, was on the ground floor of a building conveniently located next to a pub. The place was clean, well lit, and outfitted with two ranks of washers back-to-back, a spin dryer, and six large tumble dryers. Only two washers were being used, that Janet could see, but they'd been left unattended. Perhaps her laundry companion was in the restroom, whose door was closed. Or next door lifting a pint.

She sorted her clothes into two loads, figured out how many coins she needed, and got the machines going, glad for the lightened load in her pockets. Old and comfortable friends these sweatpants might be, but the elastic in the waist was beginning to go.

The other machines spun to a stop with a buzz, but no sign of the contents' owner. It might be useful, she thought, if the machines' buzzers also sounded next door. She sat on one of the hard plastic chairs with their backs against the wall below the front windows. She'd just taken the inch of contest entries out of the file folder, and the packet of sweeties Basant had given her out of her pocket, when the front door opened. A sandy-haired man held it for a sandy-colored Cairn terrier, and the two came in on a breath of fresh rain and melancholy whistling. The terrier shook the rain from its fur. The man might have glanced her way, but she didn't know. She'd lifted the contest entries so they obscured her face.

The man and dog went around the ranks of washers to the two machines that had finished their cycles. Janet put the contest entries on her lap and lifted the bag of sweeties.

"Good to see you, Rab. Would you like some licorice?"

TEN

RAB DECLINED JANET'S offer of a candy. His dog accepted one gladly.

"Is licorice safe for him?" Janet asked.

"In moderation."

"Moderation" was a word well suited to Rab MacGregor. Of moderate height and weight, with hair a moderate length for a man of…moderate years. His age, which had been impossible to tell from a distance the morning before as he sat on the harbor wall, was just as hard to guess under the cold white lights in the confines of the launderette. He'd been heard to answer the question of his age by telling people he was closer to fifty than forty. *But unless you knew him,* Janet thought, *that still wouldn't tell you whether he was on the near or far side of fifty. And it could easily be either.*

No one else came into the launderette that evening, and they spent some time in a polite smirr of small talk with intermittent periods of silence. Janet asked his dog's name. Ranger, Rab said. Ranger had the look of a lad-about-town, but he went to sit and gaze at Rab when called. *Not quite with a look of hero worship,* Janet thought; *more as an accomplice.*

Janet picked up the contest entries and started reading. The top inch she'd brought with her turned out to be some of the poetry contributions, including examples of the Skye-ku Sharon had told her about. Janet enjoyed haiku, and some of the contest poems were insightful and lovely. Rab and Ranger came to sit at the far end of the row of chairs. Rab spent equal time between tapping and swiping an electronic tablet and then writing with a pencil in a notebook. Janet didn't question the reason for that combination of using old and new technology. Ranger came over to see if she had anything more to offer. A scratch between his ears apparently wasn't a substitute for licorice, though. He went back and hopped up to sit on the chair next to Rab's. With a pang, Janet saw Rab put away the tablet and notebook and take a book from the pocket of his coat—*The Bludgeon in the Bothy.*

When her washers buzzed, she got up and made a passing comment about looking forward to using her own washer and dryer. He mentioned that his laundry machines needed parts he hadn't located yet. She asked about his availability for repainting the trim on the house. He said he would check his schedule, but he might be able to fit that in once the police released it to her, and he agreed to stop by the bookshop in the morning to discuss part-time work there.

It had been years since she'd flapped her clothes in public before tossing them in a dryer. It crossed her mind that she might not be able to make eye contact with Rab when he came in the shop, now that he was getting an eyeful of her bras and panties. And then the elastic in her old sweats betrayed her, and her pockets full of coins nearly pulled them off, giving Rab a glimpse of the underpants she was currently wearing. A lucky grab saved her dignity and his. Then she realized the potential loss was only in her mind. Rab MacGregor didn't swallow a snicker or otherwise comment. And he didn't show any embarrassment to be folding a pile of his briefs with the blue-and-white flag of Scotland and boxers with the Loch Ness monster swimming across them.

JANET WOKE THE next morning to sunshine streaming through the window of her room above the bookshop. She took that as a positive sign and got up to look out at the sky and the harbor turned blue and bright again. She hadn't made a habit of searching for positive signs in her life, having always felt strongly that she made her own luck. *Until life as I knew it slewed sideways into a ditch and died.* She rested her forehead against the cool window glass and let her eyes track a pair of kayakers in wet suits paddling out of the harbor. *Breathe in, breathe out. You're smart. You're strong. You ate the licorice allsorts the rat has forever forfeited his rights to. You're doing what you love in the place you love even more. You are exactly where you belong.*

Well, no, not exactly. She wouldn't be *exactly* where she belonged until the crime specialists were out of her house and she was in it. About *that* she was most definitely positive.

Speaking of being positive—she gathered her paraphernalia for the trip down the hall to the bathroom—a facility so small that it must have been present when the euphemism "water closet" was coined. She knew she should think of her temporary stay above the bookshop in a positive light. She should see it as useful, albeit *temporary,* research, letting her have an approximation of the sleeping-above-a-bookshop experience their future bed-and-breakfast guests would have. But the charm and adventure of the experience were wearing thin.

"En suite bathrooms," she said, passing Summer in the hall, both of them in robe and slippers. "We were very smart to insist on en suite bathrooms for the guests."

"It was an expensive addition to the plans," Summer said.

"A necessary expense," Tallie called from her room, "if we want to be competitive."

"We'll take pride in being the spoiled Americans we are," Janet said, "and not second-guess ourselves any further."

"And we'll wave rolls of toilet paper instead of the Stars and Stripes," said Summer.

"Hear, hear!" Tallie called.

"That's settled, then. The next thing we're going to settle is the murder. If for no other reason than I want the police out of my house and out of our hair."

Summer, about to disappear into her own room, stopped. Tallie stuck her head out her door.

"What?" Janet said. "Just because we have a business to run, another scheduled to start, and a third on the way, that doesn't mean we can't help Norman Hobbs do his job, too."

"No complaints from me," Tallie said. "Just wondering if you've thought this through."

"Dear, do you have so little faith in your mother?" Janet stooped to pick up the moisturizer and deodorant she'd just dropped. "I was being flip about the house," she said, straightening back up. "But we have our enterprise to think of. We need to do everything we can to make sure it works."

"Whyever would I doubt you?" Tallie said. "I should've been clearer. You usually *do* think things through, so I'm wondering if you have a specific role you'd like me to play. What can I do to help, darling mother?"

"That's my darling girl. Your Internet research skills will be invaluable. So will your nimble mind."

"There might be different search terms," Tallie said, "different vocabulary. Good. I like that kind of thing. And why don't I set up a cloud document we can all access? We can all add notes and questions as they occur to us or as we have time. I can get started on all of that this morning, if you're feeling urgent."

"Urgent-ish," Janet said.

"Then I'll run back up here and get to work on it after we watch Summer unveil her paint selections. I'll join you in the shop later."

"Good. Oh, and what about using your law background to find a friendly solicitor—one with contacts in the police?" Janet asked. "The more information we can get, the better."

"Easier to keep buttering up Constable Hobbs," Tallie said. "Besides the fact he *is* the police, I don't think we're going find a solicitor who either can or wants to be a stoolie for us. Certainly not without running up billable hours."

"I see your point."

"Good."

"But if we run afoul of the law?" Janet asked.

"Which we won't."

"No, of course not. But if we do."

"I'll run right out and flag down the best solicitor I can find."

"That's all I ask. I hereby dub you law liaison."

"I accept under the condition that you do your best, your very best, not to need my services as law liaison, especially because if I end up in the pokey with you, I won't be much good at liaising."

"But think of the quality time we'd have together, dear." Janet patted Tallie's cheek.

"And think of the wonderful human interest story I can get out of that," Summer said. "The mother-daughter angle will be so catchy. If it's all right with you, though, after we get the painters settled this morning, I want to go see the guy at the *Guardian*. The police will have already been there, asking their questions, but that's where I might have the advantage."

"How so?"

"Because I'm *not* the police. I don't know if it works the same way over here, but in my experience, it's amazing what people are willing to tell a sympathetic ear during the initial rush of relief after the big bad police are gone."

"Also perfect. While you're there, find out about their advertising rates, will you? And as long as we're being so organized, with titles and assigned duties, I'll be community liaison. I'll collect, sift, and analyze intelligence received in the shop and from various other…"

"Sources?" Summer prompted.

"That sounds more positive than 'informants,'" Janet said, "and this is a day for positivity and positive action."

"You go, Mom," Tallie called from her room. "Rah, rah!"

After showering and dressing in her bookseller khakis and blazer, formerly her librarian's khakis and blazer, Janet did go. She arrived at Paudel's Newsagent, Post Office, and Convenience in time to buy the first dozen scones Arati Paudel took from the oven.

"What kind?" she asked Basant, wanting to bury her nose in the bag he handed across the counter.

"Classic currant. Will they do?"

"I'm quite positive they will."

THE DECORATORS THEY'D hired to refurbish the tearoom arrived shortly before Yon Bonnie Books opened for the day. A middle-aged woman in a white bib-and-brace overall introduced herself as Gillian, and the identically dressed young woman and man with her as Chloe and Garth. The three made multiple trips from a panel truck. They carried in ladders, buckets and rollers, drop cloths, and what looked like a corral for small livestock.

"If they bring in sheep I'll question our wisdom in going with McVitie and McPhee," Christine said.

"Your father recommended them," Janet reminded her.

"This morning he asked if I'd like milk in my tea.

When I said yes, he gave me a splash of grapefruit juice."

The corral turned into a low scaffold before their eyes, and Christine accepted a second scone from Janet to ease her stress.

"Are you really that worried by sheep?" Tallie asked.

"Not at all," Christine said, "once they've been made into jumpers."

Summer checked the paint colors against the samples she'd chosen and double-checked their placement according to her wall plan. The four of them had debated color schemes and finally, in the interest of peace, left the decision in Summer's hands. She'd told them they wouldn't be sorry—and promised to repaint the walls herself if they were.

"'Banana cream' on the wall straight ahead," she said, pointing at the wall people would see as they entered from the street. "'Blushing' on the wall to 'banana cream's' right." She moved a bucket of that paint to the base of the wall straight ahead for anyone entering from the bookshop. "Those two will draw people in with mellow, appetite-inducing warmth."

Garth watched Summer's every move, mouth not quite hanging open. Or at least the movement of her loose, long, shiny blond hair. Christine nudged Janet with her elbow and nodded her chin toward him.

"Color groupie," she whispered to Janet.

"On the wall going into the bookshop, we have this complementary yet energetic green," Summer said. "That's 'aqueduct.' It's also reminiscent of the classic 'bookstore' green, so it'll put folks in the right frame of mind as they go into the shop, and it works well with 'banana cream' to its right. Then, on the wall along the street, it's another energetic color, 'candid blue.' It works well with the other three and brings the blue of the water and sky into the tearoom as patrons look out the windows onto the street and harbor. And with the white trim around the door and windows, we've got the blue and white of the saltire flag."

At the mention of the flag, Janet had to cough and leave the tearoom altogether. Christine followed, and as they unlocked and opened the shop for the day, Janet told her about her evening in the launderette.

"You didn't ask Rab why he rabbited off the harbor wall like that the other morning?" Christine asked. "Why not?"

"I didn't like to intrude on the dignity of his Nessie boxers."

"Good Lord. I should hope not."

"Besides, we know why he ran," Janet said. "He knew about the garbage in the house and he felt guilty for not following through when Jess hired him to clear it out."

"Did he act guilty last night? Uncomfortable? In any way uneasy? At all?"

Janet shook her head at each of Christine's questions.

"Then we only think we know."

"That's good enough for now," Janet said. "If he's coming to work for us, let's not ruffle whatever water he floats on, because that is a man who seems to be totally content with floating through life. And I think it's a quality that might be useful to us, so let's keep him on an even keel."

"What do you expect him to do?"

"You've seen sticks and branches and debris floating down the river, or caught in a quiet bend. Or boats moored in the harbor, for that matter. And what do you see happening to them? All kinds of things bump into them—flotsam, jetsam—"

"Rubbish."

"At least let me finish before you say it's rubbish."

"You misunderstood," Christine said. "I'm agreeing with you. Garbage that's tossed out or overboard gets caught up on floating objects, too."

"And that's what Rab's like. Bits and pieces of life in Inversgail bump up against him and he floats from place to place. Bits and pieces of information. He looks at them and keeps some and leaves the rest."

"Aren't we all like that to some extent?"

"Sure, but I think he's mastered the art, the way cats have perfected the art of soaking up sunshine. Think what will happen if some engineer somewhere figures out how to harness the solar energy absorbed by cats."

"Instant Nobel Prize," Christine said.

"But unlikely to happen because of lack of funding."

"Besides the cats not cooperating."

"They would never go along with it," Janet said. "And all *we* have to do is convince Rab to share the bits and pieces he collects. With us."

PAMELA AND KENNETH arrived during a flurry of pensioners on an outing from Fort William. Although the week of expertise the Lawries had promised wasn't yet up, Janet hadn't been sure they would be back. Besides Pamela saying they were ready to go it alone, and then *leaving* them alone, there'd been the incident with Sharon Davis. But Kenneth came in with his gap-toothed grin and a thumbs-up when he saw the milling crowd.

"They make the trip every few months," he said. "The tearoom will be just their cup of tea."

Pamela stood by the postcard display, greeting pensioners she recognized. After the last few had made their purchases, she went across to the sales desk.

"Nice old dears," she said softly. "That's why I didn't like to interrupt with something so unpleasant."

Janet and Christine were instantly attentive, Christine with the beginnings of a twitch in her left eyelid.

"I saw McVitie and McPhee's van," Pamela said. "Are they working in the tearoom?"

"Redecorating," Janet said. "They came highly recommended. Why?"

"Only, you see, that's why I'm shocked. They have a fine reputation."

"What are you talking about?" Christine asked.

"The bags of rubbish they hauled out," Pamela said. "They tossed them on the footpath along the back, which is both careless and negligent, not to say how it reflects on Yon Bonnie. And then some numpty's come along and slit them open, and they're lying out there like five or six fat, black trout—gutted."

Christine stared at Pamela before saying, "McVitie and McPhee didn't remove bags of rubbish."

"See for yourself. It's like a tip back there. Go on. I'll watch the books."

There are no words. Janet didn't say it out loud, not as she had two mornings before, but she repeated the horrible mantra to herself as she and Christine rushed for the back door. That door, reached through the stockroom, opened directly onto a narrow pedestrian pavement and Sculpay Terrace, the one-way street between the backs of High Street buildings and the backs of those on the next street up the hill. Janet and Christine ran out the door, Janet going left, and Christine right, and then they stopped and stood in the street and stared. There on the pavement, along the back of their building, were the slit garbage bags.

"She can't count," Christine said. "There are seven. And where she gets trout from, I can't imagine. They look more like harbor seals—"

"Don't," Janet said. "I don't want to hear what they look like. This is more of it. This is more of what's happened at the house. I just..." She clutched the top of her head. "There are no words and I don't even know what to think anymore."

"Then you don't want to hear this, either, because I *do* know what to think. This is a threat."

ELEVEN

Janet called Police Scotland's nonemergency number. The first call handler she reached at the area police service center told her that flytipping was a matter she should report to her local council, and disconnected. The second call handler Janet reached agreed that bags of rubbish dumped behind a business in Inversgail was terrible, in fact a scourge to be battled across their entire beautiful country, but not police business.

"*Murder* is police business," Janet said, with emphasis on "murder"—*salacious* emphasis, she later told Tallie—and that caught the handler's attention.

The call handler connected Janet to Constable Hobbs. Hobbs, although giving the impression he thought Janet was overreacting, said he would relay her report to the crime specialists as possibly of interest in their ongoing investigation. He didn't know when they might arrive, or when he might, but as it was a dry and not very windy day, the rubbish wasn't likely to disappear before he and they did appear. He said he'd try to be there soon. As it turned out, some of the Major Investigation Team arrived before he did.

"But it took them an hour," Janet fretted.

"And more's the pity they're here first," said Christine. "At least with Norman we've established a certain rapport."

Janet wasn't sure what that rapport was doing for them, and she clutched the top of her head again. But then the dismissive inspector from the night of the murder thanked her for reporting the "disturbance" and assured her they were taking this new incident seriously. He was sorry that a key member of their team had apparently been delayed. As had Constable Hobbs. The inspector might have ground his teeth after mentioning Constable Hobbs. Then he turned to another of his officers.

"Have you reached Reddick yet?" he asked.

"No, sir. He left word he was meeting Atkinson at the bothy. In the middle of nowhere, it sounded."

"Right. We'll make do without him."

Janet could forgive the inspector for being abrupt. Part and parcel of doing a difficult job, she assumed. And he did sound sincere. Right up until she heard him muttering to one of his men about "entitled Americans expecting police protection from rampaging bin liners."

At that point, Norman Hobbs arrived.

"Apologies for not arriving earlier, sir," Hobbs said, words and posture at crisp attention. "Attending a road accident, sir, on Tha Mo Bhàtafoluaimein Loma-làn Easgannan Road."

The inspector skewered him with a look.

"Formerly the Mull Eigg Road. It's the Gaelic road signs, sir. Difficult, but better than the Welsh. Have you and the other specialists made a determination yet as to whether there is a link between this incident and the recent murder?"

Janet thought she detected a bristle of something in Hobbs's officious words. Possibly sarcasm. From the inspector's suppressed snarl, she thought he might have detected it, too. The Major Investigation Team hadn't actually investigated the incident yet, though, so all the officers exited through the front door to do so. Janet and Christine left the books in Pamela's and Kenneth's capable and concerned hands, and for the second time that week followed Norman Hobbs toward a crime scene. Hobbs lifted an eyebrow at them, but after glancing at the blue backs marching in closed rank ahead of him, he said nothing to dissuade them. And when they rounded the far corner of their building, they were once again shocked by what lay in front of them in Sculpay Terrace—except this time it was absolutely nothing. The street, the pavement, everywhere they looked. Nothing. Not even a cigarette butt lay abandoned in the gutter.

"Mrs. Marsh." The inspector stood straight, arms at his sides. His tone of voice, though, crossed its arms and regarded her through a jaundiced, narrowed eye. "Are you familiar with the term 'wasting police time'?"

"There were bags of garbage here an hour ago. All slit open. *Six* of them."

"Seven," Christine corrected. "I took pictures with my phone."

"Bless you, Christine," Janet said. "I didn't notice you doing that."

Christine patted her back. "You were in shock."

"Right," the inspector said. "Finish up here, Hobbs."

"Sir."

"And try to answer your calls more promptly. That way you might not lose the evidence."

"Sir."

The blue backs of the crime specialists closed ranks again and marched back out of Sculpay Terrace.

"THAT WAS HARSH criticism coming from someone who'd barely arrived before you did," Janet said as she watched the specialists disappear around the corner. "Not to mention that one of his own team didn't show up at all, and you were at the scene of a road accident, for heaven's sake. I hope no one was badly hurt."

"Single car accident. Slight injuries to the driver," Hobbs said. "He'll be right in a day or two. There's a rock wall along there, and where the road turns left he didn't."

"Tcha. Distracted driving," Christine said. "On his mobile, was he? Or was he drunk that early in the day?"

"Now who's being harsh?" Hobbs asked, but his rebuke was mild. "Distracted, aye, but not by his phone, and not likely to be drinking on duty, or at least not on duty that early in the day. He'd just passed a field full of sheep, and then he saw new twin lambs with their mum on the verge. He was concerned for their safety. Then he saw the dog, but missed seeing the turn."

"On duty," Janet said.

"I didn't reckon officers in the Specialist Crime Division to be so soft-hearted," Hobbs said. "Officer named Reddick. He said the sheepdog looked like his own dog. Quantum, he calls him. He was a bit chatty, which might've been a result of the rush of adrenaline after the crash. He's a good man. His second concern was that I not say anything to the inspector before he had a chance to chat with him himself. His first was for the dog and the sheep."

"Sheep," Christine said with a shudder. "They're the woolly fluff of nightmares."

"Just don't let the fluff keep you from thinking clearly," Janet said. "We've heard that name, Reddick, before. One of the specialists told the inspector that Reddick was meeting Ian Atkinson at a brothel in the middle of nowhere. That sounds like it could be a significant development. Not a very nice one, though. Constable Hobbs, while Reddick was being chatty, did he let anything useful about his meeting with Atkinson slip?"

Hobbs looked at Janet. "Erm, did you say—"

"She meant bothy," Christine said to Hobbs. Turning to Janet, she said, "A wee hoose 'mang the heather, dear. A house, possibly a whiskymaking operation. Possibly also a trysting place, but not a brothel."

"An easy mistake to make," Hobbs told Janet unconvincingly. "The specialists are talking to Ian Atkinson, but I don't think they see him as a suspect. More like they're starstruck. The big crime writer, you see. They probably think he can solve the crime for them. My opinion, anyway."

"And sound, I'm sure," Christine said. "I must say, Norman, I admired the way you rattled off the Gaelic for your inspector. He's obviously not a believer, but you showed him how it's done. Do you speak it?"

"Sadly, not much more than signpost Gaelic. And the odd phrase."

"Nor do I," said Christine. "Funny, though, I don't recall such a long stretch of Gaelic on the Mull Eigg Road sign." She looked at him with an inquiring eye.

"Ah."

"Ah?"

Hobbs considered the sky for a moment, and then looked at them with a sweet smile. "That would be because there isn't. That was one of the odd phrases I've learnt. I'm told by my sister that it means, 'My hovercraft is full of eels.' I reckon the inspector and his mates don't have any more actual Gaelic than I do, and possibly were never fans of Monty Python or John Cleese. Now, about these bags of rubbish."

THE SKY HOBBS had so recently considered had turned gray and started dripping, so they went back into the bookshop, entering through the back door.

"You should interview Pamela Lawrie first," Christine said. "She's the one who told us about the bin bags."

"I'll hear from you and Mrs. Marsh, first, if it's all the same to you."

Janet stopped short in the stockroom. "But here, if you don't mind, and not in the shop. We don't want customers overhearing or getting the wrong impression."

"You don't think having the entire Major Investigation Team traipse in and out of the shop earlier already did that for us?" Christine asked.

"But let's not compound it," Janet said. "Nothing against you, Constable Hobbs, or the police."

"It's quite all right. Believe it or not, the uniform doesn't make friends everywhere it goes." Hobbs looked left and right at the length of the stockroom. "You've a reasonable amount of extra space here, haven't you? Deceptive from the outside."

"Like so many things in life," Christine said, "people included. All right, while you give Norman a tour of packing materials and extra inventory, I'll go let Pamela and Kenneth know we haven't given up on the idea of running a shop."

For all the extra space the stockroom provided, it wasn't laid out with gatherings in mind. The room was only as long as the building, and fairly narrow back to front. Utilitarian wooden shelves ran along the outside wall. There were several cupboards, a workbench, and a deep sink along the interior wall. Janet and Hobbs waited without speaking, with their backsides resting against the workbench.

"Christine thinks the slit bags were a message. A threat," Janet said when Christine returned and joined them in leaning against the workbench.

"Hard to know what the threat would be about," Hobbs said.

"You want more imagination, Norman," said Christine.

"Oh, aye."

"Oh, aye, indeed. I'm quite sure if you want to solve a crime like murder, you need to make intuitive leaps. You need to make connections."

"Constable Hobbs," Janet said. "The threat might be toward another life."

"There," Christine said. "You see? Connect the dots. Rubbish in Janet's house—dot one. Una murdered in Janet's shed—dot two. Rubbish behind Yon Bonnie Books—dot three. Now it's your turn, Norman. Turn it over in your mind to determine the who, the what, the where, and the when of dot four."

"Thank you," he said. "That's very helpful."

Janet thought Hobbs had a good handle on the concept of forbearance.

"About the bags," he said, "did you notice if they were all the same kind? Or did you notice if they or the loose rubbish were wet?"

Janet and Christine, on either side of him, looked around him at each other. Neither could remember exactly.

"What about the pictures you took?"

Christine showed him. They weren't much. She'd taken them quickly, and there were only three. He asked her to forward them to him, just the same.

"Now, Constable Hobbs." Janet moved around so that she was standing in front of him. She put her fists on her hips, a power stance she felt she needed when she recited the demands she'd promised herself she'd make. "I want to know what's going on with my house, when I'll be allowed to move in, and what they've found—"

Hobbs started to respond. Janet replanted her fists.

"I need to know these things so I'll know what I'm dealing with. Whether there's more of a mess than just the rubbish in the kitchen, which is bad enough. But are the police making their own mess? Is there fingerprint powder everywhere? Ripped up floorboards? I need to know. Oh! And I absolutely need to know if they've found rats in the house." Her fists left her hips as her elbows pulled into her sides.

Hobbs drew back against the workbench. "I've heard nothing about rats."

"Nor I," Christine said. "Where did you?"

"Maida Fairlie. She heard from the renters. I've never heard anything like that from Jess, and I've always liked her, but I'm beginning to wonder. Constable Hobbs." Janet's fists were back on her hips. "The success of our whole bookshop, tearoom, B and B retirement scheme rests in part on that house being livable and me living in it. I need—" Her right fist left her hip again, and her index finger drew a half dozen rapid lines between herself and Christine. "We need—" The finger made a dozen dizzying circuits connecting the three of them… "We all need answers. So what are you going to do about it?" This was the real reason Janet had wanted to hold this conversation out of the public's eye. She'd never liked confrontations, she wasn't necessarily good at putting her foot down, and she hadn't been sure she wouldn't back down or burst into tears before or after having her say. She'd done well, though, and put her fists back on her hips. The power stance felt good.

"She's made excellent points, Norman," Christine said. "What are your thoughts on all this? What steps do you propose?"

"The rats I'll check into immediately. Speak to Reddick. He owes me something, after the sheep incident this morning. For the bin bags, no doubt someone thought they were doing a good deed and cleared them away. I'll ask around. See if I can locate them."

"That's it?" Janet asked.

"You might speak to Jess yourself."

"Oh. Yes, of course."

"In the meantime." He pushed away from the workbench, and Janet and Christine stepped back. "How's the redecorating coming along? Noticing any problems with paint odor?"

"FOR WHATEVER REASON, I think the rats lit more of a fire under Hobbs than the garbage bags, don't you?" Janet asked.

"Much like finding sheep in the house would do for me," Christine said. "He's right, though. Give Jess a call. And I'll call sweet Rosie at Jess's office."

TALLIE WAS AT the sales desk when Janet and Christine returned to the shop. She was ringing up a short stack of *Recipes of the Highlands and Islands of Scotland* for a young couple bubbling over with excitement. Excitement with an accent from somewhere in their own Midwest, Janet realized.

"Christmas shopping done!" the young woman said. "Can I have a bookmark and one of those bags with your logo on it for each one? Cool. Christmas wrapping done!"

Tallie accepted the woman's high five, then, when she saw her mother, nodded toward the aisle of literature and poetry books. Janet saw who was browsing the shelf and wanted to high-five Christine, or at least nudge her with her elbow. But Christine's attention was on two figures in a couple of chairs near the fire—Pamela, snoring not so softly in one, and sitting up and watching them from the other, a sandy-colored terrier.

"Is that Pamela's dog?" Christine asked, not keeping her voice down because she hadn't noticed the man browsing the poetry, and it was obvious to anyone that Pamela wouldn't hear anything through her snores. Christine started toward the two.

Janet stopped her with a hand on her arm. "Shhh. It's all right."

"What if it has muddy paws?"

The dog turned its nose to the fire, essentially turning its back on them.

"Ranger has very clean paws," Tallie told them. "Don't you, Ranger?

Ranger lifted a desultory shoulder without looking back at them. Then he flopped down in the chair with his head on the arm.

"Rab's dog," Janet whispered to Christine.

"We're not hiring his dog," Christine whispered back.

"I'll go speak to him."

Rab had moved from poetry to the crafts section and appeared to be captivated by a book of Fair Isle mitten patterns.

"Do you knit?" Janet asked after greeting him.

"Not as well as my father did, but maybe a bit better than Ranger." He took a book of cardigan patterns from where it stood face-out on the shelf and tucked it where it belonged alphabetically spine out. He put the mitten book in the face-out position and turned to her. Then, before she could bring up the dog who'd settled in for a nap in one of their chairs, or the job she hoped he'd take, he offered an apology. Of sorts. "Jess Baillie hired me for a job at your house earlier this week. It didn't work out."

"Yes. I heard something about that. *Why* didn't it work out?"

"A phone call."

"Saying what? Who called?" Janet asked.

"Caller ID didn't work out, either, but somebody telling me not to go to your house."

"Was it Jess?"

"No." After answering, Rab moved the question around with his eyes and several twists of his lips, as though investigating its facets. "Someone trying to sound like her, maybe."

"That sounds awfully—"

"But maybe not." He shook his head. "No, she gave me that impression—that she was Jess—at first. But that made no sense, because then she said, 'Tell Jess you're sorry, but you're otherwise committed.' I didn't like to lie, so I told Jess I had a subsequent engagement."

"An earlier one, you mean?"

"No. If I'd told her it was a prior engagement, I would have been lying. The anonymous call definitely came after."

"Did your subsequent engagement pay better than Jess would have?"

Rab straightened the books on the next shelf up from

the mitten patterns. "I felt bad about it. About your house, I mean. Not about Jess. She can afford to hire someone else."

"Well, thank you for that."

"No thanks needed." He patted the spine of an origami book and then turned to face her again. "Anyway, I hope I've made up for it."

"Sorry?" She'd been wondering who could have known Jess had hired Rab in the first place. Had that person also found out about the cleaning firm in Fort William that Jess had called?

"I made up for it," Rab repeated. "Some bugger broke open your bin bags in back. But it's all right. I cleared it up and took it to the Recycling Centre."

"*Bugger*. Can you get it back?"

TWELVE

JANET'S OUTBURST CAME with enough feeling to make moderate Rab MacGregor's eyes fly wide. Then, before he could come up with a better answer to her question about getting her rubbish back than a stuttered, "Eh, erm," someone switched the music on the sound system. The mellow strings in the background were abruptly replaced by an electric, percussive exuberance that leaped into the foreground.

"Sounds like Runrig," Rab shouted. "'Alba.' Bit loud."

Janet started toward the desk but saw Tallie dive for the office, where the sound system controls were. Before she reached the door, the volume was squelched, and Christine emerged from the office looking sheepish.

"Sorry, sorry," she called to the patrons, all staring in her direction like startled meerkats. Seeing Janet, she waved. Seeing Pamela, woken from her nap, she slunk back into the office.

Janet looked to see how the sound explosion had affected Ranger. He was no longer in the chair—perhaps under it? But Ranger didn't project the image of a cowering cur, and when she stooped to see, he wasn't under the chair. She turned back to where she'd left Rab. But—

like dog, like man—Rab was no longer there, either. She made a circuit of the store without finding them.

"Bugger," she said under her breath. She hadn't often used the word and didn't intend to start using it more often now. It suited her mood, though, so that she checked ahead and behind and, seeing no one near enough to hear, said it one more time softly, but with percussive feeling. Then she called Constable Hobbs to save him the trouble of asking around about the garbage.

"*If* he was asking around," Tallie said, when Janet told her about the garbage and where it had gone.

"I think he probably was, or was planning to," Janet said. "I think he'd like nothing better than to solve this before the specialists. Remember he asked for our notes. He's taking a real interest in our contributions."

"Who's this who's interested in contributions, then?" Pamela asked, joining them behind the desk. Despite her unexpected waking to the blast of music, she appeared to be refreshed from her nap. "You want to be careful when it comes to requests for contributions. You'll find everybody and their brother will be after you for donating merchandise to one worthy cause after another. 'It's just a wee book or two,' they'll say. But when you add up all those books it's not so wee anymore. Always remember, your first business *is* business."

"Good point," Janet said, feeling as though putting more space between herself and Pamela could also be good. Or bad, depending on the message stepping away might send. She was already feeling possessive of the shop, though, enjoying the sense of ownership and control. She stayed put and used the power of her straight, white American teeth in a full smile. Unsuccessfully.

"Do you mind a private word?" Pamela asked her, moving in closer. "In the office?"

"I've got the desk," Tallie said. "Go ahead."

Pamela moved past Janet and through the door. Before stepping inside, Janet exchanged raised eyebrows with Tallie.

The office was a room about the size of a galley kitchen, partitioned off from the sales floor. There was room for two desks, one facing each long wall, each with a rolling chair and flanked by a three-drawer filing cabinet. A bookcase stood at the far end. It was Janet's least favorite part of the shop. The first time she set foot in the room, she half expected to see the ghost of a chartered accountant, hunched and rubbing its hands over a candle. She'd told Christine, who'd agreed and said they would think of some way to make the space more welcoming. When Christine saw her now, she drew her shoulders up and rubbed her hands.

"Cold in here, isn't it?" Pamela said, catching Christine's mime. "You wouldn't think it would be because it's so close. It's an awkward room, though. Tall, dark, and cramped. I think of it as Kenneth's man cave and try to stay out of it as much as possible. Do sit down, please. I'll be quick, but no point in us all standing."

Janet was tempted to stay on her feet and tell Pamela to take a seat, but the woman definitely didn't look comfortable in the room. Christine rolled a chair from one of the desks into the space between them. Janet followed suit, and they sat elbow-to-elbow facing Pamela.

"Kenneth told me about the misunderstanding over the judging committee with Sharon Davis yesterday," Pamela said. "He wants you to know that he regrets it."

"Oh, well, I'm sure—" Janet said.

"Where is Kenneth?" Christine asked on top of her.

Janet shot a glance at Christine. Christine either didn't catch it or ignored her—she was watching Pamela, studying her. Pamela must have noticed. She fidgeted with an earlobe. The interplay made Janet uncomfortable, too.

"Ken's gone for the day."

"That wasn't our agreement," Christine said.

"Unusual circumstances," Janet murmured. "Not really a problem."

"He's suffering from a bit of short-timer's disease," Pamela said with a forced laugh.

Christine knit her fingers together and brought them up so her chin rested on her knuckles, her gaze not leaving Pamela.

"It's hard, though, giving up a business we've grown and loved. You must know how it is. You've each retired from your own careers. I told him to think of himself as Andy Murray retiring at the top of his game." She forced another laugh. "Go out with a bit of topspin or whatever they call it. But do it while the business is still thriving. Well. That doesn't really make it easier for him, does it? And I think it might be best if he stays away at this point."

"Certainly understandable," Janet said. She tried to cross her legs and accidentally rolled her chair backward.

Without turning her head, Christine shot her hand out and stopped the chair, then returned the hand to nestle with its mate beneath her chin. "How do you feel about retirement, Pamela?" she asked.

"Like a million." The answer was immediate. So was the reaction to it. Pamela bit her lip, then in a rough gesture, scrubbed her lips with her fingertips. "A bit guilty, too," she said. "I don't know if Ken would have ever left if I hadn't pushed for it. That's why I wanted to tell you." She stopped, lips pursed, head shaking. "It hurt him when he wasn't asked to be on the judging committee this year. And I badgered him a bit to call and ask Sharon about it. Told him he should tell her he wanted to stay on for this last year. He's a proud man, though, and he wouldn't. And now I can't get it out of my head that if he'd been on the committee, Una might still be alive."

Christine lowered her knitted hands from beneath her chin to a place in front of her heart. Her voice was as calm and deliberate as that movement. "Do you think Una was killed because of the writing contest?"

Janet's voice wasn't quite as steady. "Have you told Norman Hobbs?"

Pamela looked from one to the other, seemingly unable to decide where to focus or which of them to answer first. Then Christine asked one more question.

"Have you told Kenneth?"

This time Pamela's short, sharp laugh sounded bitter. "I wouldn't dare tell Kenneth a thing like that, and don't you tell him, either. In fact, I already told you that you're doing a fine job, and I think it's time we both stayed away."

"Pamela, are you sure?" Janet asked, suddenly feeling...she wasn't sure what she felt. *Motherly? Hardly.*

"We'll be in Inversgail awhile yet. Busy. We'll be busy getting sorted before we're away. You won't need us, but if you do, phone me. This is best, though. I do think so."

"This really feels too sudden," Janet said. She stood up and offered her hand, ready to turn a shake into a hug if Pamela showed any signs of melting into an emotional parting. "Thank you for...entrusting your baby to us. Thank you for everything."

Christine stood, too. "If you need anything, Pamela, you know where to find us."

"Kenneth said to let you know he left something for you in the T-to-Z drawer, there. Filed correctly." Pamela nodded at one of the filing cabinets. "I meant to take a last look round the shop." She threw her head back and stared at the ceiling with an intake of breath that sounded as though it might manage to hold back tears. "Now I know I've stayed too long."

"You know where to find me at home, too," Christine said.

Pamela waved and backed out of the doorway.

Janet waited, listening for the jingle of the bell on

the door, then asked, "What was that about? *If you need us?* What do you imagine they would need from us?"

"She, not they." Christine sat back down and swiveled her chair back and forth. "A cup of tea and a friendly ear? I might be mistaken."

"You hardly ever think you're mistaken."

"Because too often *that's* the mistake." Christine had a quick smile for their well-worn joke, then rubbed her hands as though now they really were cold. "No. You're right. I don't think I'm mistaken. Were you watching her? Have you watched the two of them together? I don't know what's going on between them. They work well together, but there's some sadness behind it all."

Janet had gone to the filing cabinet and bent to open the bottom drawer. She sank to her haunches and looked up at Christine. "You don't think that comes from leaving the shop and leaving home?"

"That could be all it is."

"You're better at reading people than I am, though."

"It was even in the way she reacted to being in this room," Christine said.

"So what do we do? Tell Hobbs?"

"Tell him what?"

"That Pamela has a theory about Una's murder being connected to the writing contest. You notice she didn't answer when I asked if *she* told him."

"I'm sure she didn't tell him. I don't think she'd dare," Christine said. "She'd be afraid of Kenneth's reaction if he found out."

"But does she really believe there is a connection? Or is she afraid to find out that Kenneth is the connection?"

"That Kenneth killed Una?" Christine's lips thinned as she thought that over.

"That's so…stark. And I'm not sure that's what I meant. More like his absence from the committee put her in danger, not necessarily that *he* was the danger." Janet hadn't risen from her crouch at the filing cabinet. She shivered. "But I'm not sure what Pamela meant, and I definitely felt menace when he and Sharon faced off. But again, do you really think?"

"I'm not sure. I don't know how being suspicious of Kenneth is logical or follows Pamela's fear about the contest. But who says murder is always, or even ever, logical? Maybe we should be glad he's suffering from short-timer's disease and wants to stay away."

"There's no maybe about it. What do we do?"

"Find what he left for us in yon drawer and be prepared to make good use of it."

JANET AND CHRISTINE agreed to leave their disquiet about the Lawries in the office with the bottle of whisky they found in the filing drawer. Their questions and concerns wouldn't be appropriate topics of discussion at the sales desk. The whisky, an extraordinarily good single malt, was too precious to leave unattended in public. But now they had a trail Tallie could hunt for.

"There might not be anything as obvious as a trail for her to find," Christine said. She watched as Janet tucked the bottle back into the drawer, cushioning it like a sleeping baby with the length of woolen fabric they'd found with the bottle. "His menacing and bullying might only go so far. They might not have earned him a charge or a record."

"If it's possible to find anything, my money's on Tallie."

"Mine, too," Christine said. "I just want you to know the odds. We need to be realistic. Do you think he meant to leave that piece of tartan in the drawer?"

"The whisky was on top of it, and they're in the right drawer. T for tartan, W for whisky. It's beautiful. I love the muted blues and greens, but what'll we do with it?"

"Use it as plaidie. I wonder if it's Lawrie tartan—a memento for us to remember them by."

"If it is, then I'm less inclined to wrap myself in it. But that's being unfair to the innocent plaid, isn't it? And possibly unfair to Kenneth, because we don't know anything for certain."

"Let's go set your daughter loose on that uncertainty."

TALLIE WASN'T AT the sales desk when Janet and Christine returned to the floor. Janet thought she heard Tallie's and another voice down the aisle near the cookbooks. Perhaps another early Christmas shopper.

An uncertain-looking young woman stood in the open space before the desk, her back to it. She appeared to be waiting but didn't look entirely sure of what she was waiting for. She gave the impression of not wanting to make eye contact with any of the books shouldering each other for her attention on the shelves nearest her. She'd just cast an uneasy glance at the tall, narrow bookcase to her right, and shied away from it, when Christine nudged Janet with her elbow and called to the young woman.

"Is that you, Rosie?"

With minimal movement, the young woman swiveled on her toes to face them. She waved the tips of her fingers at Christine.

"I thought so. Good to see you, dear." Christine kept her voice low and warm, and she held an arm out as though inviting Rosie for a hug. Rosie moved several minuscule steps closer to the desk, but not within hug's reach. Christine didn't lower her arm and Janet imagined it becoming the arc of a circle creating a connection between the three of them. "Janet, I'd like you to meet Rosie. She works for Jess Baillie. Rosie, this is one of my oldest and very best friends, Janet. Not that she's all that ancient, but we're both old enough to be your gran."

"How do you do, Rosie?" Janet took her cue from Christine and kept her voice soft. She felt as though they were trying to lure a woodland creature toward them. Rosie had the delicate legs of a fawn, her russet hair styled in a waifish cut with a magenta streak over her left ear. Her shoulders were either tentative or cold in the thin blouse she wore—a schoolgirl's white blouse. This wasn't at all how Janet had pictured the chatty young woman Christine described after meeting her at the estate agency.

Like a fawn, Rosie picked her way closer, and then stopped again, still several feet away.

"You must be psychic," Christine said with a smile. "I was going to phone you. But you saved me the trouble, and now that you're here, what can we do for you?"

"I am," Rosie said.

"Sorry?"

"That's why I came. Because I am." She hugged herself, her knees below her short skirt touching, her toes turned in. "Only, I didn't realize it until this morning."

"I'm sorry, dear. It's my old ears." Christine rubbed an ear as though clearing a muddle from it. "You're here because you are…what?"

"Psychic. That must be why I came here. Because you were going to phone me."

"Didn't you know you were coming here when you set out?" Christine asked. "Where were you? At home? In the office? Isn't it likely you saw my name on a note, or remembered that we spoke?"

Janet could hear Christine's inner social worker turning skeptical. She knew Christine wouldn't be happy until she could dig into Rosie's assertion, uproot it, and expose it to the harsh light of reality. And Rosie, who'd looked hesitant and shy to begin with, now looked spooked and skittish. Janet put her hand on Christine's shoulder and gave a gentle tug backward. Christine tensed, and then Janet felt her relax and saw her give a quick nod of understanding.

"I've heard stories about second sight," Janet said,

"but I've never been lucky enough to meet someone who has it. Do you think that's what's going on, Rosie?"

"No," Rosie said with a scoff. "That's old wives' tales and stories for weans. This is different." She pulled her shoulders in, and she didn't look much older than a wean herself. "But it's never happened before."

"I'm pretty sure it would've scared me," Janet said. "What did happen? How did you know something was going on?"

"I didn't. That's the eerie part. I didn't at first. I didn't know until this morning. And then it hit me. Like a bolt of lightning. Out of the blue." Her blue eyes went wide at the memory.

"What was it that hit you?"

"That I'm psychic." Rosie pointed at Christine. "And *she* knew it, too. When I came in, she said it. But now she doesn't believe me anymore." She stopped with a yip. "Do you see how it works? That just popped into my head, but I know it's true. You can see for yourself that she doesn't believe me."

Janet still had her hand on Christine's shoulder and felt her tensing up again. Any second, she expected Christine to start gnashing her teeth.

"Rosie, dear," Janet said, "we both believe you. But we want you to tell us how you know you're psychic. What psychic…thing happened this morning to make *you* believe?"

"I knew Una Graham was going to die."

Janet's question and Rosie's answer sailed into a momentary lull in the background music. Just before that lull, Tallie and her customer had finished their conversation about traditional haggis recipes and started back toward the sales desk. Hearing Janet's question and Rosie's ringing answer, the customer—Rosie's employer, Jess Baillie—pushed past Tallie. Janet saw her first, storming toward them.

"Rosie Crozier, if you were psychic, you should have known I'd find out you left the office unattended, and you definitely would have known to keep your blatherskite mouth shut."

THIRTEEN

JANET ENJOYED WATCHING Christine toss aside her inner social worker and take control of the situation with her not-to-be-trifled-with, though somewhat amused, Elizabeth II persona. Janet didn't remember this aspect of Christine's character making an appearance during any of their fairly civilized book club meetings back in Illinois. Or at any of the more rancorous city council meetings they'd attended, either. She hoped she would remember to ask Christine later if her impersonation was some kind of natural upwelling now that she was back home and living on her native soil, or if it was a conscious transformation. If Christine could call on the queen at will, how might that talent come in handy in a real crisis?

Under Christine's direction, what might have turned into a prolonged spectacle was over in seconds. She sent Tallie after Rosie, who'd bolted down one aisle. While Tallie herded Rosie into the tearoom, Christine told Janet to hold on to Jess, though not literally, and calm her down.

"Talk to her," Christine said. "See if you can find out why she came in just now. I'll go tap into our psychic's powers."

Janet took it as a good sign that Jess hadn't stormed

out after storming at Rosie. She stood looking the display in one of the windows—local histories and historical fiction—breathing hard, but no longer hissing or spitting. Janet went over to her and pointed out which of the books she'd read and enjoyed and which were on her teetering, tottering, ever-growing to-be-read pile. Jess listened and didn't leave, so Janet told her about their plans for future displays, about the redecorating in the tearoom, and about the work to be done for the bed and breakfast. She felt she was making progress toward engaging her when Jess moved away from the window and cast the sort of appraising eye over the shop that Norman Hobbs had. The difference being that Jess had the eye of a professional estate agent and Norman Hobbs was probably just nosy. Janet thought about sharing that observation with Jess, to see if she could raise a smile, but decided against it. Mentioning Constable Hobbs might make Jess jumpy again.

Janet very badly wanted to ask Jess what she knew about the couple who'd been renting her house, but she feared the timing wasn't right. It didn't feel right for her question about rats, either. She was easing Jess toward the chairs at the fireplace, trying to come up with a smooth segue that might ease them into that topic, when Jess finally spoke again.

"I doubt this building would have worked, anyway."

"Sorry?"

"Ian Atkinson." Jess said the name to the ceiling, in the corner where it met the chimney. When she looked at Janet, she drew back suddenly as though startled at seeing to whom she'd spoken. "I must have been telling your lassie. He was looking for commercial property in Inversgail. He wants to start a boutique distillery and tasting room."

"You would've sold him this building?" Janet was appalled and didn't think she was overreacting by adding, "You would have let him…do away with the bookshop?" She'd almost said *kill the bookshop* but was able to rein in her reaction at least that small step short of jumping off the cliff into absolute melodrama. She put a hand to her lips just in case her über-melodramatic thoughts tried to get out.

"Of course I would, if I could have," Jess said. "But it was nothing to do with me. I only heard about it secondhand. He didn't work through a local agency." She sounded bitter.

"I'm glad we got our bid in first, then."

"You didn't," Jess said. "This was a year ago. Kenneth and Pamela would have been happy to sell. To anyone at all, to hear him tell it in the pub. But something didn't work out. If a local person had been involved, or could have got involved before it fell apart, it might have." She shrugged as though it had been no skin off her nose or shirt off her back, but the bitterness still came through.

"Any idea what happened?"

"Aye. One word," Jess said, near to spitting again.

The bell at the door jingled, and Summer breezed in, back from her trip to meet the editor of the *Inversgail Guardian.*

"Look who's here," Janet said, reaching for anything to keep a lid on Jess's emotions. "You haven't met our

Summer yet, have you? Summer is the fourth member of our book business cabal, and she has the absolutely uncanny ability to enter any building, from any given weather condition, looking exactly like a ray of sunshine. How do you do that?"

"It's useful camouflage," Summer said. "I disarm people with Blond Barbie Syndrome, but I never use the power for evil. I should look particularly radiant right now, though, because I've scored a coup." She laid a leather portfolio on the sales desk, spread her arms, and gave a shallow bow. "Applaud at will, because you're looking at the new Una Graham."

Except for a lively accordion version of "Laddie wi' a Plaidie" in the background, the silence following Summer's announcement deafened. Seeing Jess's face, Janet didn't want to hear how she would break that silence.

Jess stared at Summer. Her eyes might be seeing her, or they might instead be locked onto a ghost. She made an unintelligible gurgle low in her throat. Then, holding her purse to her chest with one arm as though it were a rugby ball, and with her other arm and palm in a classic stiff-arm fend from the same game, she drove for the door and right on through when Rab MacGregor, about to enter, saw her coming and opened it.

Rab watched her go, then came in, two bin bags clutched by their necks in his left fist. Ranger followed at his heels. "Had good luck," Rab said. Neither he nor Ranger appeared to be bothered by the sight or sound of Jess leaving the shop as though pursued. "Found the paper I separated when I took it to the recycle center. Brought what I could in clean bin liners."

"Is that where you went?" Janet's mind skipped across several tracks to pick up on what he was talking about. "I never thought I'd be happy to see garbage, but I am. Thank you, Rab. Do you think it was behind the shop during the rain last night?"

"Bits of paper were damp, but that's to be expected with it lying loose. But no water in the bags when I cleared up back there earlier."

"When you were clearing up, or when you were getting it back, just now, did you see anything that could tell us where it came from?"

He lifted the bags and studied them for a moment—trying to remember or running through a mental inventory. *Or maybe he has X-ray vision*, Janet thought.

"Besides addresses on envelopes? No," he said with a shrug, "but I'll think on it. Best I can say is the rubbish was fresh."

"Fresh?"

"Nothing rancid or terribly stinking."

"Oh. Interesting."

"The food waste was already gone when I got back to the center."

"Thank you, Rab. Why don't you put those…" *Where?* She didn't want the garbage disappearing again. But then she realized she didn't want it in the office or stockroom—anywhere that Kenneth might have a reason or take an interest to go. If he wandered in, which seemed unlikely, but… "Put it around the corner in the tearoom, for now, will you, Rab?" She almost added, *And I'll run it upstairs later*, but decided she didn't want to offer that information.

"I've missed something," Summer said, pointing after Rab and Ranger on their way to the tearoom. Then she pointed her thumb over her shoulder at the door. "And I was incredibly insensitive just now, wasn't I. Calling myself the new Una. What a klutz. Was she a relative?"

Janet's mind skipped to another track.

"Should I bake something and deliver it with an apology?" Summer asked. Not getting an answer, she tapped Janet's shoulder. "Janet?"

"I don't think they're related," Janet said. "It's an interesting thought, and we only have Kenneth's word that Una had no family in the area. But they do look somewhat alike." She shook herself and focused on Summer. "That was Jess Baillie. Come on back to the desk. We might still have a customer or two browsing, although it's hard to keep track with all that's been going on."

Summer took her portfolio from the desk and ducked into the office to leave it and her jacket out of the way. When she returned, Janet was ringing up a book of knitting and crochet patterns for stuffed animals. The elderly woman buying it nodded and smiled but said nothing in response to Janet's thanks or wishes for a good day. She had her own carrier bag with her. Janet offered her another, but the woman ignored her and took the book over to the chairs by the fireplace.

"Cute little old thing," Janet murmured to Summer when she was sure the woman was beyond earshot. "A comfortable chair, a good book—look at her. *This* is why I love books and why this bookshop is going to be the perfect place. Why it *is* the perfect place. Why I'm so glad we did this. Look, she's only lacking a cup of tea and a cat to be the picture of contentment. Please remind *me* to look that content ten or twenty years from now."

"We need small tables by those chairs so people can bring their cups in from the tearoom," Summer said. "And it's at least twenty years before you're her age. Those were some seriously beautiful wrinkles. Like lines of poetry on her face."

Janet raised her eyebrows.

"That's good," Summer said. "Keep that up and you'll have your own lines of poetry someday. But you're right, you know. A picture of her sitting there reading, with a cat on her lap, or a cute kid, would be a great media piece. Something to counteract the 'all that's been going on' that's been going on. So tell me about it."

"I'll tell you what occurred to me when you asked if Jess is one of Una's relatives. What if the—" Janet checked for anyone nearby before continuing. "What if the killer mistook Una for Jess? Remember that night, Tallie asked if it was Jess in the shed."

"Isn't Jess a bit taller?"

"Not by much, and not with those heels Una had on. *Did* she have them on when...in the shed? Did *you* notice?"

Summer looked at the floor, and Janet knew she wasn't seeing the polished wood, but instead was looking at Una on the floor of the shed again. "It was the same outfit," Summer said, a shade paler. "She hadn't changed. And those trousers wouldn't have worked without the heels. They would've been too long."

"And if she had the heels on, she would've been closer to Jess in height."

"I wish I could swear to the shoes. I didn't really focus on them."

"Of course not," Janet said. "But they weren't the ideal shoes for creeping around or snooping. So what was she doing there?"

"Their hair was different," Summer said. "Pretty wildly different."

"But we can find out if Una changed hers recently or frequently. To mousse or not to mousse—that might have been a daily question."

"You think Jess might have been the target?"

"I think we need to consider it," Janet said. "But I don't know. It's all a jumble with too many facts in isolation. It's too much like that massive mess of garbage in the house and the trash we found out back."

"Again, I obviously missed something this morning."

"You did. And Tallie or Christine can bring you up to speed. They're in the tearoom talking to Rosie." Janet held up a hand, preempting another question. "They'll tell you about that, too. Not that you'll be any less confused, although maybe your reporter's mind can make some sense out of it. Keeping track of all this with notes in our cloud document might get exhausting."

"It could still work. It'll help."

"In the meantime, don't worry about upsetting Jess. She was riled up before you came in."

"Her reaction was interesting, though."

"If we knew what it meant. Was that fear? Grief? Guilt?"

“And if we knew what exactly she was reacting to,” Summer said. “Was she reacting to Una’s name? To what I said about being the new Una? Or was she reacting to me?”

“Because you’re so scary. I laugh that off, but we don’t really know.”

“We don’t, although it probably wasn’t me. But what if it was the guy at the door with the garbage bags?”

“I hadn’t thought of that,” Janet said. “But again with the variables. Was she reacting to Rab or reacting to the bags of garbage? And really, who could blame her for that? Or was she reacting to the combination—to Rab *and* the garbage?” She looked toward the tearoom. Rab hadn’t come back out. Was he watching the painters? Were they all sorting garbage? She hoped not. *How paranoid is too paranoid?* she wondered. *And how many people can you be suspicious of at one time before you become a crackpot?* “Well”—she shook herself—“not everyone can be guilty. But I’m not sure it’s a good idea for you to go around announcing you’re the new Una. Not when we don’t know why she was killed. What did you mean by that, anyway? It made you happy and I’m raining on it.”

“They’ve got a nice operation there at the *Guardian*. Small, almost a mom-and-pop kind of place, but thanks to tourism it’s thriving, like the bookshop. We talked shop. James asked if I was angling for a job. He has that sad, worn-out voice you almost expect to hear from managing editors these days. I said no, I wasn’t. And then he offered me very little money to write Una’s advice column, and I said yes. Isn’t that a hoot?”

"Is it?"

"To be an agony aunt? It's at least a hoot and a half. It's a family paper, though, so I won't be answering any of the archetypal agony aunt sizzlers." She imitated escaping steam and shook her hand. "And it's a short column, once a week, answering two or three questions. No more than five hundred words. So it'll be simple, and it won't interfere with my work here, and what better way to learn about who Una was than by taking up her pen?"

"Are you sure that's a good idea?"

"We talked about this. I'm our press liaison. You rah-rahed it this morning."

"Yes, but isn't there a difference between liaising and infiltrating?"

"Not enough to matter. This is a perfect way to find out what we want to know. It's a time-honored way, Janet. It's investigative journalism."

"It sounds completely foolhardy."

"You're waffling. Where's the woman from this morning who was gung ho to solve this murder so she can get back into her own house and enjoy the marvels of modern plumbing?"

"And that sounds completely self-serving and lunatic. Good heavens, listen to me. I'm a waffling lunatic. I'm dragging my family and friends into who knows what kind of situation." *And where did the positive woman from this morning go?*

Summer took Janet by the shoulders and looked her in the eyes. "That you're worried about the situation and the welfare of your family and friends tells me you're not a lunatic. Janet, I'm a professional journalist. I probably even know what I'm doing. You, and Tallie, and Christine, and I have questions about Una's death. I'm going to try to find some of the answers."

Janet made a noise and saw that Summer accepted it as agreement. She supposed the noise *did* mean agreement, but she was feeling about as articulate as the gurgle Jess made on her rush out the door. *Or,* she thought, *the noise might be a symptom of what's going wrong, including how much harder it is for me to like Jess. Or Kenneth. Hmm.*

"Summer," Janet said, enjoying the clarity of the sibilant in the name, and the recovery from her momentary lapse into negativity, "you're right. And I'll trust you to be careful."

"That's the other goal."

"Do you think this will give you access to back issues of the *Guardian*, going back beyond what might be archived online?"

"You have a research project in mind?"

"Or a fishing trip." Janet checked for customers near enough to overhear before continuing. "Is there an equivalent term for 'disturbing the peace' over here? Is that even what it's called back in the States?" She shook her head. "It doesn't matter. It wouldn't hurt to find out what it's called here, but we should probably look for reports or mentions of any kind. Tallie's going to search farther afield online."

"Good enough. Name?"

"Hold on." Janet took her phone from her pocket and tapped her way into their new cloud document and entered

Guardian and online search: Kenneth Lawrie. Pleased with herself, she held the phone for Summer to see.

"Why limit it? May I?" Summer took the phone from Janet, tapped in *Pamela Lawrie* and *Una Graham*. "I see your one and raise you one," she said, handing the phone back.

"Two can play at that game," Janet said. She entered *Jess Baillie* and *Ian Atkinson*. "Want to see?" She held it for Summer again, but while she'd been tapping, a pair of customers had snuck up on her, and Summer had gone to help another. "Sorry," Janet said, pocketing her phone. "Did you find what you were looking for?"

The male customer of the pair dropped a book of salmon fly patterns on the desk and took out his wallet.

"He's disappointed the tearoom isn't open," his partner said, adding issues of *Scottish Life* and *Scotland Magazine* to the book.

"With luck, we'll be open by the end of next week," Janet said.

"With luck and with fresh scones and clotted cream." Summer came back to the sales desk. Her customer followed behind, carrying an oversized book of Scottish landscape photography in both hands like an offering.

"Mph." The man buying the salmon fly book and magazines handed Janet his credit card. "And the chap who's in there reading tea leaves?"

"Sorry?" Janet asked.

"It's a nice touch," the man said. "I was wondering if he'll be doing that regularly."

"I'll finish here," Summer said, catching the look on Janet's face.

WHEN JANET REACHED the tearoom, Christine, Tallie, Rosie, and the painters were gathered around a small, square table. Ranger sat under the table. At the table sat Rab MacGregor, a pair of half-glasses on the end of his long nose, so that he looked something like a scholarly hare, as he studied the tea leaves in the bottom of a pretty china cup.

FOURTEEN

"YOU WILL FIND your solution where you least expect it," Rab said. "But the answer will not come to you. You will need to look for it."

"Oh," Rosie breathed. "Is there more?"

"Oh, aye," Rab said. He tipped the teacup toward him, turned it slightly in one direction, and then in the opposite direction, and finally set it gently on the table. "There are difficulties ahead, but they will make you better, not bitter. Hard times will fade and joy will take their place."

Rosie gaped at Rab. Janet thought Christine was doing an admirable job of not gaping at Rosie.

Tallie sidled over to Janet. "Who's minding the till?" she whispered in Janet's ear.

"Summer."

"I'll go tell her about hardships making us better, not bitter," Tallie said.

"And remind her that books are friends forever, but bookmarks can be lost in a moment."

Tallie covered a snicker and left. Janet watched Rab trace his index finger above the leaves as though following a difficult line of translation.

"I see one more message." Rab looked at Rosie over the top of his half-glasses. "Would you like to hear it?"

Rosie nodded.

"Good. Do you see this, then?" He pointed to a curl of leaf that looked to Janet like a pencil shaving or…a curl of leaf. "It's your ear. And all these are your questions." He indicated a half dozen more curls. "They've arranged themselves in the center of the cup, which is round like the face of a clock, which indicates—"

"Time," Rosie breathed.

"Aye, the passage of time. The ear tells you to listen. To get the answers you seek, listen these next few days to your friends." Rab held the cup out to Rosie. She took it reverently. "Anyone else?" Rab asked.

The young man, Garth, put his teacup on the table. Rab readjusted his glasses. He gazed into the cup while slowly rubbing the palms of his hands together. Then he picked up the cup and held it near his ear. When he put the cup back on the table and said, "Someone is speaking well of you." Christine yanked at Janet's arm and stalked into the tearoom's kitchen.

Janet followed. "I've never seen anyone read tea leaves," she said to a nearly spluttering Christine. "He isn't serious, is he?"

"He's no more out there reading the tea leaves than I'm in here doing a belly dance," Christine said. "That's pure claptrap he's spouting. He knows it and so do you."

"It sounds like he's been collecting fortunes from fortune cookies. What in heaven's name brought all that on? Does Rosie believe him?"

"I have no idea," Christine said. "Between the two of them, the woo-woo quotient has been pretty high in here. But actually, Rab came to the rescue and used that parlor trick to calm Rosie down. When he arrived, she'd got herself so worked up about seeing Una's wraith walking past the cheese shop, I was afraid I'd have to throw a glass of cold water in her face."

Janet thought she might benefit from a glass of cold water in her face, too, if that could be a cure for befuddlement. "I'm not understanding."

"I'm not surprised. You're sane, so why would you understand? I'll explain in words that are simple, yet still might not help. Rosie told us that she knew Una was going to die because she saw her ghost—her wraith—that afternoon."

"And she thought that at the time? She said to herself, 'Oh, dear, there's Una's wraith. Uh-oh, she's going to die'?"

"More likely, she convinced herself after the fact."

"Are there actual facts involved?"

Christine laughed. "Possibly. She says she was in the office that afternoon, and she happened to look out the window as Una passed by. Then she heard a knock on the door. People usually just come right in, but she heard this knock and went to open the door. No one was there. She looked up and down the street. And here's where it gets spooky—"

"What?"

"Una was nowhere in sight."

"Are you kidding? That's it? She probably stopped in the cheese shop, and some kid knocked on the door just for the fun of it."

"Don't get short with me. I'm the messenger here. An earthly one, too, unlike Rosie the psychic out there, or Rab the reader. Although I should add that Una was going up the hill, not down, so she wouldn't have gone into the cheese shop. Unfortunately, that probably also means that she really was on her way to your place and to her death."

Janet pulled away from Christine. "It was never her ghost, though. Where did she get that idea from?"

"Highland folklore, which apparently doesn't fall into the same category of old wives' tales as second sight, as far as Rosie is concerned. According to the lore, a wraith seen in the afternoon betokens death. But don't worry," Christine said, "I'm sure it was Una in the flesh that Rosie saw, not her ghost."

"Lovely," Janet said. "Absolutely lovely."

They heard clapping in the tearoom, and Gillian telling the younger painters teatime was over. There were sounds of dispersal, as the decorators took up their rollers and brushes again. Rab came into the kitchen with the teacups, trailed by Rosie.

"Quite a talent you have there, Rab," Christine said. "Learned that at your gran's knee, did you?"

"Learnt the rudiments from Una," Rab said. "If you'll pardon me, I'll do the washing up." He moved past Christine and Janet, took a dishpan from under the sink, and started running water into it.

"Where's the dog?" Christine asked, looking around suspiciously.

"Guarding the bin bags," Janet said, although "guarding" was an exaggeration. From the doorway she could see Ranger lying flat out on the floor with his eyes closed and his paws chasing rabbits. She wondered if he would wake and growl when she picked up the bags to take them upstairs, or if he'd smile at her and roll over. Christine speaking gently to Rosie drew her attention back to the kitchen.

"Are you feeling better, dear?" Christine asked. "More settled and collected? You're not worried you've lost your job with Jess, are you? Janet and Jess are old friends; she won't mind talking to her and getting things sorted for you. Would you like her to do that?"

Janet was tempted to interrupt that line of helpful assistance from Christine. Rosie hadn't answered any of Christine's questions, though, even with a grunt. She aimlessly opened and closed a couple of drawers over and over. She could have been pondering the advice, or not listening at all. Then, leaving one drawer half open, she reached up and opened the cupboard above.

"My gran has one of these," Rosie said. She took a tin index file, painted in red and black tartan, from the cupboard.

"Cute," Christine said with the same enthusiasm she'd shown when meeting Rab's dog. "It was left by previous tenants. We've no use for it, have we?" Christine looked at Janet, who shrugged. "Would you like it, Rosie?"

"Can I have what's in it, too?"

"If you want the dust in the bottom," Janet said. "Otherwise it's empty."

"It's too heavy to be empty." Rosie carried the tin past her out of the kitchen, and put it on the table where Rab had been reading tea leaves. "Look, everybody—a wee tartan treasure chest."

The painters paused for this new source of entertainment. Janet tried to remember if they were paying them by the hour or the job. Christine nudged her and they joined Rosie at the table. Rab came to the kitchen door drying his hands on a tea towel.

"I love old recipes," Chloe the painter called. "Open it."

Rosie flipped the hinged lid open. "See? Not empty at all." She turned the box so they could all see the thick fold of paper wedged in the box.

"Summer must be using the box," Janet said. "Sorry, Rosie, I didn't realize."

"She wouldn't treat her recipes like that," Christine said. "Let me see." She took the box from Rosie and pulled the fold of paper from it. "Envelopes," she said. They'd been folded in half, and she let the bunch of them unfold in her hands. "Business envelopes."

"Tartan Tees and Tease?" Garth the painter asked with a leer.

"Back to work, you," Gillian said. "Nothing to interest you and your wandering eye."

"There's nothing written on them, anyway," Christine said.

"Open them," Rosie said. "They're why I was led here."

"You brought them?" Janet asked.

"No, I found them," Rosie said. "You saw me. And she knows." She pointed at Christine, who still held the envelopes and gazed back at Rosie with a clear look of *here we go again.* Rosie took the envelopes from Christine and handed them to Janet. "Go on, open them."

The younger painters were all for it.

"It might be money," Chloe said.

"Treasure trove," said Garth.

"I wouldn't." Rab spoke from the kitchen door.

His voice was so soft that Janet barely caught the tone of caution under his words. She glanced at him. He took a step forward but didn't meet her eyes, instead wiping his hands on the tea towel again. She studied the envelopes, turning them over, finding no identifying marks. They were all the same size. Some looked more worn than others. She estimated ten or a dozen. They weren't sealed. She told herself she wasn't spooked, didn't believe for a minute that Rosie was psychic, that she had been "brought" to the bookshop, or that she'd been "led" to the recipe tin in the cupboard. Even so, she set the envelopes on the table.

"Why not open them, Rab MacGregor?" Christine asked. "What do you know about them?"

He shook his head. "Not a thing."

"Well, then."

"But I'm reminded," he said, "of Pandora's box."

"The box is already open." Christine took the top envelope from the stack and slipped a folded sheet of paper from it. "A letter," she said, "and it reads, 'Dear—'" She stopped and refolded the letter. "On second thought, Rab's right." She stuffed the letter back into its envelope, scooped up the others, and left the tearoom.

"Show's over," Gillian said to her young painters.

"Och, no," Garth complained.

"Back to work or I won't have you back on my crew."

The young man leaped for his paint roller.

Rab said a soft word to Ranger. The dog woke instantly, surprised Janet by appearing to nod good day to her, and followed Rab out.

"Time for you to go, too, Rosie," Janet said. "Thank you for stopping in. It's been a, uh, a real pleasure."

"Is the recipe tin still mine to keep?" Rosie asked.

"No."

Janet took the tin and grabbed the two garbage bags, then ushered Rosie ahead of her into the bookshop and on out the front door. Rab and Ranger were no longer in sight, up or down the street. *Blast the man and his disappearing tendencies.* And where had Christine gone? Janet did a quick check of the shop, nodding to several customers, much the way Ranger had nodded to her. The old woman had pulled yarn and needles from her bag and now sat knitting. Summer was straightening a spill of books in the children's area, no doubt a result of the three youngsters being herded by their parents toward Tallie at the sales desk.

"Christine?" Janet asked Tallie.

"Office." She hooked her thumb over her shoulder toward the closed office door. "Something up?"

"What else is new?" Janet asked. "Knock if you need me." She stood at the door, hesitating, wondering what had upset her friend, not sure she should intrude. Behind her, Tallie greeted the family and offered bookmarks to the squabbling children. *Seamless customer service might be tough to achieve sometimes,* Janet thought, *and who knew it would be so hard to maintain in the midst of a murder investigation, but everyone is doing very well. Time to make sure my best friend is still holding it together.* She knocked on the door and, without waiting for an answer, went in.

Christine sat in the same chair she had when they'd spoken with Pamela. Most of the envelopes sat in a neat stack on the desk at her elbow. One envelope lay in her lap, its letter in her hand. She appeared calm and as though she'd been waiting for Janet. Janet closed the door.

"Do you think it's presumptuous of us to call what we're doing an investigation?" Janet asked.

Christine's only reaction was to press her lips together more tightly. She stared at a point on the floor beyond the top edge of the letter.

"I'll answer for both of us," Janet went on. "It isn't presumptuous, because it's human nature to give names and labels to objects and situations. I'm sure it has something to do with giving us a sense of control. Tallie came up with an idea to give us a little more control. She created a cloud document for the investigation that we can all access. We can add notes, questions, answers, theories. If we make entries as we learn things or as anything occurs to us, we'll be able to stay up to date in real time. No one will be left out of the loop. And this way we won't risk distorting whatever facts or near facts we come up with through repetition, because a game of telephone won't help the investigation."

Christine twisted her pressed lips and continued to stare.

"So," Janet said, "here I am, investigating. What's going on? What are those envelopes?" She dropped the garbage bags and set the recipe tin on the second desk. "What's in the letter you opened?"

"I don't know what the others are. I haven't looked at them. But this one—" Christine held the letter up but didn't hand it to Janet. "This is to the father of a child who's being well cared for, no thanks to that father, and despite his neglect. It starts out, 'Dear Curtis.'"

Janet's first word was lost in her outrage. The next three were crystal clear. "That bloody rat."

FIFTEEN

"If we're sticking to facts, then we don't know for certain that this letter is written to *your* Curtis," Christine said. "Or typed to him, to be completely accurate."

"That abominable rat," Janet said.

"There are enough details, though, to be reasonably sure it is him. It mentions the university. And a specific mole on his...back."

"*Putrescent* rat. Who wrote it?"

"Believe it or not, the two of you—you and whoever did write it—are on the same wavelength. The rat's ears would fry to a crisp if we read this out loud."

"Then we should," Janet said. "And the louder, the better. Let me see it." She snapped the letter from Christine's fingers and scanned it, turning it over and back again. She ended by waving it. "Unsigned? Who writes a letter like this and then doesn't sign it?"

"Or doesn't send it?" Christine said. "What's the point?"

"There's no date. No other names at all. How are we supposed to know who this child is, or how old he or she is? Or who the mother is? Oh, my God, what if it's someone I know? What if it's someone I run into in the fresh vegetables at Tesco's?"

"The mother?" Christine asked.

"Mother *or* child. Oh, my God, what if this other woman is Jess? Holy, holy cow. Rosie could've found the letters in Jess's office, read them, and then brought them here, playing her silly psychic game."

"You're getting worked up," Christine said.

"Tell me why I *shouldn't* get worked up."

"We don't know if the letter is true."

"It's believable, though, given the rat's recent history. And you believe it, or you wouldn't have left the tea-room like that. But you're right." Janet made an effort to slow down, calm down. "We don't know who wrote it. We don't know if either the mother or the child even lives in Inversgail."

"Although if neither one of them does, then why is the letter here in Inversgail?" Christine asked. "More specifically, why is it here in our business, in a tin that was empty the last time anyone looked? And what does Rab 'Pandora' MacGregor know about all this?"

"Stop it. I'm trying to be rational, but you'll send me right over the edge if you ask me to be rational about too many things at once. Okay, we don't know when this...affair happened. Ten years ago? Twenty? And we don't know if it really did. But if it isn't true, then why write the letter?" Janet pointed at the stack on the desk. "What's in the rest of the envelopes? Are they all letters to Curtis?

"Can you handle it if they are?"

"Hand them over and watch me."

There were eight more envelopes. Christine gave half of them to her, and Janet sat down at the other desk. She opened them one by one, took out and unfolded the sheets of typewritten paper they contained, and laid them side by side. Christine did the same with her envelopes.

"Each one to a different person," Janet said. "This one is two pages. This one's three."

"Here's one that's five."

"Good Lord. And all…not something I feel right reading. Are yours signed?"

Christine shook her head. "So is this someone with an unusual hobby? It's someone with an unusual mind, anyway. Who are yours written to?"

"Moira, Sharon, Scotty, Emma. No last names."

"I have Agnes, Ian, Kenny, and Tristan. They could be anyone." Christine, her lips thin and tight again, rocked slightly while she thought about that. "We might know some of them, but without surnames there's no reason to believe we do."

"Sharon isn't such a common name here, though, is it?"

"Not so much for our generation. More so for younger ones, I think. Do yours all start the way the Curtis letter does?"

"'Dear Moira,' or whoever, 'If you're reading this, it's too late.'"

"Same here," Christine said. "But too late for what?"

"Forgiveness? They look like lists of grievances."

"The Curtis letter has only that one grievance."

"Because his complete and utter rattiness left this person otherwise speechless."

"And that was no mean feat," Christine said, "because this is a person who doesn't seem to have any trouble finding words."

"Or Curtis's letter might be short because we stopped coming to Inversgail. Without Curtis here in the flesh—"

"And apparently nothing but his flesh, at least a time or two."

"Thank you for that visual, Christine." Janet closed her eyes for a moment. "Anyway, with him gone from the daily landscape, the letter writer would have lost a wellspring of inspirational irritation."

"One is out of sight and the other one's possibly out of her mind?"

"Or his. There's nothing personal about the writer in Curtis's letter. It might not be from the mother. Maybe an angry uncle. There's personal trivia in some of the others, though. Listen to this. 'You borrowed my copy of *Sunset Song* and never gave it back. I don't care if my name isn't in it; the book on your shelf is mine.'"

"I thought you didn't feel right about reading the others."

"I don't," Janet said, "but they're right here in front of me. It's like finding a diary marked *Keep Out*. That was in the letter to Scotty, so now we know three things. The writer knows someone named Scotty. The writer is missing a book. And the writer knows how to use semicolons."

"A gift so rare."

"Is it? Anyway, here's a complaint to Emma. 'You lied about having other plans for Easter Monday.' If Emma's been getting that kind of feedback, I can see why she'd say she had other plans. Here's a rap on the knuckles for Moira. 'You took credit for the Rural's fund-raising flyer and you had practically nothing to do with it. Shame on you.' But Sharon is the worst kind of wretch. Listen to this. 'You purposely gave the wrong amount of baking powder in the lemon butter biscuit recipe.'" Janet looked up from paging through the letters. "Do you think Sharon the librarian would do that? Do we *care* if she'd do that? Emma's letter is two pages long, single-spaced." She let the letters fall from her hands onto the desk.

"Tristan's is the five-pager. He's a huge disappointment. Says so right here. Poor devil."

"Most of this doesn't sink to the same level as being an unconscionable rat and fathering an out-of-wedlock child, but sabotaging recipes? Who cares and keeps lists like this? These aren't major sins. They're minor disappointments and pet peeves. Or that's all they should be. What makes them nasty is the person who wrote them."

"They aren't even *pet* peeves. They're more like stray mongrel peeves, and some of them couldn't get any more random or banal." Christine read as she flipped through her half of the letters. "'It was your fault I missed the exit for Inverness in October.' Or, 'You thought my mispronunciation of Laphroaig was funny, but you went ballistic when I laughed at your mismatched socks.' Or, 'When I needed a shoulder to cry on, you turned yours away.' Well, that last one is sad, if overly dramatic."

"This one's less straightforward. 'Recycling isn't a sin unless there's an originality issue.'"

"Someone needs to have 'suck it up' tattooed on one arm and 'get over it' on the other. That or years of therapy."

"Maybe this *is* a form of therapy. It's a lot of work, anyway, keeping lists like this and updating them. And there's a big fat clue staring us in the face—they aren't printed from a computer." Janet looked up from the page she was examining. "When was the last time you saw something typed on a typewriter?"

"When was the last time you saw a typewriter ribbon for sale?" Christine leafed through the letters again. "It does look like they've been rolled in and out of a typewriter more than a few times, though. The spaces between some of the lines are wonky—probably where the writer put the sheet back through to add another line of whine. How old does that make these things?"

"Hard to say. It probably varies from letter to letter. But some of the details are current. Listen to this one. 'You promised to Skype with me at the weekend and didn't.' Or, 'You purposely misread my response to your email about the Referendum and told people I was a traitor.' The Referendum—that was the vote for independence, wasn't it?"

"In 2014."

"How old is Rosie?" Janet asked.

"You don't think she wrote them, do you? I'd guess late teens or early twenties at most. Surely you don't think she's the mother."

"*No!* And that thought makes me absolutely sick. But could she be the child? We'd owned the house for close to ten years by the time she would've been born, and we were here almost every summer."

"It was kept awfully quiet, if she is," Christine said. "And that goes against the reputation small towns have for wagging tongues. But if she is, do you think she knows the connection between you and—"

"Her father the rat?"

"Janet, we still don't know if it's true that he had this child. All of these pages and pages might be imagined slights."

Janet held up her phone. "The easiest way in the world to find out."

"What a wonderful idea. Go ahead and make his day."

Janet hadn't spoken to Curtis in months. *Or to be fair*, she thought, *I haven't answered his calls or texts for months. That's what a good, expensive lawyer is for.* She took a deep breath, swiped her phone into action, and put it to her ear.

"Hello—"

She cut in before he could say more. "Curtis. It's Janet. A quick question—"

"Janet—"

"Don't interrupt. Just answer. Did you..." It was harder to say than she'd thought it would be. "Do you have a child by a woman other than me? More precisely, by another woman here in Scotland?"

"Janet—"

"Yes or no, Curtis."

"It's five a.m. Can we discuss this later?"

"I'll take that as a yes." Janet stabbed the disconnect icon and slammed the phone onto the desk, making herself jump. "Oh, dear." She peered at the phone. "I hope I didn't break it."

"I'm sorry, Janet."

"I'm not." Janet put her hand to her mouth, then took it away and made an effort to relax her shoulders. "This is simply a good test of my ability to face things with a positive attitude. *Another* test. But I'm up for the challenge, and here's the takeaway from this situation. It reinforces, once again, that I made the right decision when I took that rat to the cleaners."

They sat in silence for a few moments, and then Janet asked Christine if she'd known what time it was in Illinois when she made the call. Christine said she had but that she saw nothing wrong with waking Curtis from a sound sleep.

"Thank you for that, Christine," Janet said. "Your attention to detail is one of the reasons I like you so much."

"I'm a firm believer in taking pleasure in small things. Who are you calling now?"

"I forgot to ask him who the mother and child are." Janet swiped the phone into action again and waited. She crossed her legs and swung a foot. Then she disconnected. "He isn't picking up. How rude. On the other hand, I'm glad to find out that I *didn't* break the phone."

"You should've left him a message," Christine said. "I will, if you'd like. How would this sound? 'Curtis? Christine here. I need to know who you've shagged in Inversgail, and when. Approximate dates will do. Details not necessary.' Shall I? Or shall I call the new wife and ask her to find out for us?"

Janet shook her head. "She has enough on her hands just being married to him. We can find another inconvenient time to call."

"What are you going to tell Tallie?"

"This might be wrong, but for the time being nothing. When it comes right down to it, we still don't know for certain that it's true. As far as I'm concerned, Curtis answered by not answering. But it is just barely possible that being waked at five a.m. befuddled him."

"Who are you protecting with that evasion, Curtis or Tallie?"

"Maybe myself, for now. If it's true, then this is another part of my life that's changed without any input from me. When I know for sure, and whether it's true or not, then I'll tell her and call Allen."

"Fair enough," Christine said. "Here's another question. How worried do you think we need to be about finding the letters here?"

"Don't you think that depends on who wrote them, who left them, and who's going to come looking for them?"

"Or maybe it depends on what's behind that phrase, 'If you're reading this, it's too late.'"

SIXTEEN

Janet tucked the letter to Curtis in her back pocket and helped Christine put the other letters back in their envelopes. They took the recipe tin, envelopes, and bags of garbage to show Tallie and Summer—to bring them up to date and get their insights. *Although not too much insight,* Janet thought, because the letter in her pocket was making her feel less than honest. She hoped if Tallie noticed that she'd developed a case of nerves, she would assume it came from their own growing list of far from normal goings-on.

"Got enough stuff there?" Tallie asked.

"Come to think of it, there's more," Christine said. She went back into the office and came out with the bottle of whisky and the tartan fabric. "Parting gifts from Pamela and Kenneth."

Summer took the bottle from her and cradled it in her hands. "This is a nice Laphroiag."

"Is it?" Janet asked. Possibly too sharply; she'd earned a look from Tallie.

"Nothing to laugh at in *her* pronunciation," Christine said.

"Everything I know about whisky I learned at the Scotch Whisky Heritage Centre in Edinburgh. The only thing I didn't learn is to like the taste. Such a shame."

"But more for the rest of us, then," Tallie said. She took the fabric from Christine and unfolded it. It was almost as wide as she was tall. "If we don't mind cutting it, we can make it into two lap throws. Put them on the backs of the chairs near the fire."

"A wonderful idea," Christine said. "I'll see if Mum still has her sewing machine somewhere in all their accumulated detritus."

Tallie handed the fabric back to Christine and nodded at the garbage bags. "Were the garbage bags a shop-warming present from Rab? They're the ones he brought into the tearoom, aren't they?"

"You have a good eye for garbage bags, dear. Christine's going to fill you in on...everything new."

"Uh-huh," Tallie said, and Janet could see her antennae quivering. "What will you be doing?"

"I'll just run these upstairs so they're out of the way. Oh! And the meeting at the library—I nearly forgot. I'd better grab the blasted contest materials and scoot."

"You aren't late. Yet," Christine said. "You grab and scoot. I've got this."

JANET WAS PLEASED with their strategy for her exit. She and Christine had cooked it up in case Tallie's curiosity and daughterly suspicion kicked into overdrive. This way, Christine could give Tallie and Summer the few facts they knew about the letters and the garbage, and Janet would have some time alone to process the latest "glitch" in her new life. Not that she was going to keep the information about a half-sibling from Tallie or shade the truth. She didn't believe in doing either. But even a thin scab over this new wound would make it easier for her when she did tell her children. Christine wanted her to make Curtis tell them, and Janet liked the idea of making him squirm. But that would put the burden on Tallie and Allen to bring up the awkward topic with her, to let her know they knew. They didn't deserve that. Besides, she didn't trust Curtis the rat to do it.

She forced her mind away from Curtis as she climbed the stairs, thinking instead about the other letters—not quite a thought for each step she went up, but a steady progression. About lists. List making. The kind of people who think in lists. Checklists. Agendas. Personal agendas. Hidden agendas. Hiding. Seeking. Searching. When she reached her room, she put the garbage bags in the corner near the door and crossed to the window. The sky was the shade of blue she thought of as Highland blue. Small sailboats and a few fishing boats dotted the harbor, giving it the picturesque look of something staged for a movie. She saw three cats stretched out on the harbor wall. Rab wasn't soaking up the sun with them. Neither was Ranger. She wondered where else the two of them spent their time and what kept them busy—or kept them from being busy.

Janet opened her laptop and logged into the cloud document. The second part of the plan she and Christine had cooked up was for her to add the same information Christine was telling Tallie and Summer downstairs. Christine said it was an efficient use of their time. This way they wouldn't both be tied up with the telling. Janet said it was also avoidance on her part, but she was happy to multitask. She started with a note about Pamela's idea concerning Kenneth and the committee, typing in, *Pamela wonders if Kenneth had been on the committee, would Una still be alive? Is there a connection between the committee and the murder?* Then she tapped in the heading *Letters & Lists—knowns*, and followed that with her own list, leaving Curtis off, at least for the time being.

8 letters found in recipe tin (previously empty)
All appear to be typed on typewriter.
To: Agnes, Emma, Ian, Kenny, Moira, Tristan, Scotty, Sharon—who are they?
Letters are unsigned, undated.

Under a second heading, *Letters & Lists—questions*, she started another list.

Did Rosie bring them and pretend to find them?
When did one of us last look in the tin?
Who else has been in kitchen or had access? Pamela, Kenneth, unknown hikers, Una, decorators, Jess, Rab, Constable Hobbs? Any of the Major Investigation Team? (And anyone else who slipped in while the door was open for the hikers. Drat.)
Is the person who wrote the letters also the one who left them?
Will the person who left them come back for them?
Should we put them back?
Should we worry?
Rab said opening the envelopes was like open-

ing Pandora's box. What does he know about any of this?
Is it possible to determine dates through some of the details?
Is "If you're reading this, it's too late" a threat?

Under a third heading—*Rubbish In*—she entered what they knew and what they wanted to know about the garbage.

The vandal knows the connection between the house and the bookshop.
The vandal has or had access to the house.
Does the vandal have access to the bookshop?
Is the garbage connected to Una's murder?
Is the garbage a threat? To the shop? To one of us?
Rab cleared away the garbage, then brought back what he could find. What's in it? Is it the same garbage he took away?

Janet checked the time. Their plan was working perfectly. She had time for one more note. *Ask Sharon Davis if she has a recipe for lemon butter biscuits.*

She closed the document and the laptop, and slipped the brick-weight of contest entries into their Scottish Library and Information Council bag. For the next part of the plan, she would make a brief stop at the sales desk to check in with Christine and the girls. Then she would have plenty of time for the mile or so walk to the new Inversgail Public Library and Archives for Sharon Davis's dratted working lunch. And if she left soon, she'd have time to stop by Paudel's along the way to pick up a sausage roll or bridie and an apple so she wouldn't have to sit through the dratted meeting watching Sharon and Ian Atkinson eat their lunch while she had only a pencil to chew. She looked out the window again—still gorgeous, and probably warm, too. She took her umbrella and a sweater anyway, knowing how quickly gorgeous and warm could turn into cold and drenched.

She was pleased to see a short queue at the sales desk when she got back down to the shop—good for business, good for slipping out from under her daughter's inquiring eye. She breezed up to the desk, ready to wave good-bye. But just as a gorgeous, warm day might turn around and bite, so too with well-laid plans.

SEVENTEEN

Summer and Christine were handling the customers at the sales desk. Tallie was helping the old woman reach another book of patterns off the top shelf in the craft books aisle. The woman hadn't been tall to begin with, and was now quite bent. She wore dark brown trousers, a neatly tucked blouse, a fawn-colored cardigan, and a pair of ankle-high, suede, flat-soled boots that looked as though she might be hiding hobbit feet.

Tallie handed the book to her—a collection of patterns for knitted sea life. The woman leafed through the book and beamed. Then she handed Tallie a ten-pound note and a five, and with a slow, slightly lurching gait, went back to the chair near the fireplace.

"She doesn't look quite safe," Janet said when Tallie came over to her, "but she seems determined to get around. Speaking of which, I should be on my way." She patted the bag with the contest entries hanging from her shoulder.

"If you can hold on another minute, Christine wants to show you something before you go."

"Oh. Well—"

"The meeting isn't until noon, is it? You've still got loads of time." Tallie didn't appear to be in a hurry to do anything more than smile and give Janet the feeling she was onto something.

Janet returned the smile, and then practiced a mother's age-old tactic of substituting one object of interest for another. "What do you think of our knitter?" she asked, turning to look at the old woman.

Tallie turned to look, too, as Janet thought she would. "We all like her," she said, "but we don't know anything more than that. She seems sweet. She hardly says two words, though. Christine says she's a happy soul with a simple goal: she sits and she knits. That she's bought books is a plus. She adds a cozy touch to the place, don't you think? I wonder if she'd let us display some of her knitting with the books."

"She reminds me of Mrs. Tiggy-Winkle," Janet said. "And that reminds me, what do you think about carrying Beatrix Potter postcards and stationery? She had ties to Scotland."

"Perthshire, though, wasn't it?"

"But that's not so terribly far from here, and it wouldn't be such a stretch. Cards and notebooks might be popular with the tourists."

"Especially if Mrs. Tiggy-Winkle comes in with any frequency," Tallie said. "Sure. Let's go for it." She nodded toward Christine and Summer. "They're finishing up the last customers."

"Ah. Good." Janet intended to cut and run as soon as she heard what Christine wanted to tell her. She and

Tallie hung back from the desk, though, while Summer gave her customer directions to the nearest pub.

"Are we clear?" Christine asked when that customer left.

"Except for Mrs. Tiggy-Winkle," Tallie said, discreetly pointing at the old woman.

"And maybe not for long, and Janet needs to be on her way," Christine said, "so let's make this fast. We need a decision. Should we tell Norman about the letters?"

Janet stared at Christine. She'd never realized how hard it would be to read Queen Elizabeth's mind. "Have you already discussed this…to some extent?" she asked.

"We've had a bit of debate," Christine said, "with no consensus. One for, one against, one sitting on the fence."

Janet had the feeling Tallie was watching her, but she didn't check to see. She shifted her gaze from Christine to Summer. "How do you vote?"

"For. And I'm surprised there's any question. I covered a lot of criminal trials over my years at the paper, and I stopped being amazed a long time ago at the small, the seemingly *totally* inconsequential details that either make a case or derail it."

Janet almost let herself be derailed by Summer's "for" vote—astounded by it, because she'd been sure that was Tallie's position—but she made herself focus on the reasons Summer gave. "That's a valuable perspective and a persuasive argument."

But Summer hadn't finished. "And that's beside the question of why we *wouldn't* tell the police, and the question of what we plan to do with them if we don't tell the police. If we're reading them for clues, then we think they're evidence, and they belong with the police. If we're reading them because we're nosy, then ick. Bad manners."

"What if we just put them back where we found them?" Christine asked. "They're unpleasant, but do we have any reason to believe they're anything more than that? Do any of us believe Rosie was led to them in a psychic trance?"

"But do any of us believe they're totally benign?" Tallie asked. "I'm the one sitting on the fence about telling Constable Hobbs, Mom, but it's more of a yes vote with reservations. A delayed yes."

Janet chanced a look at her daughter. Whether or not Tallie had been watching her all along, she was watching her now. Not a probing or cynical look, though. Concerned? Thoughtful? Possibly a mirror image of her own face.

"But Summer's reasons are clear," Tallie said, "and they make excellent sense. So if you agree with her, and you think we should turn the letters over immediately, then I'll say yes, too."

"I want to hear your reservations," Janet said.

"Someone put the letters there recently. Since we took over the business. We don't believe Rosie's a psychic. *She* might believe she's psychic, but I think she's fitting every odd thing she encounters into that selfdiagnosis. She remembered seeing Una walking up the hill that day, and she's pairing that with folklore about what it means to see a wraith in the late afternoon. Or maybe she likes the attention she's getting for announcing her 'gift.' Who knows, but now I'm off track, and Rosie is beside the point."

"Interesting, though," Christine said.

"But it doesn't explain why you don't want to turn the letters over to the police," Summer said. "It has to have occurred to you that Una might have written them and left them here. She was in the kitchen the day she was killed."

"Also interesting," Christine said. "There have always been rumors that she wrote the letters for her column herself. Maybe they weren't just rumors. Maybe she was into writing all kinds of letters. Do your reservations still stand, Tallie?"

Tallied nodded. "But I'll sound about as flaky as Rosie. I think whoever put the letters in the tin did it either so they'd be safe or so they'd be found by someone safe."

"So take them to the police," Summer said. "Safest place of all."

"Not necessarily," Janet said.

"And that's my point," Tallie said. "Maybe they were left *here* specifically. Here, because someone was afraid of who might find them and read them. Because that person trusts us. Or doesn't know us from Adam but knows we aren't likely to talk to the wrong person. Those are huge leaps, I know."

"She's not ordinarily a leaper, Summer," Janet said.

"So I'd like a leap of faith from you," Tallie said with a smile that came and disappeared. "And I'd like a little bit of time before we give the letters to Constable Hobbs. To see if we can figure out who left them and why."

"I'm going to go along with Tallie," Janet said. "Let's give ourselves a few days."

"A few days that might be crucial to the authorities' investigation," said Summer.

"We're already halfway through Wednesday," Janet said, "and we don't know how long the letters have already been sitting there. Let's give ourselves until Friday morning, and we'll call Constable Hobbs now about the garbage. We can see what he says about that to gauge his interest in peripherals."

"Peripherals, I like that," Christine said. "Call him."

"Now? I'll be late for the meeting."

"No, you won't. Our plan was going to have you out the door way earlier than you needed to be."

The bell over the door jingled, saving Christine from Janet's best betrayed and accusing look. "Fine. You help the customer." Janet went into the office.

Tallie and Summer followed, with Tallie asking, "A plan? What plan?"

"Foiled," Janet said. "End of discussion."

The whisky and plaid were there on one of the desks; the stack of letters and the recipe tin sat beside them.

"I'd feel better if we don't leave the envelopes where someone else can find them," Janet said.

"Lock them in the desk?" Tallie asked.

"Safer than a recipe tin," Summer said, "but we don't know if the Lawries still have keys."

"We're suspicious of them?"

"Think of it this way," Janet said. "We have no good

reason *not* to be suspicious of them. And welcome to the Sisterhood of the Suspicious. Christine and I are charter members."

"I'll lock them in my computer bag upstairs." Tallie took the stack of envelopes.

Janet pulled out her phone and called Norman Hobbs. He answered, turning his name into a faint and swallowed howl with a yawn.

"Hi, Norman. This is Janet Marsh."

Tallie and Summer mouthed, *Hi, Norman*, at each other. Janet turned her back on them.

"There's been another development. Rab found some of the rubbish he cleared away from behind the bookshop. He brought it here in two clean bin bags. Will you come get it, or should we bring it to you?"

There was silence from Norman Hobbs.

Janet looked over her shoulder at Tallie and Summer. "It might be a bad connection. Did you hear me, Norman?"

"I did. Thank you for calling, Mrs. Marsh."

"What would you like me to do with the garbage?"

"I appreciate your civic-mindedness. Unfortunately, unless Rab remembers seeing anything that obviously identifies the perpetrator, I doubt it will be of any use to us. Even if we know whose rubbish it is, we won't be much further ahead. No one locks their rubbish up in Inversgail. It's free for the taking."

"I didn't think of that. Or the vandal could've brought it from another town altogether."

"That would be more work than necessary," Hobbs said, "but aye."

"Well, that's disappointing. You don't think, if you dusted, you might find fingerprints?"

"The rubbish will have passed through too many hands by now. In all likelihood we would find too many fingerprints."

"Oh, right. Fingerprints galore. By the way, did you know 'galore' is a Gaelic word?"

"Is it? I'll enjoy knowing that. Thank you. Is there anything else, Mrs. Marsh?"

"Well, yes. Rab said the garbage was fresh. Not days old. And the bags weren't wet from the rain we had last night. I think the rain stopped sometime shortly after midnight. You should be able to find out the exact time with a quick phone call, but the important thing is that he said some of the paper pieces were dampish, but none of the garbage was soaked. Those facts should help, don't you think?"

"Thank you. It's possible they will. Is that all?"

"One more thing, and then I'll let you go. I have to run myself. But here's my question, if you don't want the rubbish, do you mind if we look through it?"

"If you've a mind to."

"Should we wear gloves so we don't smear any fingerprints, in case there *are* useful ones?"

There was another silence on Hobbs's end of the conversation.

"We might have gotten disconnected," Janet said to Tallie and Summer.

"No, I am still here, Mrs. Marsh." Janet heard what might be a tic of impatience in his voice. "By all means," he said, "wear gloves to avoid smearing fingerprints, aye, but also because it is, after all, rubbish."

"YOU'RE JUST IN TIME," Christine said when the other three rejoined her at the sales desk. "I sold five copies of *The Haggis: A Little History* and two of those Gaelic phrase books. And then, all on my own, I accessed the cloud. I absolutely love the sound of that—accessing the cloud—it makes me feel like we can rise above any and all misfortunes that someone might sling or shoot at us. Now watch this. I'm going to add my first note to the cloud. Not over my shoulder, though. I can't type straight when people hang over my shoulders."

They stood back and waited until she raised both arms like a gymnast sticking a difficult landing.

"A solid ten performance," Tallie said, shaking Christine's hand. "Let's see what you've got."

They gathered around the computer and read, *What if we don't have all the letters? What if one or more was taken from the tin before we found them? What if some have been mailed?*

Janet felt as though the letter in her back pocket was glowing and turning a toasty red. Her cheeks, too. But Christine had a good point. "How would we find out?" she asked. "If you don't know if something existed, how do you look for it?"

"We don't have to find the answers to all our questions," Christine said. "The value of some questions might only be that they beget more questions. But it's all grist for the mill. Some of the notes will do that, too." She scrolled down the screen. "Like this one that you posted this morning." Christine adjusted her glasses and read, "'Pamela said if Kenneth had been on the committee, Una might still be alive.'" She turned to Janet. "She said that?"

Tallie echoed Christine. "Pamela said that? When were you going to tell us?"

"You just read it. That's the same as me telling you. Isn't that the point of the cloud? Central location, no need to repeat information and risk distorting anything, no worries about someone missing important notes, time-saving efficiency. All of that? And then some, too, I'm sure." Janet knew she was babbling, but the looks on the others' faces were unnerving. "And now I really do need to go. Dratted meeting at the library, remember? And if I come back—"

"*If* you come back?" Christine asked.

"Let me finish. I didn't mean it like that. If I come back with more leads to follow, or more information or questions, I'll add them to the cloud, and you'll all know. The magic of the Internet and the beauty of clouds, right? I can even add notes during the meeting."

"But is it safe?" Tallie asked.

"You're the one who set it up for us," Janet said. "What makes you suddenly think it isn't?"

"She's talking about your meeting, not the cloud doc," Summer said.

Tallie looked at Christine. "Do you think it's safe?"

"It's at the library," Janet said. "Of course it's safe. And the meeting will be safe, too. Even if the murder does have something to do with the committee or the contest, I'm a new member. I don't share the history. In fact, Ian Atkinson's a new member, too. Sharon Davis is the only original member. So, really, it has nothing to do with me."

"Except for the fact that the murder happened in your shed," Christine said. "And except for being the victim of vandalism by rancid household rubbish, more than once, at your house and your business. And except for the fact that you *are* now a member of the esteemed and possibly homicidal judging committee. Aside from those minor points, you're right. It has nothing to do with you." Christine turned to Tallie and Summer. "Tell me honestly, was she in there nipping at that bottle of whisky?"

"I'm actually not worried," Janet said.

"I am," said Tallie.

"But we already talked about this. Taking a larger part in the literary festival will benefit the business."

"But only if you're still alive to be part of the business," Tallie said. "Dead booksellers don't sell books. They also don't make good mothers. Aggravating ones, yes, but I'd rather have the pleasant, *intelligent* mother I'm used to. So how's this for a compromise? I'm going to crash the committee. You tell Sharon Davis that because of the short notice she gave you, you're amending your agreement to be on the committee. Your answer is yes only if we can be on it together, acting as one voice. If nothing else, I'll be able to help you get through all those entries."

"They might have bylaws that won't allow it."

"Then they'll have to ask someone else to be on the committee."

"I don't want to argue about it," Janet said.

"Being worried and cautious—"

"And pointing out the folly and the danger in a situation," Christine said, jumping in on top of Tallie, "are not the same as arguing."

"Think of it as negotiating," Tallie said. "Except that I am going with you, and that isn't negotiable."

While the other three discussed nuances of vocabulary, Summer read through the rest of the notes and questions Janet had posted that morning. "I have a suggestion," she said during the moment of strained silence following Tallie's refusal to negotiate. "It's based on what's in the cloud doc so far. Or, frankly, it's more than a suggestion. I think it should be a rule. Do you want to hear it?"

"Of course we do," Christine snapped, "because we are nothing if not reasonable people."

"Good. In that case, I'll start with the reasons. We're talking about vandalism and murder—a nuisance crime and a serious crime. And we're talking about threats—perceived, implied, veiled, blatant, it doesn't matter what kind they are; we need to take them seriously, too. And we're trying to figure out the connections between some or all of these things. For instance, whoever's responsible for dumping the garbage seems to know the connection between Janet's house and the bookshop. The problem is we don't know what the connection is or what it means. We don't know if there's a threat or where it's coming from. We don't know where or to whom it's directed. So here's the rule. Until the murder is solved we don't go out alone. We travel in pairs."

“Ha,” Tallie said. “Told you.”

“You can carry the entries, then,” Janet said, handing Tallie the bag. “And you can buy lunch.”

EIGHTEEN

"Do you feel bullied?" Tallie asked.

"By you?" Janet took her daughter's arm as they headed down the High Street toward the library. "No. I feel fortunate to have family and friends who care about me. And I think we might have been talking at cross-purposes back there. Do you know why I said I didn't want to argue about you coming with me?"

"Because you're a nonconfrontational peacenik?"

"Because I misspoke. I meant that you'd get no argument from me. I was about to correct myself when you and Christine jumped all over me. And then Summer stepped in with her rule—which I think is a good rule. A smart one. No, dear. I'm delighted that you're coming with me. Also that you'll be reading half the entries. And I'm especially delighted that you're buying lunch. Win, win, win."

They crossed the bridge over the Sgail, stopping briefly to let a photographer snap pictures of a kissing couple.

"Did Allen and Nicola have engagement pictures made on the bridge?" Tallie asked.

"No, the garden parties and romantic pictures went by the wayside when they eloped. All those grand plans would've been fun, wouldn't they?"

Tallie touched her hair. "I was looking forward to wearing a fascinator. And to seeing Allen in a kilt."

"Oh, that, yes. His knees have always been adorable. Maida's insistence on the kilt might've been the straw that broke the wedding's back, though. Here's our chance to get by."

They hurried past while the photographer and the young man tried to convince the young woman to sit on the wall gazing at the river and the bluebells.

"That's a picture I'd skip, too," Janet said. "It's a good fifteen or twenty feet over the edge into the water. I'd rather face Maida's disappointment over the elopement again than get up on that parapet."

"Or face the killer committee."

"Ten killer committees."

Basant Paudel greeted them warmly when they stopped in his shop for a takeaway lunch. While Tallie bought bridies—delicious minced steak pies with flaky pastry—and a couple of apples, Janet went looking for rubber gloves. She called the library as she scanned the aisles. A cheerful young woman answered the phone and offered to put Janet through to Sharon Davis directly, but Janet declined and asked her to pass along her apologies for running late. She might be brave enough to face a killer committee, but she saw no reason to face disappointment in her time management skills any sooner than she needed to. She picked up four sets of bright pink rubber gloves and went back to the counter, arriving at the end of a story that left Tallie laughing.

"I've given you the two finest bridies I've seen all

week," Basant said. "And these are very good-quality latex gloves."

"Basant," Janet said, "you might be able to answer a question for us."

"I always try to answer questions, and if I don't know the answer, I will make one up."

"You should've been a librarian," Tallie said.

"You would make a fine librarian, Basant," Janet said. "This is more of a phone directory question. Do you know who was renting our house most recently?"

"That I can tell you with no trouble. For several years a nice young couple lived there, Lauren and Neil Pollard. He works for CalMac Ferries and she's a weaver. She also works in the wool shop. They enjoyed living in your house."

"Thank you. I felt bad about not extending their lease, but…"

"But," Basant said, echoing her verbal shrug and adding his shoulders and a sigh.

"Do you know if they're still in the area?" Tallie asked.

"I believe they are, although I don't see them as often as I used to."

"I should stop by the wool shop," Janet said, "and thank her for looking after the house so well."

"And for starting the garden," Tallie said. "Maybe she'd like to come pick lettuce."

"A nice thought," Basant said.

"One other thing, Basant." Janet looked over her shoulder to see if she was holding up other customers—and to make sure none were close enough to overhear. "What do you know about rats?"

"Rats?" Tallie asked, and Janet realized she hadn't told her about the rats yet.

"I'm just wondering if you've heard of a particular problem with them in town."

"It's hard to find something to like about rats," Basant said. "The best I can do is recite Browning's 'Pied Piper.'

Rats!
They fought the dogs, and killed the cats,
And bit the babies in the cradles,
And ate the cheeses out of the vats,
And licked the soup from the cook's own ladles,
Split open the kegs of salted sprats,
Made nests inside men's Sunday hats,
And even spoiled the women's chats,
By drowning their speaking
With shrieking and squeaking
In fifty different sharps and flats...

"Well, you get the idea." Basant took a cloth and wiped the counter, looking thoughtful. "Rats will always be with us, but no, I haven't heard of a particular rat problem in Inversgail."

"That was wonderful," said Janet. "We should have you do a poetry reading at the shop during the literary festival." She nudged Tallie with her elbow. "What do you think?"

"A literary evening of classic poetry—would you do it, Basant?"

"You flatter me," he said, "and I have thought of one more thing about rats. The ancient Egyptians were of two minds about them. On the one hand, they bring utter destruction. On the other hand, they possess excellent judgment. The Egyptians knew this to be true, because rats will always choose the best bread. And I know it to be true, because I have seen it myself. Rats never eat the scones from the Shop Which Shall Not Be Named in the next street over."

As soon as they left Paudel's, Tallie attached her hand to Janet's elbow. "Rats?" she said. "Really? I knew you were keeping something from me, but I thought it had something to do with those letters. Mom, you can't keep things like this from me. From any of us."

Janet remembered the contrite face Tallie used to make when she was three or four and had been caught—head bowed, lower lip out, eyes big. She decided against trying that face herself. Instead, she picked up her pace so that Tallie had to drop her elbow and adjust the bag of contest entries on her shoulder. "You're right, dear," Janet said. "I should have told you. My only excuse is that there are so many other things going on, besides the fact that even the thought of rats is horrible. I've been pushing them as far from my mind as I can."

"Where are the rats?"

"Before I tell you, I want you to do something. Close your eyes and try to picture the places you've been since arriving in Inversgail."

"I'm walking. I'm not going to close my eyes."

"All right. Bad idea. But have you seen signs of rats anywhere that you've been? Have you smelled them? It's okay to take your time and think about it. In fact, the harder it is for you to answer, the better I feel."

"I don't like rats any better than you do. I think I'd rather just hear the answer."

"No, that's all right then, dear. We'll forget about them for now. Oh, but look at the new library building, will you? All those windows looking over the harbor—think of the beautiful light they must have inside."

THE LIBRARY JANET and Tallie remembered from their summers in Inver-sgail had been dark and crowded into the ground floor of a retired shipping warehouse built in the early part of the nineteenth century. Except for the musty smell, the building had given the library a wonderful vault-like atmosphere. As children, Tallie and Allen had spent many rainy afternoons there, calling it "The Dungeon of Lost Legends." A statue of Robert Louis Stevenson stood nearby looking across the harbor toward the lighthouse. The statue was one of Inversgail's landmarks, beloved by tourists, seagulls, and the knitters and crocheters who occasionally dressed it in their bright woolen creations.

There had been talk, over the years, of moving the library or raising funds for a new building. Thanks to a substantial Bricks for Books grant, that finally happened, but not until after the Marsh family had stopped visiting Inversgail. Janet and Tallie passed the old warehouse on their way to the meeting, noting that "The

Dungeon of Lost Legends" had been transformed into an upscale seafood restaurant called R. L.'s.

"Looking jaunty, R. L.," Janet called to the Stevenson statue. It wore short trousers made of crocheted granny squares and an oversized purple tam, thanks to a recent yarn bombing by a group calling itself "Your Local Knit Wits."

The new Inversgail Public Library and Archives, making plans to celebrate its fifth year, stood on the headland at the northern edge of the village. The library's architect was a young woman who'd grown up in the Gorbals, an area of Glasgow known more for its high-rise public housing and hard men than for producing women architects. As the architect had explained in her winning bid, she'd visited Inversgail and was spiritually moved by the confluence of water and land, light and air, rain and sunshine, and harbor and homes that make Inversgail what it is. At a dedication ceremony for the new building, she told the audience that she'd done her best to bring all those elements together to create a modern interior within a traditional skin. She'd likened the finished product to capturing a selkie—one of those graceful, possibly mythical creatures who swim as seals in the water but can slip out of their skins and walk as humans on land. The citizens of Inversgail enjoyed the delight she took in their town. They loved the amount of glass in the new building. They thought perhaps she hadn't actually heard or read any of the stories about selkies, but they appreciated her enthusiasm.

Janet and Tallie climbed the hill to the library but didn't take the time to admire the view before hurrying inside. They asked for Sharon Davis at the circulation desk and followed a woman to a small conference room behind the scenes on the first floor. The room was empty.

"The others will be along shortly," the woman said. "With any luck. You were smart not getting here on the dot. The rest are never on time for these meetings."

"In that case, I'm sorry I called to apologize," Janet said after she'd gone. "And I worry about her familiarity with the habits of 'these meetings.' There was only supposed to be one meeting. 'These meetings' aren't supposed to exist."

"Neither are selkies." Tallie was looking out the window. "But there's one coming out of the water, down there, right now. Nope, just a guy in a wet suit. She probably meant 'these meetings' in the history of the festival, don't you think?"

"I hope you're right."

"I hope I don't turn into a fangirl in front of Ian Atkinson."

"He'll fall all over himself, if you do," Sharon Davis said. She came into the room with the inquiring eyes and smile of someone who didn't expect to find an extra person at her meeting. But there was nothing tentative about her manner. Or about her choice of color or cologne. Her fuchsia jacket was assertive. Her scent did not hesitate. By comparison, Janet felt unassuming yet comfortable in her khakis and cardigan.

Tallie crossed the room with her hand extended. "Hi, I'm Tallie Marsh, Janet's daughter."

"Delighted," Sharon said, taking Tallie's hand. "I

would have known immediately had I seen you standing together. Wonderful to meet you. If you're hoping to catch sight of Ian Atkinson, he should be here any minute. Did you bring a book for him to sign?"

"Actually, there's been a change of plans," Janet said. "Tallie is joining me on the committee as my co-member." She turned to Tallie. "Is there such a word?"

"Let's call ourselves a team with one voice," Tallie said.

"Yes, that's exactly what we are," Janet said. She and Tallie moved to the conference table, stood shoulder to shoulder, pulled out chairs, and sat in one fluid movement, as though they'd been practicing synchronized powerposition seating for weeks. They had Sharon's attention, so Janet explained the change they wanted to make, keeping it simple and to the point.

Sharon listened without comment. Then she went to the door, looked left and right, came back, and sat across from them. "If it were up to Ian," she said quietly, "the answer would be no. He seems to enjoy being the big fish in the small pond. I hadn't realized, when I asked him to take Kenneth's place, that he would be such a prima donna." She leaned toward them. "And please don't ever tell him I said that. But he's not in charge. I am." She sat back again. "If the only way we can have you on the committee is for the two of you to come as a package deal, then welcome aboard, Tillie."

"It's Tallie, and thank you. When do you expect Mr. Atkinson?"

"Oh, please, don't call him Mr. Atkinson, or the meeting will take even longer, because of the endless preening." She leaned closer again and made a face as though she'd swallowed something nasty. "I thought getting the local celebrity author was such a catch for the committee. The man has enough hot air to blow two sets of bagpipes at once."

Janet nodded in sympathy. "I met a few like that at my library. They put a strain on one's ability to smile, don't they?"

"If I'd only known Kenneth was still in town."

"But from what you said the other day—something about close to home not working for various reasons—and from Kenneth's reaction, I assumed it wasn't his idea to step down from the committee."

"It most certainly was," Sharon said, pulling back. "Kenneth told me so himself. He said they'd sold the business and he was on his way. That's why I was surprised to see him in the shop."

From the way Sharon huffed at her remarks, Janet was afraid she'd strained the other woman's ability to breathe normally. Janet wasn't ready to let it go, though. "That's funny. I was sure Pamela told me the same thing—that he was hurt when he was dropped from the committee. I must have been mistaken."

"*My* mistake was in making that comment in public."

"What did you mean by it?" Janet felt pressure on her right foot and realized Tallie was stepping on it. But did she mean for Janet to stop asking questions, or that she should keep asking and apply more pressure?

"He didn't need to hear it," Sharon said. "That's all I meant."

Janet decided to press. "But you said close to home

hadn't worked for various reasons. What were they? There must have been something behind your comment. And you thought he was threatening you." This time Tallie's message came through sharp and clear with a kick to Janet's ankle. "But now I'm prying. I'm sorry—Oh, hello."

Tallie's ankle message might have had a dual meaning. Ian Atkinson lounged in the doorway.

NINETEEN

JANET WONDERED HOW many of her prying questions and Sharon's testy answers Ian Atkinson had overheard. His doorway pose—right shoulder against the jamb, right ankle crossed over left, hands in pockets, a quietly humorous look on his face—might have been copied from a male model. *Or is he really that smooth?* she wondered. He came into the room and as he passed behind Sharon, his foot caught a leg of her chair and he stumbled, answering Janet's question.

"Ian," Sharon said. "Nice that you could join us."

"Always my pleasure," he said. "And how absolutely brilliant to find not one, but two more lovely ladies in the room."

He stood with his hands on the back of the chair next to Sharon's, in what looked to Janet like another studied pose. The humorous look was back in place after having tripped with the rest of him over the chair leg. He was taller and younger than he looked in his author pictures. *An interesting accomplishment,* Janet thought. In her experience, authors went on using publicity shots long past the photos' sell-by dates. From the pictures on Ian's book jackets, she'd assumed he was fifty, give or take a few years, but standing in front of her he looked closer to Tallie's late thirties. His dark hair, slicked behind his ears, touched the back of his collar. Was he trying to look like a rock star? Maybe, but it tickled her to think that instead he looked more like a selkie. She swallowed the urge to laugh and felt another tap on her ankle from Tallie. Apparently she'd missed something.

"Janet and Sally are the new owners of Yon Bonnie Books," Sharon said.

"It's Tallie, actually. We're both pleased to be on the committee."

"I don't doubt it. And I'll refrain from stating the obvious, but I find the increasing internationalism of our corner of the world refreshing." He sat down and planted his elbows on the table, knitting his fingers together. "Welcome to our wee village, as we like to say."

"Ian's from Slough, just outside London," Sharon said. "He's picking up the local accent fairly well, though."

"I can do John Wayne, too, little lady."

"So amusing," Sharon said.

"Una always thought so."

"Una was under the mistaken impression she had the talent and only needed a nationality transplant in order to write the great American novel." Sharon stood abruptly. "I left my lunch in my office." She walked stiffly from the room.

"I've been told I have the comic timing of a pathologist," Ian said. "It's more of a problem when I'm under the gun with a deadline."

"Stress and grief affect us all in different ways," Janet said.

"Stress, grief, ennui, gas." He smoothed the hair over his ears with the palms of his hands. "It's terrible."

"Sorry?" Janet said.

"It's terrible being so rude. I never seem to get it right with that woman. Una and I got on better. We were compadres. She had literary pretentions and she thought I was a literary snob, but only because I told her I never talk about my work in progress. Not the best basis for a friendship, but she understood the pressure of pent-up ideas and words." He circled his fingertips on his temples, staring at the table.

Thinking about Una, Janet wondered, *or easing the pent-up pressure?* Whatever goal he'd set for his mini-massage, he met it quickly.

"But enough about me," he said, looking at them and smoothing his hair over his ears again. "I might have heard something about you. I wonder what." He didn't wonder long, though, and looked away again, missing Janet's mouth opening to tell him they were his neighbors. "I spend most of my time manacled to my keyboard. Not literally, but as good as. I don't get out much. And to be honest, the few times I set foot in Yon Bonnie Books, I didn't feel the love, as they say. I hope that will change with the new management." He smiled at them again—more correctly, he smiled at Tallie. Then he threw himself back in his chair and sighed toward the ceiling. "But that's another terrible thing about me, you'll find. I rarely buy books these days, and I rarely read. I haven't the time."

"I hope you're at least making time to read the contest entries, Ian." Sharon returned with two file folders and sat at the head of the table, leaving Ian alone on the side opposite the Marsh women. She'd apparently forgotten her lunch again.

"I'm making an incredibly noble effort," he said.

"We all feel blessed, then. Now, I promised to keep this meeting short. With that end in mind, why don't we forgo lunch and get right to the meat."

"If my nose doesn't deceive me, they brought the meat with them," Ian said. "Pasties?"

"Bridies from Paudel's," Tallie said.

"Do you recommend them? Wait—I've seen you somewhere. How is that possible?"

"You live in this town," Sharon said. "She lives in this town. People see each other."

"Yes, bravo," said Ian. "Brilliant detective work. You should write crime novels. Or try your hand at an ultra-short mystery in that benighted poetry form you're so fond of, Skye-ku."

"Tcha." Sharon snatched up the file folders. "Come to order."

But Janet, much as she wanted the meeting to start and get over with, couldn't resist jumping in and answering Ian's question herself. "It was the night of the murder," she said.

A split second later, Sharon brought the file folders down fast and hard, so that their edges hit the table with a sharp smack.

"The crack of the librarian's whip," Ian said. "A good title for a certain type of book." He spoke to the table, though, without a smirk or smile, and no sign he'd heard Janet.

Sharon made no comment, either, and the meeting got under way. To Janet's surprise, it ran as smoothly and quickly as Sharon had promised, perhaps because Sharon had snapped herself into line with her librarian's whip as much as she had Ian. She explained the rubric for scoring the entries, passing each of them a folder with ready-made scoring sheets. She thanked Janet and Tallie for stepping into the void created by the sad death of a valued member of the community. She wiped an eye.

"You're on your own at this point," Sharon said. "Read, enjoy, score, and we'll meet again in two weeks. Questions?"

Janet fought the urge to raise her hand. "I'm adding my thanks to Tallie's. We're honored to be on this committee and part of the literary festival. I have one question, if you don't mind, although it's possibly not pertinent."

"By all means," Sharon said.

"I love impertinence," Ian murmured.

"You've had previous meetings?"

Ian looked at Sharon. "Two?"

"Three," Sharon said.

"But you've just now handed out the rubric. What did you cover in the other meetings?"

"Nothing that couldn't have been covered in one quick meeting, but that was impossible to achieve, for various reasons. Thank you all for coming. Jill, it was a pleasure to meet you. We'll meet back here in two weeks."

After Sharon had gone, Janet turned to Tallie. "Tell

me, *Jill*," she said, "do you think the phrase 'various reasons' is a generalization or a euphemism? Whatever it is, she seems overly fond of it."

"DO WE ACTUALLY know your name?" Ian asked Tallie as the three left the staff area and walked down a short hall to the public area of the library.

"Tallie. A nickname for Natalie."

"That's not so difficult. But as your mother said, stress and grief play tricks with our minds. It's nice to meet you, Tallie." He maneuvered so he could take her hand, effectively leaving Janet to walk behind them.

"What *did* you cover in those earlier meetings?" Janet asked with extra *oomph* to be heard through Ian Atkinson's rude back.

Tallie stopped beside a rack of DVDs, positioning herself so Janet would be between her and Ian.

"You must be a glutton for meetings," he said. "Logistics, for the most part. I'm sure Sharon thinks I wasn't paying attention. And who knows, maybe I wasn't. But from what I do remember, she explained the database for tracking entries, went over the rules entrants were meant to follow, and the definitions of the categories they submitted to. If that's the sum total of what we covered in not two, but three meetings, then she's right. We could have done it all in one go. Mea culpa. Do people understand mea culpa in America?"

"Mostly we just yell yee-haw and go about our business," Tallie said, "because we're all, like, carpe diem."

"You're awfully jolly, Ms. Tallie. Would you like to come see my bothy sometime?" Now he was talking over the top of Janet's head, and she expected him to make himself comfortable by leaning his elbow on it at any moment.

"I say, Ian," she said, making her accent as flat as central Illinois. "Do you remember the night Una was murdered?" She'd thought that might get him to make eye contact with her. She'd been right. But she hadn't expected the rest of his reaction.

He grabbed her elbow. And because he caught her by surprise, he was able to pull her and she stumbled along with him the few yards back down the hall toward the staff entrance. He stopped at the door and she ended up backed into the corner with him looming over her.

Until Tallie came up behind him, aimed the sole of her shoe for below the back of his knee, placed it, and pushed. Just hard enough.

Ian didn't go all the way to the floor, and as he started to collapse in one direction, Janet slid away from him in the other. She joined Tallie, so that when Ian recovered his balance and turned around, he faced the combined censure of the Marsh women. The episode was over in a matter of seconds with little commotion.

"Don't move," Janet said, holding her phone up. "Speed dial."

"I actually think I'm all right—" Ian touched his forehead where it had met the wall.

"And speed foot," Tallie said, raising hers. "*Don't* move."

"That was you? I thought I'd had sudden cramp. Or a stroke." He looked at her, head cocked. "One gentle shove?"

"Next time you'll think a mule kicked you."

"No, no, no. What you did was fantastic. Effective as a kick, but not as debilitating. Genteel and gutsy, just like my protag's lady friend, and perfect for a spot she gets into further along in the new book. It'll be brilliant."

Neither Tallie nor Janet joined him in rejoicing.

"You're angry," he said.

"Shush. You're in a library." Janet, eyebrows drawn and index finger to her lips, was the perfect picture of a librarian rampant.

"And are you really that clueless?" Tallie asked. "The whole world thinks you're a genius, but right now, you're coming across as a total idiot. You accosted my mother. In a library."

"Is that going to be your refrain? 'In a library'?"

Both women put their fingers to their lips.

"Yes, yes, all right. I'll whisper. We'll carry on our heated discussion, in a whisper, in a library."

"We aren't having a discussion," Janet whispered. "I asked you a simple question and you dragged me into a corner. Why?"

"Which puts us right back where we started. Why are you so interested in the night Una died? What exactly do you know about it?" He started to loom again, and Janet raised her phone. He took a step back and sank his hands in his pockets, his shoulder against the wall. But the look didn't come together as well as it had when he'd used it in the doorway of the meeting room. Between keeping a wary eye on Janet's phone and Tallie's foot, he looked more nervous than smooth or casual.

"Tell us why we shouldn't call the police," Tallie whispered.

"Norman says he's been helping the specialists. Acting as a consultant," Janet whispered to Tallie without taking her eyes from Ian. "Was that your attempt to interrogate me?" she asked him. "Because I think there's been a misunderstanding."

"Apprise me of it."

"Mom?" Tallie nudged Janet.

"It's all right," Janet whispered. "He obviously doesn't realize we're his neighbors."

"Mom."

"We have a vested interest in everything that happened that night," Janet whispered to Ian, "because it happened in our shed. So our question is, what do *you* know about it?"

"*That's* why I recognize you," Ian said, no longer whispering. I saw you standing on the deck behind the house next door. I haven't seen you much since, though."

"We haven't moved in yet."

"No? Well, this must be one of the odder ways to meet new neighbors. So sorry if I frightened you earlier." He put his hand on Janet's shoulder, and she slipped her phone into her purse. "You're right. That *was* my heavy-handed attempt to elicit information. Una and I had our differences, but her death hit very hard. And the problem with real life, in comparison to writing fiction, is that I can't edit my own actions. I find myself saying mea culpa far too often."

Janet expected a response from Tallie. If not a restrained "Yee-haw," at least a grudging "Hmm." But Tallie had already walked away.

"Meeting adjourned, apparently," Ian said. "See you around, neighbor."

JANET CAUGHT UP with Tallie at a computer near the circulation desk, where she was filling out a membership application.

"Fill it out online," Tallie said, "and pick up your card at the desk."

"Or renew the old one. I kept mine. What's bothering you about the way that ended with Ian?"

Tallie looked past Janet toward the circulation desk, and Janet turned to see what attracted her attention. Ian Atkinson was there talking to a young woman.

"Mom, I really don't mean to criticize, but it wouldn't hurt for you to bone up on how to ask questions. How to avoid asking leading questions, especially."

"Is that what I did?"

"Yeah, it kind of is. Well, not even kind of. You did."

"And you tried to warn me. Bugger." Janet looked around guiltily.

"It's possible he'd have given the same answers anyway. But you did feed them to him. On the other hand, if he was lying, now he'll think you're gullible, so he'll be off his guard."

"An accidental ploy, but a good one." Janet kissed her daughter's cheek. "Thank you, darling. You have a gift for turning—"

"Honey into mead?"

"I was going to say cow flops into flowers, but your

way is kinder. He's over there chatting up that young woman, so on my way to get my library card I'll walk past and put him even more off guard by flashing a warm, friendly, deceptive good-neighbor smile."

"I'll flash with you," Tallie said. "For this to work, we can't play the neighbor version of good cop–bad cop. We need to be good neighbor–good neighbor. I still want to kick him, though."

"Keep your foot handy, then. You'll feel better."

They performed their smile-by of Ian on their way to the circulation desk. As Tallie finished the process of registering for membership, the young woman who'd been talking with Ian approached Janet. She looked to be in her mid-to late twenties and sure of herself. She wore her baby-fine red hair piled loosely on top of her head so that wisps floated around her face. The wisps did nothing to soften the look in her eyes.

"You're Janet Marsh?"

"Yes, and you?"

"My husband and I used to live in your house."

"Oh, how nice to meet you. You're Lauren Pollard—"

"Not nice at all."

"I beg your—"

"I wish we'd never set foot in your house."

Janet was mortified. The young woman didn't shout, but her vehemence made her hiss.

"My life became a hell," she said, "and I hope that bisom who made it so has gone there as well."

TWENTY

IAN ATKINSON CAME to the rescue, bundling Lauren Pollard out the door, but not before she hissed one more time at Janet, telling her that Una had tried to ruin her marriage by seducing her husband.

Janet let Tallie put her arms around her. "I'm so tired of people having fits and meltdowns around me," she said. "*I* didn't seduce her husband, for heaven's sake. And to blame it on the poor house? Thank goodness Ian was still here."

"Unless he put her up to it in the first place," Tallie said.

Janet shuddered.

"Come on," Tallie said. "Let's go. We haven't had our lunch yet. We'll eat our bridies in the tearoom. Or in front of the fire with Mrs. TiggyWinkle."

"I'm not hungry."

"For Basant's sake, you should eat it."

"We didn't get our library memberships."

"We live here now and have all the time in the world. We'll get them another day."

It started to rain on their way back to the bookshop. They arrived sodden and somber. Janet went straight upstairs to change, leaving Tallie to tell the others about the incidents at the library. When Tallie went up a short time later, she found Janet still in her wet things, sitting on her bed and staring at the two bags of garbage.

"I think maybe the garbage is a metaphor," she said, not taking her eyes off the bags. She'd tried calling Curtis again, then texting. He wasn't answering. "Clear away the garbage. Clear the air. Clear up the mystery of Una's death. Wouldn't it be nice if it worked that way? Fat chance, though. Or rat's chance."

"Do you want to just kick back and take the afternoon off?" Tallie asked. "It's been kind of a fraught day. One of several. No one would blame you."

"No. Work and being surrounded by books are always a good antidote for what ails me. A quiet evening and an early night sound good, but I'll get changed and go on down." She continued staring at the garbage bags.

"Do you really think the garbage will tell us anything?" Tallie asked. "We don't even know if Rab came back with any of the same stuff he carted away."

"Will it hurt to look through it, though? I might need this piece of hope. Even if it turns out to be a banana peel under my foot. Or it might be just the tiniest piece of hope the size of a crumb. But then it might be a crumb of the best bread, and we can use it to catch a rat."

"Should I worry about you fixating on rats, Mom?"

"No, honey, you don't need to worry."

"Good."

"The rats in our lives. They're the ones who need to worry."

AT CLOSING TIME, Christine announced they all needed a change of scenery and routine for the evening. "We've been working hard and there's been too much stress over the past few days," she said. "We're all going down the pub."

"You girls go," Janet said. "I've got a date with my reading lamp and my pillow." *The Bludgeon in the Bothy* was waiting for her upstairs. So were the contest entries. And she felt as though she'd been rubbing shoulders with so many people in the past few days that her shoulders must be raw.

"Nonsense," Christine said. "No one stays behind. I'll bring Mum and Dad, too. It'll chuff them no end to get out, and folks will be happy to see them. They'll want to see you, too, Janet."

"A pub full of strangers—"

"No one's a stranger around Mum and Dad. Why do you think I'm bringing them along? They'll be our entrée. Stick with them and you'll be old mates and buying rounds with the regulars in no time."

"The Fin and Feather?" Summer asked. "It's cute from the outside."

"Nev's," Christine said. "At seven thirty. No, better make it eight. Wrangling the wrinklies can be like herding cats."

WHEN BEDTIME STORIES, their B & B above the bookshop, opened it would have four rooms for paying guests. Janet, Tallie, and Summer were using three of those rooms, and that evening, in the hour before they were to meet Christine and her parents at the pub, they turned the empty fourth into their crime lab. Summer spread issues of the *Inversgail Guardian* on the floor. Janet brought in the two bags of garbage.

"Shall we just dump them out," Tallie asked, "or do you have a favorite rubbish sorting and classification method you're aching to teach us?"

"As tempting as it is to treat it like garbage and dump it out, let's take our time and sort as we go," Janet said. "Start with a rough sort into like piles and go from there."

They each pulled on a pair of the rubber gloves from Paudel's. Then Janet took hers off again to untie the knots Rab had put in the neck of each bag.

"Envelopes will probably tell us more than anything else," Janet said. "But Constable Hobbs may well be right that we won't find anything to help us identify the perpetrator."

"And he's not alone in thinking that," said Tallie. "But that won't stop us."

They emptied the bags, piece by piece, making stacks of envelopes, newspapers, receipts, church bulletins, advertising circulars, and miscellaneous, which included grocery and to-do lists. Before they'd emptied half of the first bag, Summer further divided the envelopes into preaddressed return envelopes, envelopes with residential addresses, and other. Tallie subdivided the bulletins, advertisements, and newspapers by town of origin, unless they were addressed to someone in a different town.

"Campbell Street," Summer said. "I think it's safe to say that most of this came from the Crowley and

Watson households on Campbell Street. Do you know where that is, or recognize the names?"

"We'll know where in a second." Tallie pulled the stack of envelopes toward her and typed an address into her phone. "About a mile from here. Is that useful?" She looked at Janet.

"I don't see how," Janet said. "And I had such hopes for this garbage."

"It's always been a tenuous lead," Summer said, "but let's not give up on it yet. We can walk by those two houses, and we might see something. What kind of place are we going tonight?"

"Nev's? I've never been," Janet said. "Curtis might have." She tapped her fingers on her bared teeth for a second. "Anyway, from what I've heard, it's an authentic local where locals go. David and Helen's local, I guess. They're Christine's parents. You'll like them. He was head teacher at the primary school and she was a nurse."

"Then we'll ask questions there, and we might hear something," Summer said. "We're still in the information-gathering stage, and a local with locals could be fruitful."

"Right," said Janet. "But we'll want to be careful when we're asking questions."

"Especially you," Tallie said. "You have a way of riling strange men when you're not careful."

"Only when I get excited and go off script. Let's make a separate page in the cloud for questions we might want to ask tonight. Not too many questions, though. We don't want to confuse ourselves. We'll keep it simple."

"We'll *try* to keep it simple," Summer said. "Questions have a way of begetting more questions. But if that happens, we should add them to the cloud, too. And any answers we get. If we get them."

"Good," Janet said. "We have a plan. Plans give me hope."

"I have a plan for the questions, too," Summer said. "As much as we want answers about the garbage, there aren't many questions we can ask about it in the pub without flagging ourselves as—"

"Eccentric?" Janet asked.

"That works. I wasn't going to be so polite. But it'll be natural for people to be talking about Una. If they do, listening might be more important than asking questions to begin with. Then use what you hear to prompt more information. For instance, if someone mentions a funeral service for her, you might ask if her family has to travel far to be here for it. And keep in mind what we noticed about Una for ourselves. She was on what you could call the hyper spectrum, so you might mention something about her energy and see what comments you get. She was ambitious, so you could—"

"Mention her wish to write the great American novel," Tallie said.

"Really? She wanted to do that?" Summer pushed the stacks of envelopes away. "She was obviously a woman with problems, but I wish I could've gotten to know her. I wish I could've read her novel."

"Sharon was pretty caustic about her today at the library," Tallie said. "And Ian said she had literary pretentions, which isn't exactly polite."

"And who knows how useful those tidbits will be," Summer said, "but one of my managing editors called this technique chumming the waters."

"Una asked about tension among the four of us," Janet said. "She said it makes a better story. And Jess and Pamela both said she saw herself as an investigative reporter. So maybe she made a habit of looking for tension. Or maybe it followed naturally in her wake. If she did seduce Neil Pollard, his wife might have snapped under the tension. I can understand that happening."

"Unintended consequences," Tallie said.

"But entirely predictable if people would think with their brains instead of their—"

"Easy there, Mom." Tallie put a hand on Janet's knee. "But what if looking for tension wasn't enough for her? If she set out to create tension, then *that* could've led her into trouble."

"Easily," Summer said.

"*That's* why Jess freaked when you came in today, Summer," Janet said.

Summer looked blank.

"I bet you anything that's why." Janet rubbed her hands with pleasure. Summer continued to look blank.

"It's all right, Summer," Tallie said. "It's a minor disconnect. Over time you'll get used to it. Mom?"

"Jess was telling me that Ian Atkinson tried to buy this building. He had a bid on it before we even came along. He didn't want it for the bookshop, though. He wants to start a boutique distillery. Somehow the deal got scuttled, and Jess was getting all wound up about who Ian blames for the scuttling, and was just about to tell me, when you came back from the paper. Jess freaked when you said you're the new Una. She has a real thing about Una, dating back to childhood. So when she was about to speak ill of the dead, you came in and announced you're Una risen from the dead, and her freak fits."

"And what does it mean if the freak fits?" Summer asked.

"You said we should keep in mind what we've heard about Una. We've heard that she ruined a business chance for Ian Atkinson, and we've witnessed that she elicits powerful reactions in Jess."

"Ian Atkinson, who got in your face when you asked him about the night of the murder." Tallie looked at her mother until she nodded.

"He's on your list for *Guardian* and online searches," Janet said. "Why don't you bump his name up to priority status?"

"And Lauren the betrayed, and Jess of the powerful reactions?" Summer asked. "What priority level for them?"

Janet wanted to hesitate but didn't. "Put Jess next one down from Ian, then Lauren."

"I thought you were sure Jess couldn't have done it," Tallie said. "Hobbs seems sure she didn't, and the specialists let her go."

"Yes, but the specialists are consulting with Ian, and Norman seems to think that says more about the specialists than it does about Ian." Janet drew in a deep breath, letting her shoulders rise. She held the breath for a few seconds before letting it go. It was a more positive way of affirming a decision than sighing or grinding her teeth. "Believing that someone I've known and liked might be a murderer doesn't seem right," she said. "But I'm working with what we've got. I'm listening and I'm asking questions to beget more questions, as Summer put it."

"A newswoman's tactic," Summer said.

"A lawyer's tactic," Tallie said. "I bet Christine used it as a social worker, too."

"And good reference librarians use it to figure out what information muddled patrons are asking for. So now, I'll be the first to admit being muddled about this mess." She flapped a hand at the garbage. "Do we have any reason to keep it?"

"Possibly not," Tallie said. "But as soon as we get rid of it, we'll wish we hadn't. In the meantime, it isn't in our way up here and there's nothing in it to attract rats."

"Small pleasures," Janet said. "I'll take them where I can."

"Besides, our garbage problem, here and at the house, has raised enough questions to merit its own page in the cloud. I called it 'Rubbish In,' but all I've got is questions so far, and they might not be any more useful than the actual garbage."

"Read what you have," Janet said.

"I probably could've called it 'Rubbish Out,' but I'll read it in my lawyer voice to give it some punch. 'What company did Jess hire to clear the garbage out of the house? Who cancelled it and who called Rab? Concerning the garbage out back: Did Rab really just happen by and find it? If yes, then did he find the right stuff when he went to get it back from the recycle center? How did he know? How would we know if he didn't? Did he keep anything back? Does this latest incident prove that Una didn't dump the stuff in the house? Is the garbage a threat? If it is a threat, then it's stupid, because we don't understand it.' That last note is an observation rather than a question."

"But an insightful observation," Summer said.

"I thought so."

"Add two more questions," Janet said. "Did Lauren Pollard dump the garbage? And is there a connection between the garbage and the letters?"

"Except that they're both bizarre, I don't see one," Summer said.

"Neither do I. Or I don't want to." Janet rubbed the back of her neck. "You were right, Summer. Una could have written those letters and left them here. So could Jess, Rosie, either of the Lawries, or Sharon Davis, for that matter. They all had the opportunity. Or it could've been no one we know. It's not likely that Lauren left them here, but Rab could have. It doesn't seem like something he would do, but I can't say that I really know him. Maybe he's the connection between the letters and the garbage. And do you know what's bothering me most about that? If it turns out Rab is guilty of something in all of this, I think it will break Ranger's heart."

"Then there's the bigger question," Summer said. "Are the letters or the garbage connected to Una's murder? Or are we barking up the wrong tree?"

TWENTY-ONE

THE PUB THAT Christine and most of the locals called Nev's had no curb appeal. If there had ever been anyone named Nev associated with the place, he would have been fine with that. Nev's wasn't looking for new clientele. Attracting tourists was all right for the shinier and better-lit establishments nearer the water. Nev's occupied a narrow, nondescript building several streets back from the harbor, happy in its anonymity.

Nev's neighbor on one side was Smith Funerals, and on the other the *Inversgail Guardian.* There'd been a sign hanging near the door once, with the pub's name of record—The Chamberlain's Arms—but the sign came down in a terrible, sweeping storm. Or was pulled down by rowdy holidaymakers from London. Or was removed for repainting. There were other versions of the story, several started by the publican, and the sign's demise entered into the pub's lore. Also in the pub's lore were stories about how it came to be called Nev's, none of which involved the disappearance of the sign or Neville Chamberlain.

Janet, Tallie, and Summer closed the door on their crime lab and walked to Nev's. The High Street was alive with tourists enjoying the balmy evening or on their way to dinner reservations or pints in the shinier pubs. There weren't the hordes of people that business owners hoped to see during the week surrounding the literature festival, but the number of strolling couples and parents cautioning children as they walked along the harbor wall brought good cheer.

"This?" Summer asked when they arrived at Nev's. "There isn't even an 'open' sign. I walked right past it this morning. It looks like storage for the *Guardian*. Or for the funeral home. More like a dump than a destination."

"I think that might be its beauty," Tallie said. "Are you balking at adventure?" She pulled the door open. The mingled aromas of meat pies, fried fish, and strong ale drifted out on a babble of talk and the yodel of a country and western ballad. When the other two only looked at each other, Tallie walked on in.

Janet gestured for Summer to go ahead of her. Summer gestured for Janet to do the same. Then, through the open door, Janet heard Christine greet Tallie, and Christine's mother's warm laugh, and she knew that spending the evening with these people she loved was the right thing to do. She bowed to Summer and went in.

"About time you closed the door," the barman said. "Keeps the riffraff out."

Nev's dim interior gave the impression of being smoky without the presence of actual smoke. The walls, floor, and ceiling were dark, having ripened in the preban age of nicotine fug. A polished bar ran partway down the left side of the room, with tall chairs for those who wanted to rest their feet while leaning their elbows close to the source. A bench against the opposite wall ran the length of the room, interrupted halfway along by a digital jukebox and an open doorway. Three high-backed booths against the street wall offered the illusion of privacy. And a dozen or so tables danced down the middle toward the far end, where two more of the tall chairs sat on a small stage. Janet and Summer stopped beside Tallie at the bar.

"A half pint of—"

"Try the Selkie's Tears," the barman said. "It's a new craft ale made in Dornie we're giving a try. Malty with a hint of toffee." He held up a glass of dark amber ale so they could admire the color. "It's on special tonight. Yeah? Half for each of you? And David's got this round." He nodded to where Christine and her parents sat at a table halfway down the room. "It's great seeing him and Helen in again. And Chrissie."

Janet heard something in the barman's voice when he used Christine's childhood name. He'd gone to fill their glasses, though, and she missed the look in his eye. When he handed their drinks to them, his eye had already strayed to the next customers waiting.

"Do you have live music some nights?" Tallie asked before he got away.

"Had to give it up," he said. "Brought in the tourists." He used the same tone of voice for "tourists" as he had for "riffraff."

The pub was full of people either unwinding after another day's work or in for an evening of catching up on stories and gossip. It wasn't a raucous group, but convivial and comfortable, with friends calling to each other, some sitting, some making the rounds with a sashay or a backslap, and some staring into their glasses. When Janet, Tallie, and Summer made their way toward Christine's table, an elderly trio stood up from the next table over and offered their chairs.

"We've been keeping them warm until you came," one of the women in the group said. "We're up next for darts. Great to see you out, Helen," she said, speaking louder for Helen's benefit.

"Always lovely," Christine's mother shouted back. "Oh, it takes you back, doesn't it, David?" she said after the trio had gone into the next room. "Do you remember when she lived next door?"

"She still does," Christine said to Janet from behind her hand. She got up and went around the table to lean down between her parents and speak nearer their ears. "Mum, Dad, you remember Janet Marsh, don't you? And her daughter, Tallie? And this is Summer Jacobs. We're all in the book and tea business together."

"Isn't that lovely," Helen said.

David raised his glass. "A toast to our minds and memories. May we never lose either, or only to drink." He took a sip, declared it delicious, and then reached over to hold Helen's hand.

"Thanks for the round, David," Janet said. "The next one's on me."

"Unless the first puts us under the table," he said.

"Wouldn't that be lovely," Helen said. "And two daughters, Janet, that's lovely, too."

Christine sat back down near Janet. "I phoned some folk and let them know Mum and Dad would be here. They used to come down of an evening, but that's been a while now, and a decade at least since Tony and I stepped inside. The place hasn't changed, though, except for no smoking. Danny hasn't changed."

Janet followed Christine's gaze to the barman.

"I pushed him off the harbor wall when we were eight. High tide and he couldn't swim. Had to rescue him. I think that might be what led me into social work. I seem to be a natural helper."

"Obviously born to it," Janet said.

"I can't believe you and Dad never came here," Tallie said.

"We had a couple of wild children at home, with whom I enjoyed spending my time, most of the time. And books for when I didn't. If you'd tried harder, though, maybe you could've driven me to drink. Christine, we came with a plan for sleuthing this evening. A plan with a pub-worthy acronym: CLARET. It stands for circulate, listen, ask, record, enjoy, text."

Elizabeth II regarded Janet. "I'll let you remember it. But it's good to see you back in the *spirit* of things. I knew you wouldn't stay down in the dumps for long. And I saw all the new material in the cloud. I floated up there after I gave Mum and Dad their tea, and that's why I made my phone calls. This way, whilst the oldies are occupied with friends stopping by the table, I'll be free to circulate."

"Speaking of which," Tallie said, "Summer and I are going to circulate on into the other room to watch the darts. We'll text if we hear anything or have any news."

"Check in anyway, in an hour or so, so I know where you are," Janet said.

"The place isn't that big, Mom."

"Humor your mum, Tallie," Christine said.

"Righty-oh."

"See?" Christine smiled at Janet. "Always helping. Now, shall you and I stick together or split up for maximum coverage?"

"I won't get much on my own."

"True enough."

"We could also sit here and glean what we can from your mum and dad's friends."

"Or we can do a bit of both." Christine leaned closer to Janet. "It'll give Mum and Dad a chance to complain about me if I'm not a permanent fixture at the table."

James Taylor's sweet voice finished singing "You've Got a Friend" on the jukebox, and Johnny Cash galloped in with "Ghost Riders in the Sky" to take his place. A woman sitting nearer the unused stage turned to speak to someone at the table behind her, giving Janet a view of her profile.

"Is that Jess? It is. I wonder if she thinks I'm some kind of jinx at this point."

"She's waving," Christine said.

"And her glass is empty. Shall we take her another?"

"Yes, and perfect timing. Mum, Dad, look who's just come in." Christine waved to a newly arrived couple—and their dog, a standard poodle. "You have a nice visit with Nancy and Bob. Dad, if you need me, I'll be right over there, and I'll check back in a wee bit."

"Sophie," Helen said, holding her hand out to the poodle. "Who's a lovely girl, then, eh?"

"That's fairly remarkable," Christine said as she and Janet went to the bar.

"A poodle in a pub?"

"No, Nev's has always been a dog pub. Remarkable that Mum remembered her name. That really is Sophie, and she is a lovely girl."

"Dog pub, eh? I wonder, then…"

While Christine asked Danny the barman for another of what Jess was having, Janet glanced around the occupants of the tables more carefully. Christine took the glass from Danny, and as they moved between the tables toward the stage, Janet's phone buzzed.

"It's Tallie. Ha. I wonder if Rosie would like a couple of psychic pals. Tallie says Rab and Ranger are playing darts."

"And the dog's predicting the winners, is he? Otherwise there's nothing psychic about it. Rab's one I phoned earlier. He and Mum are old mah-jongg mates."

"You're kidding."

"Only about the mah-jongg. Mum and his mum worked together years ago. Sometimes old memories are easier for her. Hello, Jess. Anyone joining you? Mind if we do? We've brought you a refill." Christine put the glass down in front of Jess, and she and Janet sat down.

"Cheers." Jess swallowed a fair portion of the fresh drink. "I was hoping to see Rosie. She comes in some evenings."

"If she comes, we can move on," Janet said. "Did she come back to the office today?"

"She might have. I didn't. I tried phoning her but

she didn't answer. I need to apologize for shrieking at her like a banshee."

"She's young," Christine said. "She can probably take it."

"Maybe. But can I? I need to get myself right in the head. Do you know what I did after running out of your bookshop? Ran straight home, put my head under my pillow, and cried myself to sleep like a bairn without her mum."

"Did it help?" Janet asked. "Sometimes we need that."

"You found me sitting alone in a pub. What does that tell you?"

"You were waiting for a friend," Janet said. "That tells me all I need to know."

"Wouldn't it be nice if that were true? It doesn't ease the guilt, though. But here's to absent friends." She raised her glass, and they clinked theirs against it. While she drank, Janet and Christine exchanged looks.

"What do you feel guilty about?" Christine asked.

"Let me count the ways. Janet's house, for one. That's why I came into the bookshop today. Did I hear right, that you're not back in it yet?"

"There's been a delay," Janet said.

"You're taking it awfully well. I feel terrible about all of it."

"None of it is your fault, Jess."

"Extraordinary circumstances," Christine murmured.

"But Ug never would have been there. She never

would have gone there at all except. Don't you see? It's the rubbish. She came back to do it again."

Janet hadn't thought of that. *Could it be? Does it come back to the garbage? But, no.*

"There's drug crime everywhere these days," Jess was saying, staring into her glass as she swirled it. "One of the lowlifes we get coming through must've been looking for an opportunity and Ug got in the way."

"I don't know," Janet said. "She wasn't found in the house, Jess, and there was no garbage in the shed. Do you know anything about her children?"

Jess found a crumb on the table. She played with it, then flicked it away, and shook her head.

"I saw Lauren Pollard today," Janet said.

"She loved that house."

"She told me that she wished she'd never set foot in it. She said Una turned her life into a hell."

"Good old Ug. Always a helping hand in the community."

Christine winced. "Jess, what about the cleaning company that cancelled? Which one was it?"

"Cosy Cleaners. I've used them before. Not for jobs here in town. Other properties, elsewhere. They've always been reliable. When I spoke to them about the cancellation, all they could tell me was that *I* phoned them, that *I'm* the one who cancelled, and their excuse is 'how were we to know it wasn't you?'"

"Who do you think it was?" Christine asked.

"Ug, of course. She liked a good 'joke.' Thought she was funny with her accents and voices. She dumped the rubbish. She thwarted my efforts to get it cleared away."

"And she picked the lock to get in the house?" Janet asked.

"As I told you before." Any mellow edge several glasses of ale might have given Jess disappeared as the furrows between her brows deepened. "She used to show off when we were girls. Learnt it from her brothers. A dodgy family all the way around."

"That would be how she got into the shed, then, too," Christine said.

"Of course it is," Jess said. "All of it. It all comes down to Ug."

"Not all of it," Janet said.

"Of course it does," Jess repeated.

"Not her death, Jess. She didn't kill herself. And she didn't dump more garbage behind the bookshop this morning."

"More?"

Janet watched Jess process that news, its progress reflected in the movement of her eyes and in the whitening of her knuckles as she gripped the table.

"That changes things." Her eyes had settled on staring into the corner beyond their table, but Jess was still thinking it through. "That means all that rubbish wasn't Ug. It was someone else. Someone else making a statement." Her voice dropped to a whisper. "It could have been the murderer making a statement *about* Ug. About Ug's muckraking. *Oh, my God.* It might have been the murderer all along. In your house. I might have been in your house with the murderer."

"Jess?" Janet called her name. It didn't get her attention. She tried tapping the table in front of Jess. She didn't dare touch her for fear of startling her. "Jess?"

Jess, still staring into the corner, scraped her chair back, bumping into a woman sitting behind her, and taking no notice. "I'll phone Norman."

"Will you be all right, Jess?" Christine asked. "Would you like someone to walk you home?"

"I'll phone Norman. Then I'll put my head back under my pillow."

Jess bumped into the woman behind her again, and then pushed her way past people who greeted her or asked her to watch it as she made her way to the door. Danny at the bar bade her good night, but she ignored him.

"That was an example of going off the extrapolation deep end," Christine said. "We should use her as a cautionary example."

"And yet the police still have my house. *Something* was going on there."

"Oh. Good point. And here I thought she was just a bit of a ninny. Strike her off our suspect list?"

Janet sipped her ale. "Maybe not."

"Gut feeling?"

"My gut doesn't know much about crime solving."

"Do you want another round?"

"Not really."

"Neither do I, but I want a word with Danny."

"I'm going to sit here for a few minutes. I'll meet you back at your mum and dad's table."

Janet's phone had alerted her to incoming texts while they'd talked to Jess. She'd glanced at her phone each time, looking for key words like "Help!" or "SOS." But not seeing anything suggesting an emergency, she'd read no further and put her phone back in her lap. When they'd made their plan, she hadn't realized how hard it would be to make herself constantly interrupt a conversation in front of her to read about a conversation happening somewhere else. She read the texts while she finished her Selkie's Tears.

From Tallie: ian sometimes drinks here. barely tolerated.

From Tallie: kenneth kicked off darts team after haggis incident. much lol, no details.

From Summer: una ace at darts. not surprised.

From Tallie: haggis inc. involved ranger. rab not lol.

From Summer: no news from u?

Then a new one arrived from Christine: una a regular. Danny no useful info.

Janet could have dropped by the darts room on her way to rejoin Helen and David, but decided to be more with it by sending her own texts while listening in on conversations at nearby tables. The music made overhearing difficult. *Probably the intent of the music,* she thought. The couples at the closest table seemed to be talking about *Doctor Who*, but then Queen started singing "Bohemian Rhapsody," and she gave up eavesdropping to hum along. She sent Tallie the name of the cleaning firm in Fort William. She texted Summer, admitting they'd muffed their chance to ask Jess what she knew about Rosie. She texted Summer again, letting her know that Christine was talking to Danny at the bar. Before she could send a second text to Tallie, she had one back from Summer.

christine not w/dan, throwing darts.

Irritated at missing a piece of real life in real time, she texted Tallie, asking her to catch Rab and officially offer him the part-time job, which she *still* hadn't done. Another text arrived immediately.

Rab & ranger gone.

She slapped her phone on the table, then picked it up and went to sit with Helen and David—where Rab and Ranger sat, too. Sophie the poodle and her couple had left. Helen and David were sharing a bag of prawn crisps. Ranger looked interested, but Rab shook his head. Janet didn't bother texting that information to anyone.

Chatting with Helen and David involved a lot of shouting and repetition. But Christine had been right that there might be an advantage to that and to having her parents there. People were happy to see them and happy to add their own shouts to the hubbub. Rab and Ranger held out for a short time, but Janet could see that shouting and being shouted at wasn't their thing.

When she caught his eye, she waved him closer so they could speak at a normal volume.

"We haven't really discussed the part-time job yet. If you're willing, we'd like to hire you."

"Oh, aye. I assumed as much."

Janet didn't quite know what to make of that answer. While she puzzled over it, Christine came back from the darts room. Her mother shouted that it was lovely to see her, and then asked when she'd got back from Panama. When Janet looked again for Rab and Ranger, the front door was closing behind them.

"Why don't you steer the conversation," Janet said into Christine's ear. "I'll be the recording secretary and the lookout, in case people of interest come in."

Christine gave her a thumbs-up and settled in for a good natter—a loud natter—and Janet settled back, ears, eyes, and thumbs at the ready.

The talk was necessarily wide-ranging and disjointed as people joined in or drifted away. Christine did her best to nudge it toward hopeful topics or pull it back when it strayed too far beyond their interests, but there was only so much she could do. Arthritis and the recent flu season kept creeping in. Politics reared its head more than once. David had been a keen fisherman, and Christine couldn't deny her father the pleasure of the latest fish stories.

But David did remember Rosie and knew her parents—her father the minister and her mother a piano teacher. Janet logged into the cloud to make a note that Rosie was not Curtis's child, when Helen brought a twenty-year-old memory into clarity.

"They said they were blessed when they were given that child to love. I always thought the child was blessed when she was given to them."

"She was adopted?" Christine asked.

"Who?" her mother asked.

Janet entered the question of Rosie's adoption into the cloud with a note to have Tallie or Summer verify it.

Christine used the topic of children to bring talk around to Una. She asked after Una's family and heard that her husband, if they were married, which they might not have been, was long out of the picture. The children were grown and gone, a woman at the next table said. Someone standing behind Helen was surprised to hear she'd had children. Those who'd known didn't know their names. Someone passing the table to get another round thought the grown children had emigrated. One and then the other, someone agreed. Maybe Australia? No one rightly knew. The family had lived somewhere other than Inversgail while the children were growing. Somewhere else was all anyone knew or remembered. Couldn't have been far. She had her column. Came to town. Came to Nev's.

The door opened and Janet saw James Haviland limp in. He waved at someone, and someone else asked if he'd fallen off anything lately. He laughed and stopped at the bar to get a pint from Danny. Janet, with a private flourish of her fingers, texted Summer. Not thirty seconds later, Summer and Tallie came out of the darts room. Summer did a credible job of being surprised and pleased to see James. She introduced him to Tallie. Tallie, in turn, introduced him to Christine.

"And you met my mother, Janet, at the bookshop," Tallie said, maneuvering a chair for him so that it would be awkward if he didn't sit down next to Janet.

"So good to see you again," Janet said. "And how nice to have you join us."

If James felt waylaid, he didn't show it. Christine ably brought him into the conversation, at the same time herding it in a direction to suit their needs.

"We were wondering if there's a service planned for Una," she said, "and how far her family might have to come."

"I assume the police were able to contact her kin," he said, "but as far as I know, there's no one left locally to really mourn her. Quite frankly, after all the years she wrote her column, I'm ashamed to know so little."

"She made our business her business," a woman at the next table said, "but she didn't share much of her own."

"She kept her personal and professional lives separate," the man with her said, "and nothing wrong with that."

Uncomfortable murmurs rose and fell around them; then a woman said she would miss Una's column. Others agreed, and then there was laughter over the old stories of Una writing the letters as well as the answers.

"The column isn't going away, though," James said. He introduced Summer, and there was some interest, and perhaps skepticism, in hearing that she was going to take Una's place.

Janet wondered again if being known as the "new Una" was such a good thing. She typed that question into the cloud, and then looked up when the door opened. Being lookout required little of her; she didn't recognize most of the people who came and went. But this time she did. Kenneth Lawrie walked in, gap-toothed smile absent, returning no greetings.

Janet texted Tallie, across the table from her.

meet me at the bar? talk to k?

"We'll keep it short and sweet," Janet said when Tallie joined her. "Thank him for the whisky and tartan."

"Ask him for haggis and an unfair game of darts?"

"Wheesht."

KENNETH SAT AT the bar with his glass, apparently more interested in staring into it than drinking. Janet and Tallie ignored the barricade presented by his hunched shoulders.

"Nice to see you, Kenneth," Janet said. "Is Pamela with you?"

"Packing."

"How's that going?" Tallie asked.

"Endless organizing. Escaping for the time being."

"That's smart," Janet said. "Big changes take an awful lot of energy. You need to build downtime into all that organizing, just to stay sane."

The door opened again, and from Kenneth's quick look toward it, Janet wondered if now he wanted to escape from *them*. The man who came in had a smooth collie with him. The man greeted Danny and took a seat farther down the bar. His dog sat beside him gazing at the occupied tables, giving the impression of being knowing but aloof.

"We won't keep you, Kenneth," Janet said. "We thanked Pamela, but we wanted to thank you, too, for the time you gave us."

"And for what you left in the filing drawer," Tallie said. "That's a great shop-warming gift. Warming in more ways than one."

"Have you opened it yet?" he asked.

"Not yet."

"When you do, raise a glass, and wish us all luck." He looked down the bar toward the man laughing with Danny. "I think we'll need it."

JAMES HAVILAND HADN'T moved from where they'd left him. He'd put his bad ankle up on an adjoining chair. His hands, fingers knitted, rested on his stomach, and his glasses had slid down his nose. He looked like someone's uncle, comfortable after a holiday meal.

"Do you know who that is at the bar?" Janet asked him. "Down at the end, talking to Danny."

James looked over his shoulder. "One of the specialists in for the investigation," he said. "Reddick."

"Huh." *Coincidence?* Janet wondered. *Or is he keeping an eye on Kenneth?*

While she pondered, Paul McCartney started into "The Long and Winding Road."

"And there's my cue," James said. "It's been a long and winding day, as so many of them seem to be lately." He swallowed the last of his drink and stood to go. "Friday afternoon?" he said to Summer.

"I'll be there."

"Good night, all."

"Mind you don't fall off the curb," someone called, and someone else called, "Good night, Scotty."

James turned in the doorway and waved.

TWENTY-TWO

LEAVING NEV'S TOOK some effort and the last smile of patience Janet had. But she didn't want to leave Christine on her own to get Helen and David to the car park. They were tottery at the best of times, and after a convivial evening, they were more dangerous. And Helen had become unhappy with "that bossy woman who's been following us." Tallie finally convinced Christine to bring the car to Nev's door while the rest of them got Helen and David safely moving.

"She might even give you a tip," Tallie said, "if she thinks you're a valet."

"How will you manage when you get them home?" Janet asked.

"One foot forward and one old dear into the house at a time," Christine said. "And a nightcap for the valet."

After they'd driven off, Christine with a wave that made Elizabeth II look hounded but resolute, Janet uncorked and let herself flow.

"Reddick!" she said. "It must mean something that he's in there. Otherwise, how did he even find the place? He came in very soon after Kenneth, and Kenneth gave him a look. A look like he knew something was up. Like he's being watched and knows it. But James! He must be the Scotty in the letters. And his attitude did a one-eighty when he saw Reddick. Comfortable one second, up and out the door the next. Reddick didn't follow, though, so my bet's that he's watching Kenneth, who said something very interesting and dark about needing luck. Oh. But I wonder if Reddick does plan to follow James. But it's too late. He's nowhere in sight. If we go back in, I wonder if we can get him to tell us anything."

"Who?" Tallie asked

"Reddick. Who did you think I was talking about?"

"Several people. Let's walk while we talk."

"But—"

"Less likely to attract attention," Summer said.

Janet put a hand over her mouth, then took it away and said, "Attention of the wrong kind." She put her hand back on her mouth and started walking, going the long way around the block, past Smith Funerals rather than past the *Inversgail Guardian* building. None of them spoke again until they'd turned the corner. "I have a lot to learn about investigations," Janet said then.

"For someone who wanted me to text my whereabouts while I was in the next room," Tallie said, "yes, that was a curious lapse of judgment back there."

"I warned you about what happens when I get excited."

"No apparent harm done," Summer said.

"Reddick, though," Janet said. "I'm sure it means something, and that James bolted when he showed up."

"Hardly bolted," Summer said. "Or the same could be said of us. He arrived. We left."

"You do think James should be considered a suspect, though, don't you?"

"I'm just saying that not everything is cause and effect. Besides, do you really think he could've killed Una with a…in that way? Wouldn't his ankle make it hard for him to sneak up behind her or overpower her?"

"Maybe that's why he's limping," Janet said.

"He fell off a stage."

"So he says. Maybe he twisted his ankle fleeing the scene."

"I think there were enough witnesses at the ceilidh to prove it," Summer said.

"Sometimes it takes a day or two for an ankle to get really sore. Maybe he knows that from experience and he's using it."

"But how would he benefit from killing Una?" Summer asked. "Her column was hugely popular."

Tallie had stayed out of the argument, instead acting as guide for the two bickering behind her. But their voices rose as they approached the High Street, and she put up a hand, like a traffic warden, to stop them.

"We won't exactly be buffeted by crowds when we turn the corner," she said, "but if I might make a suggestion? Either keep your voices down, or pretend as though you're discussing a book you've read so you don't alarm or libel anyone. Throw in words like protagonist and villain and we should be good. Agreed?"

"That might be a technique to use in the shop," Janet said. "I wonder if that could work, or will people want to know the title so they can buy it?"

"Maybe we should try writing it," Summer said.

"Come on, you two."

Janet tried out the book discussion scheme immediately. "On the surface of it—of the story—James, as the villain, didn't benefit. But that raises the question of why any of the characters had it in for the victim. Who did benefit? Was she killed because of advice she gave?"

"No, sorry," Summer said. "This won't work for me."

"She's right," Janet said. "Besides, who's the protagonist?"

"Beats me," Tallie said, "but it got you to stop arguing. Do you want a tot of something when we get back?"

"I'll pass," Janet said. "I want to read the letters more carefully. We had a Kenny and a Scotty at Nev's tonight. I'm going to keep looking for answers."

"Summer?" Tallie asked.

"It's an invasion of privacy."

"I meant do you want a tot."

"It isn't an invasion of privacy," Janet said, "because the expectation of privacy was lost when the letters were left in the recipe box."

"But we don't know if the person who wrote them is the person who left them," Summer said. "If they aren't one and the same, then the person who wrote them deserves to have his or her privacy protected until which time the letters can be returned."

"In which case we should read them so that we can make a good-faith effort to get them back to whoever *did* write them," Janet said.

"I think I deserve two tots for putting up with both of you," Tallie said.

ALONG WITH SO many other new things in Janet's life, since the move to Inversgail she had a new morning routine. Back in Illinois, she'd read the paper or scanned online news, cup of coffee in one hand, breakfast utensil in the other—if she'd had time to eat. She'd checked the weather on several sites, read the front page, scanned the obits, hurried through the op-ed, slowed down for the few book reviews she ran across. What she absorbed from print or screen before rushing out the door to join the stream of other drivers running late often set the tenor for the rest of the day. A day spent hemmed in by the books she loved, but with very little interaction with the sky.

By contrast, Janet's morning routine in Inversgail consisted of getting out of bed and looking out the window.

The morning after their visit to Nev's, after gazing her fill at her new world, Janet felt a centering balance in her life. Her view of sea and sky refreshed her enough that she only barely begrudged firing up her laptop, rehashing the questions of the night before, and adding new ones. Maybe another look and a refreshed perspective would give her a balanced view of their suspects. She wasn't sure that thinking of suspects on a balance board was the best way to look at them, but for now, with no clear evidence against any of them, it seemed to make sense. It was like balancing pros and cons before making a major decision.

Weighing down one end of the balance board were Ian Atkinson, Jess Baillie, and Lauren Pollard—each with a reason to be angry, if not violently furious with Una. Ian's efforts to start a distillery had been thwarted by her. Jess felt personally bedeviled by her and thought she posed a threat to her real estate business. Lauren blamed her for ruining her marriage. Janet had seen clear signs that Jess was teetering on the edge, and it was easy to believe she might snap. But Jess's reaction when she suddenly realized the murderer could have been in the house with her seemed completely genuine. They had a letter written to an Ian, but it didn't contain enough details for Janet to be sure it was written to Ian Atkinson. They hadn't found letters to Jess or Lauren. But what if there had been and they'd been removed? How could they know? And the garbage—either Jess or Lauren could have dumped it.

Balanced in the middle were Kenneth Lawrie and James Haviland. At first glance, Kenneth was likeable. But he had a temper and he threatened people. At Nev's it looked as though he might have attracted Reddick's interest. The letter written to Kenny included a list of inconsequential, almost laughable sins, but also the lines "The one time I asked you to be there for me, you suddenly had better things to do. Taking a day trip to Aviemore isn't better than helping a friend in crisis (especially as your trip wasn't with your wife)." The Kenny of the letter might not be Kenneth Lawrie, but Pamela had called him Kenny on at least one occasion. James also came across as a pleasant fellow. But he'd worked with Una for close to twenty years yet didn't know the names or whereabouts of her children. What did that say about him, her, or their working relationship? The letter to Scotty, which now seemed likely to have been written to James, talked of bitterness at being passed over for promotions and mentioned his "fear of crossing lines, including lines in the sand," and "being a grass when it counted most to be loyal."

Opposite the heavy end of the balance board were Sharon Davis, Rosie Crozier, and Lauren Pollard's unfaithful husband, Neil. But they were such featherweights on their end of the board that in the bright light of day, Janet wondered why she didn't remove them and let the board tip… Except this was information, and in her experience, information helped light the way toward answers.

Sharon shed tears for Una one day and spoke contemptuously of her the next. The letter to Sharon complained that she'd purposely given the wrong amount of baking powder in a recipe for lemon butter biscuits, and several people in Nev's had remarked on the quality of the lemon biscuits Sharon Davis served at library functions. Janet didn't think for a minute that being chastised for a purposely inaccurate recipe would incite anyone named Sharon to murder, but the detail confirmed for her that the letter was addressed to Sharon Davis. As for Rosie, unless she'd put the letters in the tearoom herself, didn't finding them there point to her innocence? Because if the letters shed any kind of light on the murder, then why would the murderer want them found? And except for the knowledge that Neil Pollard worked for the ferry and was susceptible to older women, he was an unknown quantity.

All of this pointed only to the fact that they were woefully short on motives. Before closing her laptop, Janet typed four more questions into the cloud. *Was Una killed because she was in the shed? Because of ad-*

vice she gave (and/or the way she gave it)? Because of something in one of the letters? Who had opportunity?

There was one question bothering her that she didn't add to the cloud—could their infant partnership withstand the stress of looking for a murderer? She knew Tallie and Christine and was sure of them. But after arguing with Summer on the way home from Nev's, she felt less sure of her. Were the arguments a sign of the tension Una had asked about? How much tension could they take? The arguments hadn't been terrible. But any cracks appearing in the foundation of their partnership should be cause for concern, and tended to. There was too much at stake for all of them, financially and emotionally, to do otherwise.

Janet listened for any sound of Tallie or Summer stirring in their rooms. Hearing none, she went back to the window to reboot her morning.

"IT'S ABOUT TIME you came down," Tallie said. "We've been up and doing for more than an hour. Summer made scones."

Telling her about the scones hadn't been necessary. Janet had knocked on their doors, thinking she was waking them from a sound sleep, and then smelled the scones as soon as she'd hit the stairs. She'd followed the heavenly scent to the freshly painted tearoom, where she'd found Tallie and Summer and a table set for three with the scones and a pot of tea. Summer smiled as she poured Janet a cup.

"I'm glad to see your smile this morning," Janet said,

"and overjoyed to see the scones." She took an appreciative sniff of the pastry Tallie put on her plate.

"Test-driving the kitchen might as well start today," Summer said. "Plus, it occurred to me that we should've searched it after Rosie found the envelopes. We came down to do that."

Janet looked toward the kitchen.

"We didn't find anything," Tallie said. "So we walked to Paudel's and bought ingredients."

"When we told Basant we were making scones, he printed off three recipes." Summer pushed them across the table. "I started with the classic. I'll branch out from there."

"How did the kitchen test-drive?" Janet asked.

"I need to spend more time in it," Summer said. "Do some production baking. Get Christine in there, too, so we get used to moving around each other, but I think it's going to work. We should be ready in time for an inspection and then a soft opening before the lit fest. But I'd like to hire out for a deep cleaning."

"That makes sense."

"I thought so," Tallie said. "So I called Cosy Cleaners."

"Oh, very good," Janet said. "And you asked about Jess's cancellation?"

"Yeah, but I don't know why I thought we'd get a different answer than Jess did. As far as they're concerned, Jess called and cancelled. They're coming to clean the tearoom; otherwise, it's a dead end."

"I wish you wouldn't say dead end, dear."

IAN ATKINSON, IN A tweed jacket complete with suede elbow patches, graced Yon Bonnie Books with a visit that morning. His presence didn't cause a minor stir with the browsing customers. Whether he'd hoped it would, Janet couldn't tell. It didn't cause a stir among the staff, either. Janet was the only one who saw him come in. Christine and Summer were working in the tearoom, door closed so no one thought they were open for business. Tallie had just come from the tearoom and was offering tea and scones to Mrs. Tiggy-Winkle. Janet had wanted to watch the old woman's reaction, but instead she greeted Ian. For another customer, she might have come out from behind the sales desk, but after her experience the day before, she decided she liked the desk as a bulwark between them.

"Good to see you, Ian."

"You're kind to say so. I've come to apologize for my abominable behavior yesterday." He stopped short of the desk by five or six feet and cast a few glances over his shoulders. No one had come to gawk.

"You apologized yesterday. It's fine. Water under the bridge."

"I've also come to apologize on Lauren's behalf. She's been under tremendous stress lately." He'd moved closer and lowered his voice to a level of grave concern.

"Thank you. She was certainly very upset. How is she doing?"

"I should probably phone her and find out, shouldn't I?"

"You mean you haven't? Does she know you're here?"

"No, but I feel I can speak for her, as her neighbor of several years, as a friend. I was by way of being a mentor to Neil, her husband. He's a young man who dreams of writing. How could I not?"

"How indeed?" Janet looked for Tallie. She was reaching another knitting book down for Mrs. Tiggy-Winkle. They really should think about moving all those books down a few shelves. A young man approached the desk and stood to one side. "Ian?" Janet said, indicating the customer.

"Please, go right ahead." Ian waved the customer forward. "I'll take myself on a browsing tour, shall I?"

Janet rang up a book of Wodehouse short stories for the man, and then rang up the knitting book for Mrs. Tiggy-Winkle.

"Did you enjoy the tea?" Janet asked.

The woman smiled and nodded, took her change, and went back to her chair.

"She had a sip of tea," Tallie said quietly, "but she wrapped the scone in the napkin and put it in her purse."

"Did she say anything?"

Tallie shook her head; her thumbs were busy with a text. "I was going to hang out with Summer and Christine for a while," she said when she'd put the phone away, "but when I saw our friend, I decided to stay. I let the kitchen help know, though, in case they want to come out and gawk."

Ian strolled down an aisle toward the desk, hands in his pockets, and did a double take that wasn't quite believable. He'd found his books and rocked on his heels as he looked at them. He took four from the shelf and brought them to the desk—two copies of *The Bludgeon in the Bothy* and two of an earlier title that hadn't sold as well, *The Halberd in the Hostel.*

"Nice to see you again, Tallie."

"Glad you stopped in."

"I am, too. It's such a delightfully cozy atmosphere you've got going on here, right down to the plump old dear with her tea and knitting. Do you have a cat or two nestled somewhere to complete the picture?"

Janet thought his remarks made him sound like the cat. Then she regretted that thought; it maligned cats. She brought his stack of books closer to the cash register. "Will this be cash or credit?"

"Sorry? No, my mistake. I'm not buying. I wondered if you'd like me to sign them."

"Oh. But yes, of course. That'll be great. Do you need a pen?" But he'd pulled one from his breast pocket. Janet picked up one of the books and flipped it over to read the back. She glanced between the book and Ian; it appeared he was wearing the same tweed jacket. Not that there was anything wrong with that; it was a good-looking jacket. She handed the book to him after he'd signed the others. "Are you working on a new novel?"

"That's what I keep telling myself." He looked up with a chuckle. "I'd rather not talk about it, though. Chases the muse away."

"Don't let that happen," Tallie said. "Quick question, though, Ian, just to be clear. Sharon said something that made us think you might not be okay with an extra person on the committee."

"You do realize that wasn't a question, don't you? But to answer it anyway, the ways of Sharon Davis are strange and sometimes tedious. I'm perfectly fine with any number of people being on the committee."

"Good."

"Then as long as we're clearing the air," Janet said, "and because we're going to be next-door neighbors, I'd just like to say that we heard about your failed bid on this property, and we hope there are no hard feelings."

"Hard feelings?" Ian looked at her with a narrowed eye. "What exactly was your role in that debacle? Were you working in the background with Una?"

"What? No." Janet stepped back. Tallie was immediately beside her.

TWENTY-THREE

"Poor joke." Ian raised his hands. "Really, just a bad joke. I warned you yesterday about my regrettable sense of humor."

He backed away from the desk, his hands still raised. Janet knew it might be contrition, but his backing away also made room for several customers. By the time she and Tallie had rung up the purchases, her heart had calmed down, and Ian's hands were back in his pockets.

"To make up for my poor taste and bad judgment, would you like to hear my own theory for the origin of the name Inversgail? It involves whisky, which I had such high hopes of distilling in this very room."

"Sure," Janet said, not sure at all.

"The debate is quite fascinating, in terms of the literary festival and for me as a scribbler and true lover of whisky—the water of life."

"Um, sorry." Tallie waved to catch Ian's attention. "I'm just going to help—" She pointed down an aisle he couldn't see from where he stood—or he would have seen there wasn't anyone who needed her help—and she weaseled away.

Janet watched her daughter go and planned the sour look she would give her later. As soon as she glanced back at Ian, he started in again.

"I'm sure you've been a good little incomer and read the tourist bureau brochures, yes? Well, you can forget all that havering on about 'river mouth' and 'confluence of waters,' and the Sgail, Skail, Sgeul schools of nonsense. My own theory does account for the importance of stories in this, the storytelling capital of Scotland, and the flowing of our little river, but more importantly, my theory takes into account that other great product of our region. Are you ready?"

Janet could hardly wait.

"When whisky flows, so do the stories."

"Ah."

"Short and perfect, don't you think?" Ian asked. "I'm toying with the idea of using it as the slogan for my Inversgail Distillery." He framed the name with his hands.

"Very catchy," Christine said, coming up behind him and catching him by surprise with a hand clapped on his shoulder. "Christine Robertson. Pleased to meet you. And this is Summer Jacobs. We're the tearoom half of this operation. Open for business in about a fortnight."

Tallie slipped in beside Janet behind the desk again. "Fetched emergency backup," she whispered. "In case of terminal bloviating."

Janet turned thankful eyes on her daughter. Ian only had eyes for Summer.

"Janet," he said without taking his gaze from Summer, "did I tell you what I was doing Monday? Why I didn't see anything going on next door? I was out at my bothy, getting it ready to put on the market. I wish I *had* seen something that could clear up that terrible crime." He heaved a sigh in Summer's direction. "Have I told you about my bothy?"

"What's a bothy?" Summer asked.

"It's actually an old croft house," Ian said, "and not your traditional bothy for ploughboys and whatnot. I bought it as a writing retreat, and it served its purpose well."

"Cool. Where is it?"

"Out in the heather-covered hills." Ian maneuvered so he could lean artfully against the end of one of the taller bookcases. "Even cooler, I could tell the place had been used by someone making illicit whisky. That was the spark my imagination needed. I blew on the spark and came up with the idea for my Single Malt Mysteries. So the bothy is where my muse and I got together, as it were, and my first best-selling thriller was born."

"A place with a storied past, then," Christine said.

"Ha-ha! Yes, exactly. I say, if any of you are interested," he said directly to Summer, "would you like to see the place? The view is divine."

Summer looked over at Janet and Tallie and shrugged. "Sure. It'd be nice to take a walk in the hills, and I've never seen a traditional croft house."

"You understand it's quite rustic."

"But charming, I'm sure," Summer said.

"Absolutely," said Ian. "Completely full of the old R and R—rusticity and romance."

"But by rustic, you mean no plumbing; isn't that correct?" Christine asked.

"Sadly, that is one of the drawbacks, and one of the reasons I'm looking to sell. But it's a gorgeous location up there in the hills. What do you say—one evening, before the gloaming sets in, will you come with me?"

After Ian left, the other three women told Summer that under no circumstances was she to go to the bothy alone. Tallie and Janet, however, said they wouldn't mind seeing it, too. Christine wasn't interested. It was bound to be surrounded by sheep.

Norman Hobbs stopped in soon after Ian departed. He'd stopped in and made a solemn circuit of the shop each day since the murder, and Janet wondered if they'd become part of his patrol. *But if so, why? Because of the case? Because the Lawries are no longer here? Because Rab MacGregor so often is? Should we be more worried about the threat from the garbage—whatever it is? Or is he here today because he's been keeping an eye on Ian? So many possibilities.*

"Oh, you're buying a book?" Janet said. That possibility hadn't occurred to her.

"My youngest niece, who gave me the pink princess notebook, is having her own birthday." Hobbs handed her his credit card and a copy of *The Pink Princess Cookbook*. "I thought I should return the favor."

"A perfect choice," Janet said. "She's a very lucky girl. Does she live here in Inversgail?"

"Inverness."

"If she ever visits, you should bring her in for tea." She completed the sale, slipped the book into a bag, and handed it to him. "Any word yet on the house?"

"I'll be sure to tell you as soon as it becomes available."

"I HAVE A PROPOSAL," Tallie said as Christine locked the door behind the last customer that afternoon. "As long as two of us are reading contest entries, and acting as one judge, why don't all four of us read them? This is a lot to churn through. We'll still act as one judge, but this will spread the joy."

"Oh, joy," Christine said. She eyed the manuscripts Tallie held. "If we're dividing them by category rather than weight, I'll go for the poetry."

"We did quite a bit of the poetry already, but here's the rest." Tallie set the stack on the desk, took a good two inches from the top, and handed the pages to a gaping Christine.

"I might back out," Christine said. "Honestly, there are this many poets in the area? Where did they all come from?"

"Most of those are Skye-ku," Janet said, "but your critical eye will flatline if you try to read and rate all of them. Why don't we each take some from each category, so we don't bog down? Pick your favorites from each category and we'll go from there. And unless anyone else wants to read the novels, I'll keep those as punishment for getting us into this."

"I'm game for a novel," Christine said. She subdivided the stack of poetry, and then leafed through the chunk she'd kept for herself. "Good heavens. Who knew there were so many ways to talk about hills, heather, and rain in seventeen syllables? Here's one with a water horse, though. I'll read these to Mum and Dad. They'll enjoy them."

"I don't mind taking a novel, either," Summer said.

She sat on the high stool behind the sales desk, already drawn into the first manuscript in the stack Tallie had handed her. "I'm glad to see they have a creative nonfiction category, but—" She looked up. "There's an introduction to this one and it's kind of disturbing. The essay's called 'Ferry Boat,' and it goes on to talk about working the boats between the islands, but listen to this. 'Lose hold and you sink, and you know that the only way to save yourself is by grabbing the outstretched hand of your rescuer and pulling. Pull, man, pull yourself from the depths, but always know there's a very real possibility you'll unbalance your rescuer, and she's the one who'll lose hold and sink into the violence below.' I'm not really sure what that means, but—"

"But it's not your typical boat ride to Mull," Christine said.

"Neil Pollard works for CalMac, doesn't he?" Tallie asked.

"Ian said he's been mentoring him," Janet said. "How disturbing is it, Summer? Enough to call Norman?"

"Or are we jumping at shadows at this point?" Tallie asked.

"And losing perspective," Summer said. "Call the police? Really? I only said it was kind of disturbing. And you'd call Hobbs about this, but not about the letters? Think about it. This essay was written and turned in weeks ago. Weeks before Una was killed. It isn't a blueprint for murder. Or a confession."

"I'm only trying to think things through in my own stumbling, bumbling way," Janet said. "I didn't mean to upset you."

"Yeah, well, it's been a long day."

"You don't have to make it longer by reading those if you don't want to."

"No. It's fine. I said I would." Summer stood up. "But I'm going to do it quietly, alone, in my room."

After she left, Janet looked at the others. "Did it sound like I was calling it a blueprint?"

"Don't worry about Summer, Mom. I'll check on her later. But yeah, you kind of did."

Christine put her arm around Janet. "But that's all right, because we're all wondering if it might be."

CURTIS THE RAT finally got back in touch that evening. Janet thought she handled his call well for someone prone to stumbling and bumbling. She listened through his apologies—*there hasn't been a good time; my new in-laws were visiting.* She didn't ask leading questions, and she kept her voice steady and under control. Mostly.

"This is so difficult, Janet."

"Go on."

"I had an affair. In Inversgail. With a young woman named Emma."

"Go on."

"There was a child."

"Was?"

"Is. I've been paying for it. I mean, I've been paying child support."

"Emma?"

"Do you know her?" He sounded…eager.

Janet gave in to a moment of being human and vindictive. "Which Emma are you talking about, Curtis?

There are so many of them around these days, for all I know you've had more than one."

Curtis didn't say anything right away. She waited.

"Emma Graham."

Janet's words and voice were back in check. "Emma Graham?"

"Do you know where she is?"

"You don't?"

"I've lost track of her," he said. "And the child. A girl. Her name is Lucy."

"But you're sending support. How does that work?"

"She wanted nothing to do with me. I don't know where she is. Or the child."

"Lucy. Her name is Lucy, not 'the child.'"

"I made arrangements through Lucy's grandmother."

"Her name. The grandmother's name."

"Una Graham. Janet, do you remember when we'd read the paper and laugh and the jokes we heard wondering whether or not she was a real person? Well, she is."

"Not anymore."

TWENTY-FOUR

JANET WANTED TO scream at Curtis. She didn't. But she did give in to the urge to tell him Una's murder was entirely his fault for buying the horrible garden shed. Then, because she'd been reading so much bad poetry for the literary contest, she told him, "That wasn't fair, but I don't care," and then she hung up and turned off her phone. It gave her a wonderful feeling of release. She turned the phone on again to quickly text Christine the details of the rat's perfidy, then turned it off again, and she slept better than she had for days. At one point, she thought she heard Tallie come to the door and call softly, but then she was surrounded by selkies singing lullabies and she drifted back out to sea in a teacup.

The next morning she once again felt mature and turned the phone back on. And found a commiserative text from Christine. And another from Tallie. She sat up in bed. There was a soft rap on the door and Tallie came in.

"I was listening for the bedsprings. When Dad couldn't get hold of you last night, he called me."

"He told you?"

"And I told him that he isn't to call and ask you to forgive him. That you might offer it, but it isn't his to ask."

"Will you forgive him?"

"He didn't ask and I didn't offer. Someday I probably will. He said he would call Allen, too."

"Let's call Allen ourselves."

Allen answered with a quick hello; then Janet pulled the phone from her ear as he spoke firmly and loudly to Freddy, telling him to return the Marmite to the counter and leave the cat alone.

"Sorry," he said, "trying to get them organized and out the door. Mom, Dad called last night."

"One more thing to rock your world."

"I'll deal with it. How are you, though? How's Tallie? I want to make sure you're okay."

"We're okay." She looked at Tallie, who nodded. "We are. I am. And I'll continue to be." She disconnected with smooches and hugs for all of them, and realized she really was okay. Curtis and his messy affairs were something separate from her now. *Maybe I'm compartmentalizing my problems,* she thought, *but it works. I am putting this one on a shelf with the other discards going to the used-problem sale. I don't need it anymore and good riddance.*

Janet shrugged into her bathrobe and went to look out the window. Not a clear day. Swathes of rain-heavy clouds moving in. "Interesting that no one we've talked to has mentioned a granddaughter."

"No one in Inversgail seems to know much about Emma. I'll see what I can find." Tallie joined Janet at the window. She looked out, looked at Janet, the windowsill, out the window again. Janet recognized it as a regression to childhood habit—vacillating over an awkward question.

"Did you want to read the letter?"

"If you don't mind."

"I've been carrying it around in my back pocket. I like the symbolism of asking him to kiss my—well, never mind about that. The trousers are on the back of the chair."

Tallie took the letter from Janet's pocket and read it, her left eye narrowing as she did.

"He said he'd lost track of Emma," Janet said, "so my guess is that Una wrote that. The rest of the letters, too. It all fits. She carried grudges, she looked for the tension in situations, she invented letters for her column, and in her own, odd way, she saw herself as helping people with their problems."

Tallie continued staring at the letter.

"I'll add this bit to the cloud," Janet said. "It clears up who Emma is, at least. I wonder if she really emigrated?"

"I wonder how she and Una got along? I can imagine a few scenarios where a child could want to kill."

JANET ASKED THE others to meet with her an hour before the bookshop was due to open. They sat in the chairs near the fireplace. She told them she didn't want anyone dancing around her because of the letter and the situation with Curtis.

"Please don't think of it as an awkward situation," she said.

"You're a better woman than I would be," Christine said.

"Nope. Just one who's moved on in more ways than

one. I'll call Norman Hobbs and give him the letters. Thank you, Summer, for not saying, 'I told you so.' By keeping them, we've lost Norman valuable time with them. We, on the other hand, have been asking questions and turning over theories about them, and maybe *those* can help him. So I'd like us to go over our theories and questions, type them up, and give him the letters and our theories."

"I've got my tablet," Summer said. "I'll type. He can have a printout if he wants, or I can send it."

"Thank you. Okay, the situation with Curtis gave us another piece of information, so let's see how it changes things. It seems likely, now, that the letters are Una's. And if that's true, then it seems less likely that Jess was the target and Una was killed by mistake."

"That never seemed likely, anyway," Tallie said. "Or that was a really inept killer who gave up after that one mistake."

"Kind of like us," Janet said. "A stumbling, bumbling amateur." That earned a smile from Summer, and Janet was glad for that smile's resilience.

"I wonder if we could just ask one of the people the letters are written to if they've ever gotten a nasty letter from Una," Summer said.

"Which one?" Christine asked. "The least dangerous looking? No, I still think we need to sit Rab down and sweat him until he coughs up what he knows about the letters. Because maybe he doesn't just know about them; maybe they're his."

"Um, Christine?" Tallie waited, scratching her ear until Christine snapped at her.

"What?"

"Speaking as someone who doesn't want to end up as your lawyer, let's avoid strong-arm tactics."

"I was being colorful. I'll tone it down. But I still like the idea that the letters are his. Janet, your theory for how he floats through life, bumping up against people and places and collecting bits and pieces of information, could explain the letters and how they're constructed. They're an accumulation. He accumulates."

"That was true of Una, too," Summer said. "But instead of placid floating, she was more like Muhammad Ali—stinging like a bee."

"And Rab doesn't strike me as the kind of guy who has a beef with anyone," Tallie said.

"Because he puts his beefs in the letters," Christine said, "and goes about his placid way. Maybe he's creative about it, too. He wrote each one to a different person, so maybe each one is 'from' a different person. I'm just brainstorming here, but think about it. How does he manage to make a living doing...whatever it is he does? Maybe he has a vast web of intrigue and blackmail spread throughout Inversgail."

"That's so..." Janet wondered if she should be worried about her old friend.

"Why do you have it in for Rab?" Summer asked. "He seems so gentle."

Janet, Tallie, and Summer regarded Christine—whose brows and lips were as contorted as the hands wringing in her lap.

"Because if the letters are Una's, I hope you both realize"—the hands stopped worrying each other for a moment and one pled with Janet and the other with Tallie—"then we have to consider Curtis a suspect. You've been phoning his mobile, Janet. How do you know you've been phoning him in Illinois? Or he might be back there now, but where was he Monday night?"

"Is *that* all you're worried about?" Janet said.

"All?" Christine and Tallie both said.

"Unfortunately, he's out of the running. I know for a fact that he hasn't left the States…lately. It seems I inadvertently, and by that I mean with spite aforethought, packed his passport. It's somewhere in the shipping boxes. Possibly at the bottom of the one marked 'open last.'"

Christine closed her eyes. "May I just say that your organizational skills are without compare? All right." She opened her eyes again. "That theory's down the drain. What else have we got? Anything that ties the letters to the murder?"

"Back to the letters-as-therapy idea," Summer said. "What if they were never meant to be delivered or read by anyone else? Curtis knows about his child, but not from the letter. Maybe they were meant to be delivered at the author's death. The author having the last, nasty word."

"That *would* be nasty," Tallie said. "I've heard of nasty video wills, though. So it's possible. And if the letters are Una's, if for whatever reason she put them in the tin, then that's why Rosie found them. Una expected to come back for them, but…didn't."

Christine nodded. "Plausible."

"Here are my questions, though," Tallie said. "What

if we don't have all the letters? What if one or more was delivered at some point? What if someone found them in the recipe box earlier? How would we know if one is missing?"

"Theory," Janet said. "What if the murderer found the letters on Una, read through them, and realized their discovery would direct attention to others? Could that be why they were 'hidden' in the tearoom? What if the murderer left the rest as a nest of red herrings?"

Summer stopped typing. "A *nest* of red herrings? That's an icky image that I don't want in my kitchen cupboards. But to add onto that, if there was a letter to the murderer, of course the murderer took it."

"And again, how would we know?" Tallie asked. "I can think of a lot more questions, too."

"We probably don't need to put down every single question," Janet said.

"No," Christine agreed. "There's no need to boggle Norman's mind. Oh, *bugger*. I've just thought of a work-around for Curtis and his passport. He *hired* someone."

Janet and Tallie laughed. Elizabeth II frowned at their hilarity.

"Oh, Christine, I know you'd like him to spend time in jail, for my sake," Janet said. "But no. He couldn't have done that. Curtis never balanced the checkbook. He never did his own taxes. He was incapable of filing insurance forms. Putting out a contract on Una would be way beyond his ability to plan something and then carry it through."

"Plus that would be an awfully up-close-and-personal way to make a hit," Tallie said. "I think we're looking for someone who was out for personal revenge or who felt an imminent and very personal threat." She looked at her phone. "Almost time to open."

"I'll call Norman," Janet said.

"What about the letter to Curtis?" Christine asked. "Do you want to keep it back? I think everyone will understand if you do."

"Absolutely," Summer said.

"No."

"What about Christine's suggestion that he might be guilty?" Summer asked. "Shall I keep it in the notes? I can delete it."

"Keep it. Not because I want him to twist—any more than I've already enjoyed watching him twist—but because it's bad enough that I didn't turn the letters over immediately, and we do want the murderer caught."

CONSTABLE HOBBS FOLLOWED Janet and Christine into the tearoom, looking much like one of the lowering clouds Janet had seen out her window that morning. He brightened briefly, as the morning had, when he took in the new paint job. But like the day, his dour look returned when they showed him the cupboard, the recipe tin, and the handful of envelopes.

"Rab MacGregor was reading tea leaves," Hobbs said, "and Rosie Crozier had a psychic episode. And you say that you opened and read these letters. All of you."

"Minus Rab and Rosie," Janet said.

"And as I'm sure you would have, Norman," Christine said, "had you found anything so unusual in your kitchen cupboard. But whilst these letters were in our care, we had time to consider and discuss the possible reasons and…" Christine hesitated and looked to Janet.

"Ramifications."

"Thank you, Janet, yes. And we formed various theories. We've made note of them here." She handed him one of the pages Summer had printed out. "And here is a separate page with some rather good questions which might trigger thoughts of your own."

"You seemed to appreciate our notes last time," Janet said, hoping to see a lightening of Hobbs's spirits.

"Thank you," said Hobbs, not perceptibly lighter. He put the papers on the counter, folded them into meticulous thirds, in half again, and tucked them in his pocket behind his pink notebook.

"We think we know who most of the letters were written to," Janet said. "That should save you some time—that I know I wasted for you, and I'm so sorry about that. One of them is to my ex-husband, Curtis. It's all in the notes, but did you know that Una has a granddaughter?"

Hobbs made no comment but took his pink notebook from his pocket.

"But we'd be happy for any input or insight from you on the identity of the others," Christine said. "For instance, do you know who a Moira, an Agnes, or a Tristan might be?"

"I have no comment at the moment, Mrs. Robertson." Neither did he write anything in his notebook.

"Of course, you can read our thoroughly thought-out theories at your leisure," Christine said, "but the big questions remain. Did Una leave the letters here, and if she did, why?"

Hobbs remained silent. Possibly contemplative, but silent.

Janet felt worse and worse that she hadn't turned the letters over to the police immediately. She also felt this meeting wasn't going as well as it might. Christine was doing a fine job, but her own contributions were paltry. Surely there was some part of discovering the letters or a detail from the interview with Una she could recall to redeem herself. And then, in a flash of remembrance and inspiration, she surprised Christine and Constable Hobbs—as well as herself—by breaking into song. "The texts, the texts are calling me."

"Janet?" Christine asked. "Are you ill?"

"That's what Una did just before she left here Monday afternoon. She looked at her phone, and to the tune of 'Danny Boy,' she sang about texts calling her. That's why she left. Norman, do you know who sent the texts?"

"I have no comment at this time."

"But the police do know about the texts?"

"They do, Mrs. Marsh. Looking at texts and phone messages is part of what police do. That's the kind of thing that police do in a timely investigation."

"Then you must have a suspect," Janet said.

Rather than answer, Hobbs asked another question. "How did she react to the texts?"

"She ended the interview. Prematurely, I thought. She looked around the kitchen, acting like a victim of advanced ADHD. I didn't actually see that, though. Summer brought her in here and I stayed out there.

She was getting on my nerves by then. It sounded like she opened and closed every cupboard and drawer. She never stopped talking. She turned on the water and left it running. But it was all misdirection, wasn't it? So she could leave the letters. Finding the tin was probably a bonus. Now it's your turn, Constable. What do you know about the texts?"

"I have no comment at this time."

"Well, you're making it very hard for us to help you."

"Information from an ongoing investigation is not always mine to give, Mrs. Marsh. But I can tell you this. Mrs. Graham received more than one text Monday afternoon, and those texts came from more than one person."

Janet's hand flew to her heart. "It was a *gang*? Oh. No. I see what you mean. If they'd all come from one person, it might have been like a giant red arrow trailing a banner that said 'Number One Suspect.'"

"If the murderer even sent her a text," Hobbs said. "Wouldn't it be nice if things were that easy?"

Janet glanced at Christine. She appeared to be deep in thought, running the tips of her fingers over her lips. But Hobbs's mood had improved, and Janet was encouraged.

"I see your point, that this isn't exactly an information-sharing session, Norman."

"I'm glad you understand. I find it's often the case between local and specialist police, as well."

"That's just so silly and it's one of the reasons we're trying to help. Well, that and to get the specialists out of my house. But that's some of the information they're not sharing. Irritating people. We saw Reddick in Nev's the other night."

"He's a decent chap. Does his best. I'll pass the letters along to him as from an anonymous source. Keep you and the bookshop out of it."

"Thank you. That's very kind."

"Not kind, but with all the commotion in here, painters, baking, and whatnot, and with the four of you passing the letters around, there won't be any useful prints or evidence left."

Hobbs and Janet both sighed. Christine was still far away.

"Here's something that might help, then," Janet said. "I met Lauren Pollard Wednesday. She's the young woman who was renting my house."

"I'm aware of Mrs. Pollard."

"This was at the library. She was upset. Upset to the point where I could picture her being violent. She said Una broke up her marriage by seducing her husband. She said she wished she'd never set foot in the house and Una turned her life into a hell. I felt terrible for her. It was disturbing."

"I imagine it was."

"Ian Atkinson was there and he calmed her down. But she could be the one who dumped the garbage—literally trashing the house. And no one would think twice about seeing Lauren or Neil there. Motive and opportunity. It made me wonder, have the police looked carefully at the Pollards?"

"Alibis."

"What?"

"They both have alibis for Monday afternoon."

"*What* alibis, Norman?" Christine asked, back and invigorated from her thoughts.

"Solid alibis. A private matter."

Tallie knocked on the door frame, interrupting a nose-to-nose confrontation between the constable and the queen.

"Do you need me?" Janet asked.

"No, it's quiet out there. But while it is, and while Constable Hobbs is still here, I've got a couple of quick questions, if it's okay?"

Hobbes turned to Tallie with a wary smile. Her warmer one didn't prompt his to let down its guard.

"The night of the murder," she said, "after telling us that Jess wasn't guilty, there was something else you didn't think we should hear. Can you tell us now?"

"I have no comment to make."

"But there is something?"

Hobbs remained silent.

Tallie nodded. "Okay, moving on, we have another mystery." She told him about their frequent knitter, leaving out the name Mrs. Tiggy-Winkle. "We aren't even sure if she speaks much English. Maybe Gaelic? Anyway, we haven't found anyone who knows who she is. Do you?"

"You've been asking around?" Hobbs said.

"Out of curiosity."

"Is she bothering you or other customers?"

"Not at all. We like her. In fact...we've been thinking of her as Mrs. Tiggy-Winkle."

"A hedgehog. I see. Well, if the hedgehog isn't bothering anyone, then my advice is to leave it well alone. I'll go out the back door, shall I, and make sure the area behind is free of vandals. Good day."

"I think he has a soft spot for hedgehogs," Janet said after Hobbs closed the tearoom's back door.

"Who doesn't?" Tallie said. "But I want to know what he doesn't want us to hear."

"I think I know one thing Norman doesn't want us to hear," Christine said. "And you provided the clue, Janet. One of Una's Monday afternoon texts must have come from Danny at Nev's."

TWENTY-FIVE

Mrs. Tiggy-Winkle added a bright spot to the bookshop that Friday morning—literally, as the skeins she took from her carrier bag were neon shades of purple, blue, and green. Brisk business kept Janet and Tallie at the desk or in the aisles helping customers, an excellent problem to have. But it meant Janet caught only glimpses of the knitting and she couldn't figure out what the yarn was turning into. Christine and Summer were perfecting their choreography in the kitchen and making noses lift in the bookshop as the warm smell of shortbread slipped under the tearoom door. Tallie slipped into the kitchen during a lull and brought tea and a shortbread petticoat to Mrs. Tiggy-Winkle.

"Still can't tell what it is," she told Janet as they traded places at the cash register. "And she wrapped the shortbread and put it in her bag. Maybe there's a Mr. T-W at home."

"It looked like a sleeve and then it didn't."

"It might not look like what it is until it's closer to being finished."

"That might be how this case turns out, too." Janet bounced a pencil on its eraser and then pointed it at Tallie. "We haven't asked Rab or Basant if they know who she is. One of them is bound to."

"Or the Lawries? They just passed the window. Maybe they're stopping...and yes, here they are."

Janet looked at the door in time to see a transformation. At the moment they reached the door, Pamela and Kenneth glowered. When the bell chimed as they came through, their personal clouds lifted and gapped teeth shone. However briefly.

"So nice to see you," Janet said.

Kenneth's smile disappeared. "I'm surprised you're able to say that."

Janet glanced at Tallie. She appeared to be frozen to the spot, but calm. Janet hoped she looked calm, too.

"What he means," Pamela said, "is that we had a misunderstanding. About the week of our time we were giving you. Kenneth thought you'd told us we weren't needed, and that's why we haven't been coming in."

"It's what you told me," Kenneth ground out between his teeth.

"I never did," Pamela said. "There, you can see he feels badly."

"I do," Kenneth said. "But here's your first weekend in the shop coming up, and if you'd like extra help, you've only to ask. Or if you have any questions."

"One question." Janet motioned them closer. "Do you know who that woman is?"

"Can't say I've ever seen her before," Pamela said.

"No, not familiar," Kenneth said. "So would you like us to come in tomorrow?"

"I—" Janet looked at Tallie, who shrugged. "I think we really will be all right."

"Aye. Right, then. Phone if you change your mind.

One more thing, though. I left a length of tartan in the office. Do you mind if I get it?"

"Oh, dear. We thought—"

"Christine has it," Tallie said.

"Why?"

"Another misunderstanding, I think," Janet said. "We'll see that it's returned."

"Thank you," Pamela said. "He isn't happy I forgot it. It's nothing to worry about, though. It's not, Kenneth."

The two left, glowers firmly back in place.

TALLIE HAD LUCK in one of her searches that morning. She found an Emma Graham online, with references to Scotland in her profile and sympathy expressed over the recent death of her mother. From there, she found Emma's sibling—Tristan—and evidence that he and Emma had immigrated to Australia. Tristan left first, seven years earlier. Emma followed a year later.

"Why couldn't Norman just tell us that?" Janet asked.

"Because there was no good reason to. Once I had Emma's name, it was easy enough to find them. But Hobbs has to worry about privacy issues whenever he tells us anything."

They rang up one of the signed copies of *The Halberd in the Hostel* and answered questions about the smell of baking.

"There's no record of a child traveling with Emma," Tallie said, "and I can't find Lucy in the local schools. And I looked, but I didn't find a death notice for her. I didn't know that would make me so emotional."

Janet held her daughter for a moment, and then told her to go sit near Mrs. T-W and read.

"Are you sure?"

"I'll get my break when I go with Summer to the *Guardian* this afternoon. But if you're feeling guilty, read contest entries."

"Oh, goody."

A SHORT WHILE LATER, Janet saw Tallie searching the shelves in the folk and fairy-tale section. She came back to the desk, holding pages of contest entries under her arm and paging through a fat paperback of traditional travelers' tales.

"I thought I'd heard this or read it before," she said, taking the manuscript pages from under her arm and putting them on the desk. "This is a short story called, 'Blind, but Now I See,' and here's 'The Wily Auld Carle.' It's a murder ballad about a woman who wants to kill her husband but ends up being outwitted by him. It's supposed to be a comedy."

"Told the other way around, it might be," Janet said.

"So is there a rule in the contest about fairly transparent retellings? There's no author's note with the entry to say where the story came from."

"I'll ask Sharon."

JANET HAD WORRIED that Summer would find an excuse for going to the *Inversgail Guardian* alone that afternoon for her first day as the new gossip columnist. True, Summer was the one who'd voiced the rule about none of them traveling alone, but in practice it had the awkwardness of walking a grown child to school. *And there's the awkwardness over the arguments after Nev's and that dreadful contest entry...*

"Did Christine tell you that the Pollards are completely in the clear?" Janet asked as they walked toward Paudel's to pick up something for lunch along the way.

"I scratched them off the great suspect list in the cloud."

Did that really merit sarcasm? If we're like this before the first week is out, we'll soon be at an end. "Summer—"

"Do you know what bugs the snot of out of me?" Summer stopped short, crossing her arms and looking anywhere but at Janet. "I was right there. In the kitchen. Watching her. And I didn't see her put those envelopes in the tin. Not in the tin, not in the cupboard."

"It's still possible it was someone else."

"That's not what I'm saying. I'm agreeing. I think it *was* Una. But what kind of observant reporter am I, that I missed her playing that shell game? She totally snowed me and it's been making me pissy and pick at everything."

"Don't be so hard on yourself. Una seems to have been an expert at games like that."

They went into Paudel's and each picked out a meat pie. Janet asked Basant to add a small bag of sweets to the order.

"What kind?" he asked.

"Surprise us," she said, and while he wrapped the pies and then studied the jars of candy, Janet described their frequent knitter. "Any idea who she is?"

"She rings no bells," he said over his shoulder. "But is she a comforting presence?"

"Yes, I guess you could say that."

"More comforting than the rats we spoke of, anyway. And she comes to your bookshop, to your hearth, so she is clearly wise. I think she must be good luck." He handed the meat pies to Summer and the bag of sweets to Janet. "Pink and white sugar mice. They bring better luck than rats."

THE NEWSROOM FOR the *Inversgail Guardian* was bigger than it needed to be. The paper probably hadn't ever needed an entire fleet of desks and clattering typewriters, but the room Janet and Summer walked into looked almost abandoned, and they heard the hushed pattering of only a few keyboards.

"They sound like the ghosts of newsrooms past," Summer said.

"It smells like the dust of newsrooms past, too," said Janet.

James Haviland greeted Janet cordially and accepted curiosity as her reason for being there with Summer. To demonstrate her curiosity, she asked him how his ankle was and then why he was sometimes called Scotty.

"On the mend for the ankle, and insider's joke for the name. I had the great good fortune to intern at the *New York Times*, thirty-five years ago. I came home to this job with a love for kosher pickles and a personally autographed picture of James 'Scotty' Reston, patron saint of the *Times*. It's on my desk, pride of place. Haven't had a good garlic dill since."

He didn't introduce them to the other two people in the room—a man typing and a woman staring at the ceiling. Neither the man nor the woman seemed to expect him to. *Which no doubt accounts for why he doesn't know the names of Una's children,* Janet thought. He took them across the room to Una's desk—wooden, two sets of file drawers, cigarette burns. It faced the wall. She'd taped a variety of quotations to the wall over the desk, arranged in a circle with a single typed line, "Creep up from behind!" in the center.

"I have my patron saint," James said. "She had her motto."

"It's okay if I use her desk?" Summer asked. "I'll have something set up in my flat, eventually, but for now—"

"Free to use. The police have been through it. They had to break the lock. She liked things under lock and key. Part of her persona, she said, because people entrusted her with their deepest, darkest secrets."

"Did the police take anything away with them?" Janet asked.

"Her laptop."

"She had that with her at the bookshop Monday afternoon when she interviewed us. Did she stop back here after that?"

"She must've done."

"You weren't here?"

"Home with the ankle. They took some files and papers, too, but as you can see, they left plenty of, uh, stuff behind."

He took a newspaper from a knee-high stack to the

left of the desk. There was a similar stack flanking the other side of the desk, and Janet leafed through the top several papers in it. They were mostly American papers, some with address labels on them—to libraries and individuals—in Inverness, Fort William, Oban.

"Some of these are decades old," Janet said. "How did she get them?"

"Scrounged, collected, stole—kidding. Mind you, everyone has their ways and their sources. She called these her reference library. She was interested in American news and American crime. She was writing a novel and she said these gave her story verisimilitude. I haven't had the time to bother with clearing them out yet."

"Have any new letters come in for the column?" Summer asked.

"One."

"Is that typical? How did she fill the column?"

"Ah. The eternal question. Mind if I put the ankle up?"

He rolled a chair over from a nearby desk and propped his foot on the nearest stack of newspapers. Janet sat on the other stack, shooing Summer into Una's chair.

"Una loved being called an agony aunt. She believed that role made her a power for good, a voice answering and calming the yowl from the wilderness. Her words, honest to God. And—I'm letting out a trade secret here, so keep in mind the old joke, 'If I tell you, I'll have to kill you—'"

Janet had never seen the color drain from anyone's

face before, but James aged ten years before her eyes. He took his foot from the newspapers, put his elbows on his knees, and leaned his forehead against his steepled fingers.

"That was undeniably the most insensitive thing I've ever said in a long life of not caring what anybody really thinks of me."

"This is going to sound rude," Janet said, "but—"

"Open season," he said into his hands. "Your rude won't measure up to mine."

"How do you know what Una thought of being an agony aunt or that she was writing a novel, and yet you don't know the names of her children?"

"It's the work." He made it sound as though she should have known the answer. "For her, for me, it's always been the work. That goes back to what I was going to say, when I so rudely interrupted myself. She did make up letters for the column. A good portion of gossip columns probably do. But Una's letters were part of her personal crusade to improve people—or to needle them. The woman had a singular ability to hold a grudge. Una—the one, the only. Again, her words."

"Grudges against anyone in particular?" Summer asked. She'd found a pencil and twirled it in her fingers.

James watched the pencil and nodded. "Una never turned off her inner reporter, either. But you're here for the column. I don't need you for a story."

"It's a story that happened in my garden shed," Janet said. "I'm *not* a reporter. But stories have been my life, as a librarian and a bookseller. And this one is having an effect *on* my life."

"Then I wish I could tell you. But Una held a lot of grudges—and new ones every week. You might find something in the desk the police didn't want. Notes for the novel, maybe. It hung around her neck like a millstone, but she was also writing an article about agony aunts. She was always working on something that would be her breakout piece. Now I've taken up enough of your time. And you mine."

"Thank you, James," Janet said.

He didn't answer, and they watched him limp away.

"Do we pretend to be working on the column," Summer asked, "or be honest and do the nosy thing?"

"I think he expects us to be nosy. You take the left side. I'll take the right."

"What are we looking for?"

"Anything like the letters in the tin. Or anything like the novel or the article he mentioned. Any kind of writing that might be considered extracurricular. If the police didn't take it all."

There were two file-size drawers on each side of the desk. Janet took the chair that James had vacated and opened the bottom drawer on her side. She found three pairs of shoes and two umbrellas. The upper drawer held a framework for hanging files, but no files—or none left. "I'm a whiz," she said. "Done on my side. Any luck on yours?"

"Mph."

"I'll do the middle drawer, then." She slid the kneehole drawer open. It held the usual hodgepodge of office supplies, including a stack of envelopes—empty and unused. There were also three books. She took them out and laid them on the desk—*Scottish Ballads*; *Dear Auntie: A Social History of Agonizing Answers*; and *The Claymore in the Cloister,* the first book in Ian Atkinson's Single Malt Mysteries—valuable if it was a first edition.

Janet opened the book to see. First edition, yes, but discarded from the Orkney Public Library and Archive and full of underlining in pen and pencil. *Dear Auntie*'s pages bristled with sticky notes. She opened it to one of the marked pages and found two paragraphs highlighted in pink. There were sentences or paragraphs highlighted on each of the other marked pages as well. It reminded Janet of college days and cramming for exams. The book of ballads, a paperback, had a cracked spine. She picked it up and it opened to "The Wily Auld Carle," the ballad Tallie had recognized as the source for the contest entry she'd read that morning. And now it seemed it was also the source for the quote over Una's desk. The last wry lines of the ballad were, "Eggs, eggs and marrowbone/Will drive your old man blind/But if you wish for to do him in/Creep up from behind!" She glanced over at Summer.

"You're reading the newspaper."

"The *Virginian-Pilot,*" Summer said, "from July 28, 1994. But only part of it. And parts of the other two that were sitting on the desk. And I've just learned that I can save myself a lot of time by writing Una's column the way she did." Summer smacked her hand against the paper.

The woman who'd been staring at the ceiling when they came in had left, but the typing man looked over the top of his glasses at them. Then he went back to typing.

"*Maybe* she made up letters," Summer said, "but she also copied them from old columns in papers from the States. I've been reading her recent columns online, to get the flavor of her answers. They are these exact columns; I'm sure of it."

"Why would she do that?"

"It took almost no time or effort, there was zero chance of being caught because she stole from decades-old columns, it gave her loads of free time to pursue other writing projects, she got paid—take your pick."

"Does he know?" Janet tipped her head toward James's office.

"I don't know. My guess is no. He's a newspaperman. You heard him. It's the work that matters to him. Una might've been a newspaperwoman once, but she was trying to be something else. And this makes it look like she really was something else."

Janet glanced toward the office again. "What if someone found out? What if there's a slippery slope to her plagiarism? Letters, columns, articles, short stories, novels."

"And what would James do if he found out?"

"Or the person she stole from."

TWENTY-SIX

"Phlegmatic," Janet said. It was the first word she or Summer had spoken since leaving the *Inversgail Guardian* office. "I was trying to think of the word for James. It's phlegmatic."

"I'll give that plagiarizing phony some phlegm," Summer said. "*I* feel betrayed and I barely met her. Through all those years at the paper, I reinvented myself every time the newspaper world shifted. Write the community engagement column? Sure, I can do that. And I went to PTA meetings, city council meetings, and every single pancake breakfast and fish fry. Take over the business and finance section? Show me the stock charts and the suits and I'll sip a three-martini lunch with the best of them. And when they moved me to the food column, I couldn't boil an egg without making it explode. But do you know what I did? I played your *why not* game and I asked myself, why not learn to bake cakes instead of burn them? What I *didn't* do was steal someone else's words."

"He's phlegmatic and you're simmering," Janet said.

"I'm boiling bloody mad."

Rab MacGregor was puttering among the bookshelves when Janet and Summer got back to Yon Bonnie Books.

He appeared to be dusting. Possibly rearranging. Janet wondered if they'd gone over a job description of any kind with him. Possibly not. But with Schubert's "Trout Quintet" playing in the background, the shop was an oasis of calm. Mrs. T-W knitted, Christine chatted with a customer and didn't seem bothered that Ranger napped in a chair across from Mrs. T-W's. But Summer still simmered, and she'd told Janet she was going straight to the kitchen to work it off. She steamed straight past Tallie, who greeted Janet with worried eyebrows.

"Trouble?" Tallie asked.

"Developments in the case."

"At this end, too."

Tallie told her she'd found evidence online of Ian Atkinson's rocky relationship with the community. He'd tried to buy another building, before Yon Bonnie Books, and that also fell through. There were rumblings about him suing people. "But last week he made an offer on another building, and so far, so good."

"Is it too soon for anyone to know or protest?" Janet asked.

"Or is it that Una's gone? I found a couple of interesting stories in the *Guardian*, too." The first was a report of Kenneth involved in a loud disagreement outside the Chamberlain's Arms, Nev's apparently going by its formal name in the press. The second was of a road accident that had claimed the life of their daughter, the Lawrie's only child, ten years earlier.

"Heartbreaking," Janet said. "I can't imagine waking up every morning and facing that loss again and again."

"But I can imagine a tragedy like that changing someone. What happened at the paper?"

"Why don't you and Christine go in and let Summer tell you. I'll be fine here. It'll be good for her to spew and I need the nearness of books."

"You're misquoting that, if you're doing *Charlotte's Web*," Tallie said. "It's the nearness of rats."

"Then let's hope the rats aren't nearer than we think."

"I HAVE A couple of questions, when you get a minute, Rab," Janet said.

He set down a stack of books she hadn't expected to see him carrying and came to the desk.

"Do you have any idea who Ranger's friend over there is?"

"Here's the only place I've seen her, and only this week," he said.

"Huh. I was sure you'd know."

"She's got a nice pair of Nessies, though."

"I beg your pardon?"

"What she's knitting. Loch Ness monsters. With fins." He paddled his arms. "Anything else?"

"Two things. We should talk about your hours and the sort of work we expect. And I thought you'd like to know that I gave the letters Rosie found in the kitchen to the police."

"To Norman Hobbs?"

"Yes."

Rab looked thoughtful. He took a small pen and scrap of paper from a back pocket, made a note, and returned them.

"*Do* you know anything about them?" Janet asked.

"Letters unsent." He shook his head. "Never a good sign."

He stepped aside to let her wait on customers. She remained busy. When a lull came, she looked for him so they could discuss his hours and duties, but he and Ranger were gone.

"WE HAVE MOTIVES and possible motives galore," Christine said toward the end of the afternoon. "We need to zero in on opportunity. We eliminated the renters from our pool of suspects because of opportunity. We need to find out who else we can cross off."

"Strictly speaking, we didn't eliminate the Pollards," Janet said. "Norman did and told us later."

"We won't quibble."

Speaking of opportunity, Janet thought. She saw that Mrs. Tiggy-Winkle was packing away her knitting—including a flock of neon blue, purple, and green monsters. The old woman hoisted herself from her chair and steadied her legs. Then she put her carrier bag on her arm, nodded and smiled as she passed the desk, and left.

"Trundles," Christine said. "She actually trundles."

Janet counted to twenty, told Christine she'd be back, and she went out the door, too. The old woman was just going around the corner. Janet followed, but drawing on her vast experience of watching TV detectives tailing their marks, she hung back until she saw the woman turn the next corner into Sculpay Terrace. Then Janet hurried to that corner and looked around it, arriving in time to see the woman get into the passenger side of a car and be driven away.

THE FOUR OF them sat down by the fire again that evening. They each had a miniature quiche, thanks to Summer's need to work off her anger at Una.

"Speaking as a retired social worker," Christine said, "spinach quiche is a much healthier way of dealing with anger and frustration than murder. I'm glad we had the opportunity to give you this delicious outlet. Now, on to the opportunities our suspects had. Which of our suspects had the opportunity to kill Una? In a shed—true—but both Una and the murderer went there in broad daylight."

"Opportunity will tell us a lot," Summer said, "but so will knowing why she was there. And even if we can't get into her mind, we know some of her actions."

"So she could've been looking for Neil Pollard," Tallie said. "Maybe she didn't know they'd moved out."

"That still doesn't explain the shed," Janet said. "'Opportunity' and 'why' come together at the shed. The dreadful shed."

"Possibilities," Christine said. "She was spying on Ian Atkinson. But how could she do that from in the shed? If he didn't see her, she couldn't see him. Next possibilities. She was looking for something. She was leaving something. She was meeting someone. *That* makes the most sense."

"A timeline," Tallie said. "Una was here, she got a text, she walked past Jess Baillie's office, where Rosie saw her—"

"She dropped her laptop at the newspaper office," Summer said. "So why didn't she leave the letters there? The desk locked. They would've been safe there. Safer."

"We're back to the murderer finding the letters on her?" Janet said. "Then we need two opportunities. The murder and planting the letters."

"Here's another way to look at opportunity," Tallie said. "It *was* broad daylight, but it would be good to know how easy it is to move around there without being seen. Want to take a field trip?"

THE FOUR OF them got into Christine's car and stopped first at her house with spinach quiche for her parents' evening tea. Christine told them she would be back later that evening and left as her mother complained loudly to her father about the au pair who spent all her time out clubbing. They then drove to Argyll Terrace.

"But let's park at the corner and walk," Janet said. "We don't know if the police are there or watching it."

"If they're watching it, I would hope they'd notice the four of us creeping up on it," Tallie said.

They parked at the corner anyway.

"This is only the third time I've been here since we arrived in Inver-sgail," Janet said. "And each time the circumstances have been unusual."

"Third time's the charm," Christine said.

"If the murderer is someone with the opportunity to come and go without being remarked, that pretty clearly points to Jess or Ian," Summer said.

"But we don't know who's been coming and going while the Pollards lived here," Tallie said.

"True," said Summer. "I'm keeping an eye out for Ian anyway."

Janet pictured the four of them walking abreast down a dusty, high-noon Argyll Terrace toward her house. In fact, they walked two-by-two on the sidewalk and it was early evening, but her senses were alive to the drama. A bird twittered and then sang in the garden next door. A warbler? She didn't know, but she decided to make sure Yon Bonnie Books carried guides for birders, and maybe some of those book-and-CD sets for identifying birdsongs. She heard a child across the street calling and another laughing.

They stopped and she looked at the front of her house again, at the front door and windows trimmed in the same blue as the sky. She looked at the front garden, not much bigger than a welcome mat, but offering warmth and welcome all the same. A house she loved. Her house.

"I've asked Rab to find more of that blue and touch up the door and trim. It looks fine, though, doesn't it? I've missed it these five years. Jess always put a picture of it in her Christmas cards. That was such a nice touch. It's been like seeing photos of a distant relative."

They went around to the back, as they'd done Monday evening, opening and closing the garden gate with care, then standing for a moment to listen. They went to the bottom of the garden and stared at the shed.

"It's not such a bad-looking shed." Christine tilted her head sideways as if that improved it from "bad" to "not so bad."

"I'd like to burn it," Janet said.

"I'll hand you the match," said Summer.

"It's a quiet neighborhood. Walls around some gardens." Tallie turned in a circle. "Four of us just came in the side gate and didn't cause a hullabaloo. If someone really tried to sneak in, it'd be a cinch. Standing here, I can see Ian's windows." She went to stand at the shed's door. "Now I can't see his house, so he can't see me. And I don't see any windows in the houses around that would have a clear view."

"So the murderer knew that?" Summer asked.

"Or Una did. She might've picked the spot," Tallie said. "Considering Lauren's reaction to the house, Neil and Una probably—"

"Ugh," Janet said.

"And that is her name," said Christine. "Ug might have chosen the spot and called her murderer to her. Where are you going?"

Janet didn't want to look at the shed another minute. "The house. As long as we're here, I'm going to snoop. See what they're up to or what they've done to it." She walked up the rise to the deck, and hesitated before putting a foot on it. Creeping seemed to be in order, but she decided against it, for the same reasons they hadn't crept on Monday. This was her house and she belonged here. She stepped up and crossed the deck to look in the window.

And experienced a moment of the same shock she'd felt Monday morning when she and Christine had looked through the kitchen window—except this time garbage wasn't the surprise. The lounge was spotless, and there was Mrs. Tiggy-Winkle, sitting in Janet's chair, knitting a neon purple Nessie.

Janet pulled back from the window. Should she knock on the door? But if the woman didn't speak English, what would that accomplish? Seeing the others about to join her on the deck, she waved them off. She went to join them, and this time she did creep.

"What is it?" Tallie asked.

"The last thing I expected." She explained the situation to them. Then she called Norman Hobbs. "And come quietly," she warned him, "so you don't scare her."

JANET STOOD JUST inside her front door. Norman Hobbs, at uncomfortable attention, stood beside her waiting. She let him wait, not out of spite, but because she needed to calm herself. While she did, she looked at the embroidery hanging above the door. Curtis had loved the coincidence of the house being built in 1880, the same year that William McGonagall, the Scots poet famous for overly dramatic doggerel, wrote his ripped-from-the-headlines poem "The Tay Bridge Disaster." Janet had embroidered the last lines of the poem on linen and had the piece framed for him. "For the stronger we our houses do build/The less chance we have of being killed." They'd hung it over the door, half for a joke and half as a talisman.

"My grandmother has always been fond of McGonagall," Hobbs offered.

"Which grandmother would that be, Norman? Another one? Or Nana Bethia, formerly of Inverness, now knitting Nessies in my lounge?"

Christine, Tallie, and Summer had stayed in the lounge with Bethia Ferguson—Nana Bethia, as Hobbs called her—who was surprised but happy to see everyone. But Janet had insisted Hobbs come with her to explain exactly what he'd done. Explain in private, because she didn't want to chance losing her temper in front of an apparently blameless grandmother.

"She's been staying with my sister there, you see," Hobbs said. "But my sister can't keep her any longer. We've arranged for a sheltered housing flat in Ballachulish, but there's been a delay. I couldn't keep her at my place, because—"

"Because you wanted to make the right impression on the Murder Investigation Team. You're unbelievable."

"It's a temporary situation."

"Unbelievable. Does she speak English?"

"Perfectly. But her dentures are being fixed. In the meantime she has trouble speaking clearly and thinks she looks gormless if she opens her mouth. I do beg your pardon, Mrs. Marsh. I think I must have lost my head."

"Another temporary situation? If she's your grandmother, how come no one knows her?"

"That would be due to the myth of small towns—that everyone knows everyone else's business. If that were true, there'd be no need for police. My grandmother only visited Inversgail once. She didn't like it."

"Was that you picking her up on Sculpay this afternoon?"

"I borrowed a friend's car. I didn't want to use my official vehicle for private transportation."

"Of course not. Unbelievable."

"Would it help for you to know that my father was a distant relative of Stuart Farquhar, who started Yon Bonnie Books?"

"No, that doesn't help. You're using my house as a hostel and my shop for elder care. Not that we mind having her in the shop. She's no trouble and she adds to the ambience."

"And at least there aren't any rats in the house, or signs that there ever have been."

"That *does* help. Unless you put that idea into Maida Fairlie's head in the first place to keep me away."

"It would never occur to me to do something like that."

"But it didn't bother you to ask for my keys and postpone the locksmith? Did it ever occur to you to ask me if I would put your grandmother up for a few days?"

"I didn't feel I knew you well enough to ask."

"Unbelievable. Ask me now."

"I beg your pardon?"

"Never mind," Janet said. "The answer is yes. Your grandmother can stay until her space is available in the home. I happen to like her. But she'll have company, because I'm coming home. And Norman, guess what. You owe me. Oh, boy, do you owe me."

TWENTY-SEVEN

JANET DECIDED AGAINST moving home that night. She needed time to decompress. And Hobbs needed time to move his grandmother from Janet's bedroom into Allen's old room. But she, Tallie, Christine, and Summer did go back to the bookshop and open the bottle of whisky.

"To our business and our friendship," Christine said. "Our homes, new and old."

"And to our new collaboration with the local constable," Janet said. "I should tell him the story about Una and the slippery slope of plagiarism."

"And who she might've encountered at the bottom of it," Summer said. "Hey, I think I'm finally getting the hang of whisky."

"That reminds me," Janet said. "The whisky was for us, but not the tartan. Kenneth came looking for it today, Christine, and he wasn't happy. I hate to ask if you've cut it already."

"Thank goodness for procrastination, then," Christine said. "It's still in the car. Remind me and I'll bring it in the morning."

"He wanted us to raise a glass for him," Tallie said.

"I'd rather not," said Janet.

"Me neither. But he also mentioned luck." Tallie

raised her glass. "So here's to luck in solving this case, and to my sister, Lucy, and luck in finding her."

"Our friend Norman might be able to help with both," Janet said, "*Sláinte*."

"AM I GOING to regret my mistake for the rest of my possibly shortened career?" Hobbs asked the next morning when Janet called and asked if he could find Lucy for them.

"Don't let that thought even cross your mind. Although I guess it just did. But don't worry, Norman. We'll help you solve this murder and let you have all the credit. *Do* the specialists have a suspect or a theory?"

"From what Reddick tells me, they think it's drugs and they're looking at someone in Glasgow."

"Oh. That didn't even occur to me. Do you think they're right?"

"I think that's another part of the myth of small towns—the stranger did it. But they like their modern retelling—the stranger did it and drugs."

"Interesting that you mention retellings, Norman." She told him about the plagiarism and the books on Una's desk. "But it might mean nothing at all."

"Or something. I'll let you know what I find out about Lucy."

"Thank you. How's your grandmother this morning?"

Hobbs was silent.

"How's your grandmother? Norman? Does she know I'm moving in? Moving *home*?"

"She does."

"But?"

"She thinks she's staying in an Airbnb. She doesn't mind more guests arriving, but she doesn't understand why she should change rooms. I'm sorry, Mrs. Marsh. She's my grandmother."

"YOU LEFT IT at that?" Christine asked. "You're soft."

"It's a small thing to do for her," Janet said. "None of this is her fault and she can move into the facility on Monday."

"Softhearted."

HOBBS CALLED BACK shortly after the bookshop opened. Lucy Graham was a five-year-old special needs child living in a care home in Crieff, about sixty miles northwest of Edinburgh.

"Thank you, Norman. Will Bethia be coming in today? Oh, I see her coming now. Talk to you later." She hoped she hadn't just heard him groan.

Janet and Tallie called Allen. They told him the good news about moving back into the house, but didn't tell him the story of Constable Hobbs and the lodger. Then they told him about Lucy.

"I'll see if they'll let me visit her. Maybe even today. It's gorgeous here. Good day for a drive."

"Why don't you and Nicola and the boys come over for the literary festival? I'll babysit one evening so you and Nicola can get out and about."

"Sounds like fun. We'll talk and let you know. It could get tricky if we stay with you and don't see enough of Maida, though. We don't want her to feel left out."

"Of course not."

"Have you got another minute? Nicola wants to talk to Christine."

Janet handed the phone to Christine, and her end of the conversation was odd in the way that conversations about toddler behavior can be.

"She's asking my advice," Christine whispered to Janet. "Yes, Nicola, still here. Just making Janet jealous… Twice is hardly a rash… Crying breaks my heart, too, but he's only a year old… *Three?* But still an infant, really, so it's not alarming at all… Don't ask him if he did. Tell him you know what happened, and don't give him the chance to make another mistake by lying… He'll be fine; he has me in his life… My love to your wee delinquents." Christine disconnected and handed the phone back to Janet. "Oh, sorry. I could have let you say good-bye."

"What was that all about?"

"Professional advice. One of their rascals has turned klepto. I didn't like to tell her that they start by taking keys and end up driving getaway cars. It's all over now for the poor little chap."

"You're terrible."

THEIR FIRST SATURDAY operating the bookshop on their own was busy, but not busier than they'd planned for. Christine and Summer took the day off from prepping the tearoom to help with book sales, and the steady flow of customers through the door was nothing they couldn't handle. That's what they told Pamela when she called, and it was the story they stuck to even when

Janet heard Kenneth in the background questioning what Pamela was relaying to him.

"I keep forgetting to bring his length of tartan out of the car," Christine said. "I'll phone later and let him know I'll have it for him Monday."

Bethia knitted in her spot near the fire, no more communicative after their visit the evening before, but no less pleasant, either. By then, she'd knitted an entire armada of Nessies. Tallie slipped into the kitchen to make her a cup of tea. Janet missed calling her Mrs. Tiggy-Winkle.

Maida Fairlie came in during the early afternoon.

"Shall I tell her that her grandchild is doomed to a life of crime?" Christine whispered to Janet.

"Don't you dare. Hello, Maida. I talked to a couple of giggling grandboys this morning."

"I was in Edinburgh yesterday. I was going to tell you they send their love. I guess there's no need, now."

"Never too much love. What can I do for you?"

"I'm here to see a Ms. Jacobs."

Summer looked over from ringing up a stack of postcards. "I'm Summer Jacobs. What can I do for you?"

Maida handed Summer a business card. "You called to arrange for a cleaning team? I'm here to assess the job and make sure that we'll be providing you with adequate staff for your needs. I understand you're preparing for a health inspection. We want to ensure that you pass."

"Sure," Summer said. "This is great. Come on and I'll show you around. Christine, you want to come along? You guys can do without us for a few, can't you?" she asked Janet and Tallie.

"Of course," Janet said. "Why don't I put the card in the file."

Summer looked at the card in her hand, shrugged, and handed it to Janet.

"What file?" Tallie asked after Summer and Christine left with Maida.

"'Affiliated Cleaners,'" Janet read. "Affiliated with whom?" There were two numbers on the card. The first was local. She called the second.

TALLIE SAID SHE could handle the desk and told Janet to go. Janet hurried upstairs to their makeshift "crime lab." She swept their piles of sorted envelopes, receipts, and miscellaneous papers back into the bin bags Rab had brought them in. Then she ran back down the stairs. In the meantime, Tallie sent three texts. Summer and Christine received theirs, and when they saw Janet at the door of the tearoom, they excused themselves and left her alone with Maida. Christine pulled the door almost closed and stayed there to listen, and to charge in if necessary.

Janet was only slightly taller than Maida, but she felt as though her eyes were boring down into the other woman's. She was a snake hypnotizing a mouse. Mousie Maida. Maida's eyes kept shifting to the bin bags, and Janet didn't need any further confirmation. But her phone buzzed with an incoming text, and what she read clinched it.

"From Nicola," Janet said. "The key they thought Wally took and put back—twice—is their copy of my house key. They've been worried about him turning into a liar and a thief, because he said he didn't do it. He's three. And he's your grandson."

Had she thought Maida would crumple? Her beady eyes glared back at Janet.

"And Jess Baillie. Do you have any idea what you put her through? Jeopardizing her business? Letting her believe Una Graham was out to get her?"

"Go ahead and despise me."

"Despise you? Why on earth would I?"

"I've got eyes."

"Use them and look in a mirror, then. There's nothing wrong with you but what you see in yourself. Come on, now. Your daughter loves you and your grandsons adore you."

"You didn't mention your son."

"Allen loves you because they love you. Mind you, he's still leery because of the kilt you were going to make him wear—oh, my gosh. I was joking about Allen and the kilt, but you aren't. Really? You're still upset about the wedding?"

"My only daughter. Her only wedding. Do you know how much money I put into it? How much I borrowed? And then you told them to elope and I lost it all."

"Maida, I didn't tell them to elope."

"You said you supported it one hundred percent."

"Of course I did. They'd already done it and were perfectly happy."

"YOU TRASHED HER DREAMS, so she trashed yours?" Christine asked.

"She said her behavior surprised her, too, and she's never done anything like it before."

"And yet she did it three times and fabricated rats out of whole cloth. Did she at least apologize?"

"Not really," Janet said. "But I think she's been kind of out of touch with reality lately."

"Oh, no. She's in touch with reality, all right. It's just her own version of it."

Janet pictured Maida's beady eyes as they'd blinked back tears. "She might have had a nudge back to our reality from the Presbyterian ancestors who always look over her shoulders. Or maybe that's a reality she's finally laid to rest."

Elizabeth II looked askance. "And then you told her we still want her cleaning crew for the tearoom before the inspection?"

"Because that's part of the myth of small towns I will continue to believe in. We have to try to get along."

ALLEN CALLED JANET that evening. He'd driven to Crieff and visited Lucy. A sweet girl, he said, who likes fairies and country and western music.

"Her favorite song is 'Don't It Make My Brown Eyes Blue,' but she doesn't understand why her eyes don't turn blue like her mummy's when she sings it. She has a picture of her mother on her bureau."

"She can't have two blue-eyed parents," Janet said, thinking of Curtis's handsome, lying blue eyes.

"I just got off the phone with Dad. He accepted Emma's word for it because he felt guilty and assumed he was the only one. He never followed through with the paternity test."

"Typical."

"Anyway, she's a sweet girl, it's a cheerful place, and she does get other visitors. She chattered on about Auntie Jess, who always brings her a fairy cake when she visits, and she asked if I want to be her daddy, too. Twisted my heart a bit."

Janet disconnected and sat by the window watching the tide run out. Then she went down the hall and knocked on Tallie's door.

"She told Allen that Auntie Jess has brought her about eleventy-teen fairy cakes in all. The other night, at Nev's, Jess told me she didn't know anything about Una's children. I guess, technically, she wasn't lying because I didn't ask about grandchildren."

"Who do you think the other daddy is?" Tallie asked.

"I don't know, but I think I should call Norman Hobbs."

"Go ahead. Maybe those are stray pieces of the puzzle. But if there's nothing in it, there's no harm done."

"I hate being suspicious of everyone," Janet said. "Do you know what that does to a nice retirement?"

"You're hardly retired."

"Well, it's disturbing."

"Then let's get this crime solved so we can get back to our quiet, bookish lives."

TWENTY-EIGHT

YON BONNIE BOOKS had always kept shortened hours on Sundays, and the new owners kept with that tradition. The free morning came as a welcome breathing space. Christine took her parents to church. Tallie and Summer rented kayaks and went to look for harbor seals. Janet spent the morning reading. She started out being virtuous, by picking up the contest entries, put them aside to finally start *The Bludgeon in the Bothy*, then gave up and sank into pure enjoyable escapism with an M. C. Beaton Hamish Macbeth mystery.

They opened their doors at one that afternoon. Bethia arrived with her knitting. And Pamela Lawrie arrived without Kenneth.

"Did he stop by?" she asked. "He hasn't been himself lately. He left in a huff early this morning. He didn't come home for his dinner. I can't phone him because I have his, and mine's not working." She glanced around as though she might find him lurking or tucked on a shelf.

"He hasn't been in," Janet said. "Did any of you see him this morning?"

Pamela watched them shake their heads. "I'm worried," she said.

"If we see him, we'll tell him," Janet said.

When she'd gone, Christine remembered the tartan fabric again. "She has an interesting look to her 'worry,'" she said. "I'm just as glad the tartan's still in the boot. If I'd given it to her, she might use it to strangle him."

It was a quiet day in the shop. Summer and Tallie rearranged the craft books, moving knitting and crochet down several shelves and leather and woodworking up. Even if Bethia was leaving, the new arrangement made sense.

Sharon Davis came in halfway through the afternoon. She approached the counter with the same selling smile she'd worn the first time Janet met her. Janet braced herself.

"How are you, Sharon?"

"Wonderful on a wonderful day."

Oh, boy. "And what can I do for you?"

"It's more what I can do for you."

Oh, boy.

"Would you like to appear on my *Book Blather* show on Radio Nevis tomorrow? It'll be a great plug for the shop."

"I hate to admit it, but I don't know anything about the program."

"Actually, I'm not surprised, but it's fun. We talk books—any kind, as far ranging as we want. Read excerpts, debate favorites, talk about new releases, anything goes, because it's my baby. A couple of librarians letting loose. I've been doing it for three months now, and I love it, but filling an hour on my own is demanding."

"No kidding. When and where?"

"We can do your portion over the phone, if you like. The station's in Fort William, so understandable if you can't get away. But if you can come over with me, that would be grand. Live is, well, livelier."

"How long would we be gone?"

"And that's why you might prefer phoning in. It's a time commitment, but while I'm there I treat myself to a meal out and get some shopping done. I leave here at four and I'm usually back by eight or half past."

"You should do it," Christine said.

"Is that a yes, then? Oh, sorry." Sharon's phone tweedled with an incoming text. She took it out, and as she read, her eyebrows rose steadily higher. "He's pathetic," she said, shaking her head, which returned her brows to normal. "Ian. Sounds to me like he started on the whisky a little early and thinks he's one of his own characters. Pick you up tomorrow, then? Great. See you."

"Tallie?" Janet asked.

"Already checked," Tallie said. "She was on the air on Monday."

"And we can scratch her off our list of suspects," Christine said.

Janet's phone buzzed. "Also from Ian," she said. She started reading it to herself, but stopped. "Watch my eyebrows, girls, because this is a lulu. 'I have absolute proof and the evidence to back it up in the murder of Una Graham. It's at the bothy, but I do so like a clever criminal so I'll give you one hour to collect it and make it disappear. When the hour's up, I'll call in the police.'"

Before she'd finished reading, Christine's phone

buzzed. "Mine's the same. How absolutely annoying. It means he's solved it, and he's beaten us."

"No, it doesn't," Janet said. "And he hasn't. It's a ploy. He's using a shotgun—scattershot. He doesn't know who he's trying to snare. And who knows how many of these texts he's sending."

Tallie and Summer had their phones out, waiting. And waiting. Waiting. They put them away in disgust.

"Aren't we shifty enough?" Tallie asked.

Janet patted her cheek. "You two are obviously the more upright, responsible, trustworthy members of our business."

"I'm insulted," Tallie said. "I want to be just like you."

"You two will need to hold down the fort while we go out to the bothy," Christine said.

"Oh, no, no, no, no, no," Tallie said. "What makes you think you need to go out there? If he's set some kind of trap, then it's going to be dangerous. When there's danger, you're not supposed to run toward it."

"We won't be running toward danger," Janet said. "When we get there, the killer will already be in custody. This will be a way to have closure so we can get back to that quiet, bookish life we talked about last night."

"Or you might run into the killer retrieving the evidence," Summer said, "and that might be a different kind of closure."

"Do you believe he *has* evidence?" Tallie asked. "What if he's the killer and he's going to pin the evidence on whoever shows up? Can't you leave it to the police? Please, yes, leave it to the police."

"We will," Christine said. "We'll wait for that hour, and then we'll go out when the police do and let them do the dirty, dangerous work. But Janet's right. It will be good to be there to lay this to rest."

"What makes you think he'll really call the police?" Summer asked.

"Because he's going to catch the villain," Janet said, "but he'll need them to make the arrest and congratulate him on his success."

To make Tallie and Summer feel better, Christine called Norman Hobbs. He told her he knew of the situation because, being the local police, he tended to be in the loop on most local police matters. Christine, in an aside, told Janet he sounded testy. Hobbs then asked how they knew of the operation. Christine told him Atkinson considered them suspects.

"Is it possible to hear someone rolling his eyes over the phone?" Christine asked Janet.

Tallie made Janet promise to text her and let her know when it was over.

THE DRIVE TO Ian Atkinson's bothy took them along the Sgail until the river leaped over some rocks and turned wild, running away into a glen that disappeared into a gorge. The road took an easier route, climbing the hills and circling around until it came out with a view of the sea, the mountains, and the tops of the trees in the Sgail Gorge woodlands. Ian's bothy sat in the sun near the gorge in a spot of breathtaking beauty. Janet and Christine got out of the car and saw no one.

"I knew it," Christine said.

“That we’d miss it?”

“No. Sheep.”

“What a disappointment,” Janet said. “Let’s at least look around.”

“You go that way.” Christine pointed toward the watching sheep. “I’ll go away from them.”

Janet walked toward the sheep thinking they might back up and she could save Christine from her somewhat silly fear. The sheep parted as she approached. A good start. But then they went around her and toward, rather than away from, Christine.

Christine, in the meantime, had approached the edge of the gorge and peered down at something, and called. Janet couldn’t hear what she said. Then Christine turned toward her, calling her name, and at the same time saw the advancing sheep. She took a step back. “Whoops,” she said, and slipped from view.

Janet ran toward the gorge, and so did the sheep. The sheep stopped at the edge. Janet stopped several yards from the sheep. The sheep parted again and started back up the hill. Janet, terrified, inched her way to the rim and looked over.

Christine had slid fifteen or twenty feet down the side of the gorge—part slope, part bluff, with loose soil where the slide occurred, decaying leaves, fallen branches, rocks. Christine, on her back, rested on her elbows. Janet whimpered and wanted to follow the sheep back up the hill. “Christine,” she called.

Christine looked up. “I’m all right. But Janet—Reddick was here. And his dog. I heard him calling for help. When he saw me, he said, ‘You were on the list. She wasn't.' And then I slid down, and he went over an edge below me. I'm going to try crawling along that log and see if I can see him." She moved toward the log and slid down a few more feet.

"Don't move again, Christine. Can you hear Reddick?"

"No. The dog didn't go over, though. I think he's found his own way down farther along there, and I think I can—"

"Don't you dare move. I'll get help."

Janet backed away from the gorge and called Tallie. "It's Mom. I need you to listen. We're okay. We need help at Ian's bothy. Call nine-nine-nine, tell them where we are, that a policeman has fallen into the gorge; he's probably badly injured. It's Reddick. Call now. I need to help Christine and won't be able to stay on the line with them. Love you and see you soon."

Janet disconnected and ran to Christine's car. She got the tartan from the trunk and ran back. "Christine, I'm going to let the end of this down to you. Reach for it carefully and hold on to it." She tied one end of the tartan around her waist and then pitched the length of it down the slope. The weight of the woolen fabric carried it close enough to Christine that she was able to get hold of it.

"Are you okay up there?" Christine called.

"I'm going to sit down so I can't see how far down it is."

"I think this is a good omen, though, Janet," Christine called. "We've faced the twin terrors of sheep and high places. We have nowhere to go but up."

"For your sake, let's hope so."

NORMAN HOBBS ARRIVED with a scatter of gravel. Tallie and Summer arrived on his heels—in Rab MacGregor's small pickup. They'd left Rab in charge of the shop. Janet took the tartan from around her waist and gave the end to Hobbs.

"He and the dog went over?" Hobbs asked.

"Christine thinks the dog found a way down," Janet said.

"I would've followed if I could," Christine said.

"I'm glad you didn't. I'm going to help you climb back up, Mrs. Robertson. It shouldn't be too hard."

"Hold your end and let me get closer to the edge first, so I can check on Reddick."

"No. If the edge gives way, I can't hold you."

"I hope you're not insulting my weight, Norman."

"I would never."

"Then help me up."

WHILE THEY WAITED for the rescue personnel, Christine told Hobbs what Reddick had said. "A woman who wasn't on the list. The list of suspects, I'd assume. But does that tell you enough to know who he was talking about? And did she come out here and spring the trap?"

"I don't know. Ian Atkinson might have had his own personal list."

"Let's find out who *was* on his list," Janet said.

"SORRY TO HAVE included you in my dragnet," Ian said when Janet called. "No hard feelings, I hope. That was Plan A, which was rather crude in detail."

"If by crude, you mean a fiasco, I agree. Reddick is—" Janet's throat caught. "We may have lost him."

"That was never my intention. It was also a fiasco because the real culprit was getting himself sozzled in Nev's and never read my text. I dropped in there to celebrate my success, found him blitzed, and realized not only had he never gone to the bothy, but he could hardly walk straight. That's when Plan B hit me; and that's B for pure brilliance. I got him in my car, drove to my place, and locked him in the garage. No muscle required on my part because he'd passed out, not that I couldn't have supplied muscle, if he'd put up any kind of fight. This will be a brilliant piece of publicity—'Author of Single Malt Mysteries Bags Villain for Police Scotland.' *He'll* know it's brilliant, too, when he wakes up. I texted him with the whole scenario so he'll know he doesn't have a chance."

"Who are you talking about? Who have you got?"

"Kenneth Lawrie. Oh, and I say, here comes a fascinating turn of events up my front path. A coincidence like this would never work in one of my books. I think things are about to get interesting."

Janet couldn't tell if he'd disconnected or the phone had gone dead.

TWENTY-NINE

"Ian Atkinson just set himself up for disaster," Janet said. "He's lured Pamela Lawrie to his house and doesn't realize she killed Una. Norman, you need to get back there."

"You need to come with me. You can tell me along the way why I'm arresting her."

"Tallie, go with your mum," Christine said. "She needs you. Summer and I'll wait here for the responders. Go."

"Can you listen and drive fast at the same time?" Janet asked.

"If the story's good enough."

"Then, put the pedal to the floor, Constable. Ian sent his text to Kenneth as one of his suspects. But Kenneth didn't get the text, because he didn't have his phone. Pamela had it, and she read the text. She went out to the bothy, but there was no evidence, only Reddick. I don't know what happened there, but something did, and Reddick went over the edge. And he told us who was responsible. Sort of. 'You were on the list. She wasn't.' Pamela wasn't on the list."

"Why didn't he name her?" Tallie asked.

"He could've been in shock. We don't know how badly hurt he was before he fell the rest of the way."

"Jess might not have been on the list, either," Hobbs said.

"But it comes back to Pamela," said Janet. She told them about Ian's Plan B. "His plan is going to backfire. No question. But what's ours, when we get there?"

THEY PULLED UP in front of Ian Atkinson's house, and for all the trauma and drama that had taken place in Argyll Terrace during the past week, everything appeared peaceful and calm. Another, or perhaps the same, warbler sang. The sun shone on the houses and gardens. Janet glanced at her own house and pictured Hobbs's nana Bethia sitting in the family room knitting Loch Ness monsters.

"I'm just saying, Constable, that you don't know what kind of situation you're walking into, and if you will just let me have your tire iron, and let Tallie have the jack, we can go in as your backup. You going in alone is just plain foolish."

"No weapons," Hobbs said. Again.

"Look," Tallie said. "There's Rab waving to us from Ian's front door."

PAMELA LAWRIE SAT in a chair at Ian's kitchen table, staring at nothing. Maida Fairlie stood behind her with a cast-iron frying pan, flushed and triumphant, as though she'd aced all the lessons her ancestors had been whispering in her ears down through the years.

"I always let myself in to make Mr. Atkinson's tea,"

Maida said. "Quiet as a mouse so I don't disturb his writing. Only tonight when I came in, she was holding a knife on him, so I grabbed the frying pan and hit her. I must've left the door open, because the dog came in."

Ranger's nose was raised; he smelled something on the kitchen counter.

"Rab came over to get the dog after walking the old lady home to your house. He said you gave her free bed and board. That's lovely, Janet." She'd told the story when they came in with Hobbs. And told it twice more after he'd put handcuffs on Pamela and cautioned her. But the story put more life into Maida's beady eyes than Janet had ever seen, so she didn't mind hearing it again.

"You did a brilliant job, Maida," Janet said. "Pure brilliant. We'll just go through and check in with Norman."

"Aye, you go on, then. I'll keep an eye on this one." Maida slapped the frying pan in her hand.

"That's the most I've ever heard Maida say," Tallie murmured as she and Janet went to join Hobbs.

"It's either adrenaline talking or she's found her niche," Janet said.

They found Hobbs with Ian, Rab, and Kenneth across the hall in the lounge. Neither Ian nor Kenneth looked well. Janet wasn't sure what was wrong with Ian. Pamela hadn't actually attacked him, so physical injury didn't account for it. Kenneth's brown eyes were bloodshot, and he was no doubt hungover. But he wanted to talk.

"I've been carrying around a burden," he said. "Hiding it. Letting it eat at me. Letting her get at me. Is she all right in there?" He shook his head. "It doesn't matter. She'll blame me." He told them that he and Pamela never got over the death of their daughter. “And my way of not getting over it was to have an affair with Emma.” He said he never knew Emma was pregnant. Never knew about Lucy. “When Una heard we were leaving the country, she said she felt she needed to tell me about the little mite.”

He was shocked, then angry that he hadn’t been told, hadn’t been asked to do anything for her. “Una told me that’s because it was easier to hit up someone she didn’t see face-to-face. And she didn’t know which one of us was Lucy’s father, until I took the test.” He’d told Pamela about Lucy. And he told her maybe he wouldn’t go to Portugal after all. Maybe this was his wake-up call. “I thought it might be my way out.” The tartan fabric was some he’d bought for their daughter and put away for her wedding. Now he wanted it for Lucy.

“We’ll get it back to you, Kenneth,” Janet said.

“What’s he telling you in there?” Pamela called from the kitchen. “What are you telling them, Kenneth? I want to see him.”

They heard a chair scrape and indignant sounds from Maida, and Hobbs was immediately there.

“You’ve been cautioned, Mrs. Lawrie,” Janet heard him say. “I would advise you to wait.”

“I want equal time. You let him talk. I’ll talk.”

“He’s not under arrest.”

“I want to see him.”

Hobbs came back into the lounge with Pamela. His hand on her elbow would have looked like a friendly gesture if not for her wrists handcuffed behind her back.

“*She* should’ve been under arrest,” Pamela said. “Ug

should've been. She was going to ruin everything. She *had* ruined everything. She wouldn't tell Kenneth not to stay. She wouldn't tell him Lucy wasn't his. I dug around and found out she had someone else paying for the child's care. But Ug said it was too late."

"It was," Kenneth said. "It wasn't just Una's word. I had the test. Lucy is my daughter."

"And Una had a copy and she waved it in my face," Pamela said. "I only wanted to talk. To tell her to leave him alone. Because I knew she was trying to take Kenneth from me. I sent her a text from his phone, and she thought it was him, and we arranged to meet. She knew a private place."

"My shed?" Janet asked.

"I didn't know who's shed. But she used to meet someone else there. And when she saw me instead of Kenneth, she laughed and said Kenneth would do anything she asked and she waved the test in my face. She gave me no choice."

"So you killed her, Pammy?" Kenneth said.

"She gave me no choice," Pamela repeated.

"Did you take the letters from her, too?" Janet asked.

Pamela looked at Janet, then looked away. She didn't say yes, but she didn't ask what letters Janet was talking about. She told them she'd been working on Kenneth, to wear him down.

"So he'd come to Portugal with me after all. A few more weeks are all I needed. You'd have done it, wouldn't you, Kenny?"

Kenneth, head in his hands, made no response.

"And you weren't worried about someone else, someone you know being accused or convicted?" Maida asked. She sounded scandalized and tempted to use the frying pan.

"No," Pamela said. Then she made a guttural, dismissive noise. "Incomers and strangers. It's a known fact they cause most of Inversgail's problems."

Janet's phone rang. It was Christine with the news that Reddick had been found, unconscious but alive, and expected to live, his fall broken by foliage. Quantum was by his side when the responders reached him. Janet relayed the news to the others.

"Where is Quantum now?" Hobbs asked.

"Christine is bringing him to you, Norman."

"Thank you."

"CONSTABLE," TALLIE SAID, stopping Hobbs after he helped Pamela into his vehicle, "now that it's over, will you tell me what occurred to you the night of the murder that you didn't want to tell us?"

Hobbs studied Tallie's face for a moment, and then nodded. "I hoped I might get together with Jess because I know she has a good heart. That she's been visiting Una's granddaughter is further proof of that. But it isn't easy for a policeman."

"Especially one who just moons around and won't speak up," Tallie said. "Or one who lies and sneaks old ladies into other people's houses."

Hobbs nodded again.

"PAMELA'S ATTITUDE IS IRONIC," Janet said as they watched Hobbs drive away with her, "considering the bookshop does well because of tourists, and her dream was to become a stranger and an incomer in another land."

"Mm," Tallie said. "You know, though, after this adventure with murder, the book business is turning out to be more exciting than I thought it would be."

"That?" Janet said. "That was a typical day at the library. And a tame one, in some cases."

THIRTY

One week later

"It's a decent crowd," Janet said as she and Christine surveyed the audience gathered in the library auditorium.

"Nice to see," Christine said. "And a nice culmination to the festival. But we'll hope they don't all get wind of the reception at Yon Bonnie Books and show up there this evening."

"We'll cope if they do." Janet gave Christine a nudge with her elbow. "She's going to announce first place."

"I can't believe she wouldn't tell us beforehand."

"Wheesht. It's more fun this way."

"And finally, as chair of the Inversgail Literary Festival writing contest, it is my great pleasure to announce the first-place winner. For his short story 'Tea Time at the OK Corral,' Rab MacDonald."

"A lovely gathering," Ian Atkinson said to Janet and Christine that evening at the bookshop. "Thank you for inviting me. Ah, there's Rab. Is he going to read his story?"

"According to Sharon," Janet said.

"I must go congratulate him. See if he'd like any pointers."

"Rab saw him coming," Christine said as they watched Ian try to catch up. "And there's Danny coming in the door. I'll just go say hello, shall I?"

Janet heard the infectious laugh of her grandsons and turned to see Tallie and Maida playing peekaboo with them. Allen and Nicola had brought the boys up from Edinburgh for a long weekend. They were staying in the rooms above the bookshop. Maida waved at Janet and then picked up a carrier bag and brought it over.

"Some books I'd like you to have," Maida said. "I found them in a house one of my crews cleaned out. Payment was anything we liked that we hauled away."

Janet took half a dozen antique volumes from the bag and set them on the sales desk. She opened the first and then the second. "Oh, my goodness, Maida." She opened each of the others. "Do you realize what you've given me? They're first editions by Ian MacLaren and Lewis Grassic Gibbon."

"Aye, and I can't think of anyone who'd like them more."

As Janet hugged her, she heard a familiar throat clearing behind her. Norman Hobbs, his grandmother beside him.

"Nice to see you again," Bethia said, smiling with a mouthful of teeth. She took two of the ginger pear scones Summer was passing. She ate one and gave the other to Jess.

Janet saw Basant talking with Reddick. Reddick's collie, Quantum, sat at attention by his side. The policeman was still convalescing but his doctors expected him to make a full recovery. Summer stopped and offered the tray of scones to the men. Basant took one and, after taking a bite, raised the scone to Janet.

"Perfect," he declared.

Sharon Davis was the only one who didn't look happy. "Where's Rab?" she asked Janet. "I gave him a five-minute warning for reading his story."

"Change of plans," Tallie said. "He and Ranger just went out the back door."

"It's all right, though," Summer said. "We've got this." She and Christine passed cups of Atholl Brose for the adults and lemonade for the kids.

"Mom," Tallie said, "a toast?"

"Me?"

"No one better."

Janet looked at the smiling faces around her and reflected on the happily-ever-after dream she'd embarked upon. "To friends and books," she said, raising her glass, "and friends in books, may our stories be long and our friendships longer."

* * * * *

ACKNOWLEDGMENTS

Stories come from so many more places than just one person's head. For this story, the elements span decades and continents, and for all I'm grateful. Thanks to Kristina Hoerner for the launderette; Evelyn Shapiro for the new paint in the tearoom; Cammy MacRae for the correct Gaelic (any incorrect Gaelic is my fault); Sharon Davis and James Haviland for their names and good humor; Basant, Arati, and Puja Paudel for friendship and amazing spirit; Ann Campbell and Caroline Wickham-Jones for reading with Scottish eyes; Linda Landrigan for the inspiration for the Single Malt Mysteries; Claiborne Hancock for taking a chance; Cynthia Manson for continuing to believe in me; Chris Thompson, Marthalee Beckington, and Nancy and Bob Lawson for Ranger, Quantum, and Sophie; and always for my Mike.